I0777527

Perfidy

Christian Apocalyptic Science Fiction
Futuristic Fantasy

The Debacle Series
Book 1

Ardith A. Price

AJAP Heavens Edge
Ardith Arnelle' Price
CHRISTIAN
AUTHOR

Published by AJAP Heavens Edge, P.O Box 141076, Detroit, Michigan 48214

Website: https://drmozart18.com

Bookbrush Book design & Cover by Ardith A. Price, Stock art: Pixabay, GB Taylor & Pixabay popmellon

Editor: Stacy Juba

First Edition - August 2024

Library of Congress Control Number: 2024915479

ISBN (print): 979-8-9862956-1-9

ISBN (e-book): 979-8-9862956-2-6

Printed in the United States of America

Publisher's Cataloging-in-Publication Data

Names: Price, Ardith A.

Title: Perfidy : the debacle series, book 1 / Ardith A. Price.

Description: Detroit, MI : AJAP Heavens Edge, 2024. | Series: Debacle series ; book 1. | Summary: Carmen Northrop and her teammates as they emerge as humanity's hope against a Nephilim invasion. A skilled engineer, Carmen discovers an ancient holographic bracelet with supernatural abilities. She must use these powers to thwart the aliens and save humanity from impending destruction.

Identifiers: LCCN 2024915479 | ISBN 9798986295619 (pbk.) | ISBN 9798986295626 (ebook)

Subjects: LCSH: Extraterrestrial beings – Fiction. | End of the world – Fiction. | Supernatural – Fiction. | Women in engineering – Fiction. | Colorado – Fiction. | BISAC: FICTION / Christian / Fantasy. | FICTION / Christian / Futuristic. | FICTION / Science Fiction / Apocalyptic & Post-Apocalyptic.

Classification: LCC PS3616.R53 P4 2024 | DDC 813 P75--dc23

LC record available at https://lccn.loc.gov/2024915479

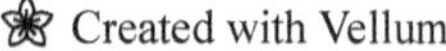 Created with Vellum

*To the Triune God (Father God, Father Son, and Father Holy Spirit),
who gives me the knowledge to write the books for them. To my
husband, who has always been my number one fan.*

Foreword

While the prequel is a work of fiction, it incorporates elements of the Scriptures, God's name (Messiah Yeshua), and prayers. I sincerely hope this unique blend will captivate you and inspire you to read the first book in the series PERFIDY, experiencing the transformative love of Jesus Christ, our Messiah and coming King. Shalom.

Shaalu Shalom Yerushalayim, "Pray for the peace of Jerusalem!"

If you enjoyed the novel PERFIDY, get on your cell phone or computer and write a positive review on Goodreads or Amazon.
https://amzn.to/3qxKHRM
Stay in the Loop
Don't miss the next book in the series.
Click the web page link: https://bit.ly/39n3RlO to join my mailing list.

Contents

Perfidy

Chapter One

Marsh Harbor, Colorado, Spring 2033

PEALS OF THUNDER EXPLODED, shaking the bedrock of our home perched on steel poles. I tried to relax on the patio lounge chair overlooking the reservoir in Marsh Harbor. The sound of the waves splashing against the shore was soothing. The once cloudless sky transformed into a foreboding hue. Beneath the thunderclouds, the heavens trapped a mysterious golden light, its origin a puzzle that added to the growing sense of unease. The light created an eerie glow, a sight both fascinating and unsettling. A deep, rough voice emerged from the galaxy's far reaches, echoing around me. Its origins are a puzzle. A wave of panic washed over me as the ground quivered beneath my feet. The sinister speech in the shadows accused someone of being a deceitful conspirator. The words oozed with malice, each syllable a bone-chilling threat that hung in the air, refusing to dissipate.

"What on earth was that?" I screeched, my breath coming in panicked gasps. A persistent creaking noise accompanied the clatter of dishes on the table as the house adapted to the unstable landscape. As I scanned the deck, my hands clutched the armrests, feeling the smooth texture beneath my fingers as the noises grew louder. I searched

Noah's face for any sign of danger. My heart pounding in my chest, my mind racing with fear.

Noah paused his browsing on the tablet and fixed his stare on me, his concern palpable. His brows furrowed in confusion. "Carmen, what's wrong? There's nothing but laughter, children playing, and the house creaking. You're scaring me. What did you hear?"

My husband of twenty years, Noah, sat at the outdoor table across from me. He displays a generous set of pearly whites and a crown of curly brown hair. While engrossed in his work, a law brief, he never took his eyes off me, attempting to comfort me as my unease grew. Noah's hand caressed mine, a testament to our years together and the life we built with our three triplet boys. Despite this, Noah's job required him to be away for weeks, causing him to miss precious family moments with me and the teens. It always saddened me to see how his obsession with wealth and power overshadowed the love and connection he could have had with his family.

With a nod, skepticism clung to me, refusing to let go of his hand. My heart raced, gasps of breath quickened, and a shiver of tension ran through my body. Calming myself, I tilted my head to glimpse the setting sun. But the enigmatic whispers and screeching noises persisted. My worry remained as the unusual outcry continued to disrupt the silence. Noah didn't notice the disturbance in the air, and his affidavit consumed his attention. Yet, I could tell he cared from his body language - his lips formed a pout, and his eyebrows lowered.

Once more, the screeching sound echoed around us, and I questioned Noah if he had heard it. "Did you catch that noise?"

"No, my love, but please alert me if you detect any more noises. Carmen, I hate surprises, especially frightening ones." He leaned closer to rub my hand, and his tender touch assuaged me.

Chaos erupted as barking dogs filled the air, screams pierced the stillness, and people dashed from the lake. As I peeked over the brick wall, my anxiety lingered. I saw nothing, but I was sure a sound or something terrified my neighbors enough that they fled. Something lurking in the water filled my neighbors with fear, prompting their unexpected departure from the beach. The water roared and crashed, reaching heights above the average. I had a perfect waterfront view with the shore just a few feet away. Despite the circumstances, many neighbors defied the odds and continued their routine, taking their dogs for a walk along the beach.

Fierce wind gusts carried the unsettling energy of panicked and confused voices. With each air gust, sky-to-ground lightning bolts flashed across the heavens.

A robust breeze wailed with an unmistakable foreboding, hinting at an impending storm. My fingers fastened around the armrest as the forceful breezes whipped against my skin, bringing respite to the sultry air. Over the canopy, lights tinkled and swayed. Shimmering sunlight on our outdoor deck formed a detailed pattern of lively orange, yellow, and red tints.

Unmarked, sleek, black police hovercrafts raced across the sky with a hum, increasing my panic that something forbidden existed in the airspace. To ease my fear, I paused and inhaled, the tempting scent of the lasagna wafting through the air, triggering my hunger. The casserole dish sat on the metal table warmer. Noah and I needed to finish work assignments, so we agreed to delay our meal by thirty minutes.

Our home defies the laws of physics as it hovers above the ground, supported by robust columns. The round platform and pool glimmer with a soft glow of white lights, casting a magical ambiance. Many flower pots filled with vibrant lilacs, azaleas, and peonies adorn the perimeter, depicting colors and scents.

Luminous lights and bone-chilling screams resonated within my mind. With a quick change to my posture, I evaluated my surroundings, taking every view into account. The sound of scraping footsteps, high-pitched cries, and frantic wails from an unknown source only intensified my fear and uncertainty. What was causing the mysterious sounds that whispered only to me?

In a desperate frenzy, I spun around, my senses heightened as I tried to pinpoint the origin of the action. Then, silence in the heavens, as if someone had pressed a mute button. In the fading light of dusk, I strained to glimpse hovercrafts, but the only illumination came from our gazebo's gentle, sparkling glow.

After catching a peek at Noah, his fingers pounded on the screen of his tablet. His forehead creased, and his lips squeezed together in a tight line, radiating intense frustration. I sensed a sudden, overwhelming darkness descending upon me. The blurred boundaries between reality and illusion made me question my sanity. Goosebumps crawled along my arms when another outcry of terror shattered across the stillness of twilight. My gasps and heartbeats quickened.

"Noah," I wailed. "Did you catch those spine-tingling screams and shouts?" His fingers paused on the keyboard, and his lips pursed. Then he straightened his frame.

"No, my beloved Carmen, you must be mistaken. Maybe what you perceived was part of a dream. Regrettably, I gleaned nothing resembling what you have described. Instead, kids playing and the occasional yapping of dogs, although the cries at the beach have shifted. Someone needs help. Sweetheart, you need to pause and rest. You have spent excessive time on that computer application. Hydrate yourself and try to nap."

He turned back to his project. The tightness in his jaw and furrowed lines on his forehead increased. Despite his lack of awareness of the commotion, I took solace in the refreshing gusts of wind. He was right. It must have been a dream.

Exhaustion won, and my eyelids closed, swept aside by the faint noises. Once more, I shifted in my chair and relaxed. The humid evening breeze caressed me. The melody of reservoir waves crashing on the shore, the melodic songs of night creatures, and the mingling aroma of fish and lilac surrounded me. Then sleep covered me.

Out of nowhere, a roar came closer. A chilling sensation crept up my spine, signaling wickedness nearby. Dread overwhelmed me, and my eyelids popped open. Then I saw Noah's composed face.

"Carmen, are you okay? My love, you keep jerking in your seat."

My entire body trembled as he leaned over, touched my outstretched palm on the table, and settled back into his chair. He flexed his muscles and sighed as he dragged his tablet closer to his frame.

"Sweetie, are you sure everything is fine with you?" His wrinkled forehead and his piercing glare bore into my face.

The only break taken since morning was to prepare a romantic dinner. And a pre-nap before wrapping up my computer code. My eyeballs grew tired and strained from prolonged screen-staring. My stare met Noah's, and without hesitation, I responded to him.

"Yes, I'm sleepy," I yawned. "I guess the noise came from hover jets overhead. Give me ten minutes to rest, code my last line, and then supper."

"Sounds good, a solid plan."

My hand trembled when my fingers dragged my laptop from across the table, but my attention veered to the laptop screen. What if exhaustion wasn't the cause, but my paranormal gift was activating instead?

I kept my unique talents hidden from my unsuspecting husband, which was crucial, as I feared he'd question my mental well-being. His commitment to Jewish traditions prevented him from delving into metaphysical concepts. Yet he knew I had heavenly powers. He had seen the ethereal blue aura that enveloped me.

Given his skepticism, I refrained from pressuring him to have faith in my superhuman powers. My parents embraced our Jewish identity, and the supernatural gifts granted by the Holy Spirit to explore beyond the surface. Self-doubt whispered in my senses, and then fatigue. More booms echoed in the sky, causing me to shake my head and take a breath.

Out of nowhere, the air buzzed with energy as a dazzling swirl appeared before my eyes. The sight made me shiver, and my mind raced with potential danger. Enthralled by the portal's pulsing, magnetic presence, I pushed aside my apprehension and resolved to explore its enigmatic depths.

"Noah, sweetie, do you see the spiral hovering over me? I realize sleep has evaded me, but I need to be sure I wasn't seeing things." As I questioned him, I wrestled with my inner conflict, longing for proof to confirm my vision. He stopped typing and answered me.

"Honey, I don't see a portal. The blue light from your computer must be affecting your eyesight. Hurry and complete your project, and then we can eat. I don't want to have dinner without you."

"I will hurry." Noah once again focused his attention on his legal brief. When he glanced in my direction, I saw suspicion in his eyeballs, and when he squinted and tilted his head, a quiver formed in my stomach.

Immediate memories of my mom telling me stories of alternate universes flooded my thoughts. She warned me our universe possessed evil and godly entities. Mom told me to be careful and pray before entering strange portals. You have abilities of sight and discernment, she often reminded me. The gifts passed through generations in our family allowed me to perceive things beyond the ordinary.

Once, after stumbling upon a shimmering gateway arch exuding otherworldly energy. A divine force blocked me. But today, this alluring entrance beckoned me to step inside as it resonated with the essence of my being.

Ten years ago, a portal opened before me. Nervous and terrified, my hands pressed forward, but a white-robed being motioned for me to stop. I froze, and the realm melted away.

As the evening wore on, I caught sight of Noah's grim face as he tightened his fingers into a fist and stiffened his jaw. He saw the mesmerizing sight of the swirling light. He looked over at me but remained silent. His face twisted as his mouth dropped open, and his eyebrows shot upward. I was relieved he didn't question the mysterious blue glow that filled me with wonder and excitement. He paused, his glare more intense, before shifting his attention and tapping his tablet. My forehead glistened with beads of excessive perspiration, a chilling reminder of the impending danger lurking in the shadows.

Overwhelmed by a moment of grief, Mom's memories consume my spirit. Mom's wisdom and guidance were necessary for me to navigate these mysterious paths. But her absence left me feeling vulnerable, devastated with despair, and lost.

My eyes fixed on the arch. Time froze, and the moment felt profound. It made me wonder if my mother had ever experienced a similar sensation or encountered a celestial entity clothed in glorious white attire.

Her chilling reminder remained with me, and I couldn't forget her words:

"Evil demons often enter a passageway intending to provoke trouble for saints blessed with God's supernatural strength."

Meanwhile, on this balmy evening, after gathering my courage to glide into an arch to understand the portal's power for the first time. With fists clenched, my voice trembled with frustration. A challenging threshold lay beyond the arch; it demanded answers to its mysteries. My fingertips touched the mystical white corkscrew, and a powerful force snatched me, leaving me breathless.

THE SWIRLING SPIRAL yanked me inside, and I gawked and struggled to gain my breath. A surge of electricity coursed through my hands and body, enveloping me with thrill and apprehension. The surrounding air was alive with energy, compelling me deeper into the twisting vortex.

When I stepped through the fractured entryway, it wrapped me in a vibrant whirlwind of colors. A whole new world stretched out before me, unfamiliar and strange. Panic surged through me as I goggle at the swirling lights and wispy mist pulsating with an unsettling energy. My heart raced as the gravitational energy lugged me further into the spinning vortex. My mind struggled to handle the incredible speed at which I was hurtling forward, leaving me gasping for air in awe of the sheer force propelling me ahead.

I remembered the lessons my mother imparted to me. She shared her knowledge of ancient wisdom and personal anecdotes with me. She exposed a hidden method to use when encountering a supernatural doorway.

Mom said, *clench your fists to unlock hidden power.* Her voice echoed in my reflections and enabled me to access a parallel universe, boosting my senses and energy once inside the portal.

She had taught me that in times of danger, I could invoke the word

'*Azar*,' a Hebrew word meaning help me. This directive will cause a blue aura to appear, covering me and anyone I sought to protect. The blue aura manifested power, signifying my superhuman abilities and protection.

My spirit glided further into the portal as I prayed and clenched my fists. The blue cloud enveloped me as I followed my mother's guidance. It manifested in my protective power, shimmering around me, an obvious sign of my supernatural abilities. It pulsed with a gentle light, and I could sense its protective energy radiating from my body, creating a shield against potential threats.

Mom advised me that my aura is visible in the physical but not in the spiritual realm. Yet I am hidden from danger unless the entity is demonic, but they have no power to harm me. My blue mist protects me in a portal, and I can travel to other realms. She explained that this was a heavenly gift, a power that demanded caution and responsibility. She warned that misuse or lack of control could lead to failure or danger. *Faith and prayer*, she said, may be necessary for the blue mystical energy to work. Fortunately, I am proficient with both.

A spectral presence circled me as a massive planet materialized. My mouth fell open, and I gasped in anticipation when I spotted an alien twin planet, a sight both overwhelming and majestic. This scene provoked a growing anticipation within me. With my arms set tight against my sides, the powerful force of the protective blue energy pulled me into the mystical world. I stood tall and proud as I sailed, feeling the wind whip through my curly reddish-brown hair. The electricity from the portal slowed my ascent. As I approached, the surrounding noise grew louder, intensifying the atmosphere. The planet's greatness stretched before me, its vastness too immense to put into words, making me appear minuscule.

I was in awe as I saw the enormous Nephilim slicing through the winged Nephilim creatures with their glowing light sabers, creating an electrifying buzz in the night. Fear turned into horror as I looked up at the towering giants. My eyes widened in surprise at the sight.

"Kill them," rang out a harsh voice from a huge gold-colored Nephilim who charged toward a hybrid Nephilim. The anguished cries echoed through the forest, producing an eerie atmosphere as the hybrid-winged Nephilim succumbed to the hot terrain. I couldn't believe what I had seen—a Nephilim flying in the heavens with gold wings, bulging muscles, and skyscraper height. The sight was so immense that I shuddered from the fear of the beasts.

The clashes brought back vivid memories of when the golden Nephilim visited Earth three years prior. Yet they were docile and helped our planet's technology and ecosystems. Were these the same creatures known for their kindness? I shook my head in disbelief. Still, I always sensed evil from their beings.

The hybrid Nephilim bird beings engaged in combat with the golden Nephilim, with their unique blend of features. "Shoot them if they take flight, ensuring they have no chance to flee." The shining yellowish Nephilim stood out, radiating power and ferocity, as they snatched, chased, and bludgeoned the hybrids when caught with dangerous devices.

The moment I saw the aliens in combat, I was sorrowful. I couldn't help but support the magnificent hybrid bird Nephilim, whose graceful, colorful wings fluttered. The hybrid resembled those of an eagle; its wings were a stunning mix of vibrant hues. As they fell to the ground with a heartbreaking cry, their short-lived flight came to a tragic end. The red laser beams cutting through the land turned the once serene landscape into a horrifying scene of blood and destruction.

First, the celestial beings known as Nephilim arrived on Earth with a radiant aura, but as time passed, their behavior shifted. Upon watching the brutal attack on their kind, their demeanor took a darker turn from their once mischievous antics. Although they tried to be diplomatic and provide support, I hesitated because of the Nephilim's counterfeit motives toward me. Their sudden show of kindness, when our society crumbled, fueled my suspicions of their ulterior motives. I never trusted the beasts.

Second, the commander of the golden Nephilim didn't care for me. Whenever he focused his words on me, I recalled the sharpness of his speech. His unsettling transformation of his eyes went from gold to a chilling shade of red. Every day, the memories of my terrifying experience with the commander haunt me, as do the potential consequences if I defy him.

A sigh of relief washed over me when they disappeared from our world without explanation.

Meanwhile, I couldn't bear the harsh and grating voices of the alien Nephilim. The energy from the spiral slowed and glided me over the topography. What caused the portal to force me to this awful galaxy?

Now, I direct my attention to the voice and action on the planet.

"Move fast and stop attacks on the hybrids. Focus on targeting and eliminating Zerus."

With confidence, the military Nephilim commander brawled his instructions: "Halt, reversal, but continue moving towards the ridges."

"Kill everything that moves." In rapid motion, the hybrid golden beings stopped, their attention drawn to the vibrant forest. Without missing a beat, they resumed their journey in perfect harmony, heading toward a distant range of mountains.

Tears crept from my eyeballs. I blinked and shook my frame to gather my thoughts and analyze the scenery before me. I didn't understand why the aliens killed their hybrid aliens unless they revolted against the political power. Driven by the spiral energy, the coiled mist dragged me towards the forest again.

The planet's vast landscape was a masterpiece of nature, with lush vegetation, looming palm trees, and futuristic constructions levitating above the surface. The intense heat radiated from the planet as drops of sweat fell from my face. I cruised over a dried-up stream while floating above the ground, with only a few large bubbling lagoons formed by the volcanic pumice flowing into the waters.

Many erected buildings rested on stilts and towered into the heavens. Seeing the odd-shaped edifices adorned with floating builds of different shapes, such as multi-diamond, oblong, and quad-circular, filled me with wonder. Heavy moss hung from the base of the constructions, and tree limbs twisted and wrapped around the legs of build with strange palm tree foliage. Strange columns supported the erected buildings that sat on the terrain. The square poles, made from scales and wood, had gnarled roots plunged into the ground. These towering buildings reached several feet above the planet, their tiny windows emitting a warm, golden light.

The sporadic volcanic eruptions were my most significant concern, their unpredictable bursts of lava and ash filling the sky with a pungent, sulfuric smell. I had no desire to be launched into space by a volcanic eruption. They cast a fiery glow and billowed smoke across the transformed environment, setting the towers erected on the planet on fire. I focused on the inhabitants as they marched across the terrain toward a colossal, mountainous range.

Meanwhile, another mob of hybrid and golden Nephilim marched toward the regal Nephilim with a crown on his head. The Nephilim man dashed back and forth to avoid the lightsaber's rays.

"Fire again, and don't stop until Emperor Zerus dies," the lightsaber wielder warned.

A burst of cheers and alien words filled the air.

"Zerus knew the black hole was sucking both planets, yet he didn't say a word to us. Kill him, don't relent," the commander spoke.

A tall, cruel-faced man stood amidst chaos and leaped across the terrain. The crowd targeted him. Red fire bursts shot across the dense green forest.

The crowd cheered and screamed while they stomped in rhythm, chanting, "Kill Zerus, Kill Zerus!"

The giant Nephilim wielded glowing lightsabers and aimed towards a cave, where one Nephilim raced across the rugged terrain. They taunted the man with each strike, referring to him as Emperor Zerus. A red mist swirling around the portal filled me with dismay, and a palpable sense of danger hung in the atmosphere. My body, a mere speck in the chaotic scene, blended with its environment and remained hidden.

When I approached the golden Nephilim, who had a blend of human traits, including impressive height and muscular physique, and faces from Greek mythology. I noticed a range of complexions. They were the mutated bird people who mated with the ancient Nephilim and became the dominant golden Nephilim.

Both men and women wore futuristic gold jumpsuits that hugged their figures, with lightsabers, boots, and otherworldly weapons.

In my vision, I watched and listened to the Nephilim's insurrection. The garbage stench and planetary heat grew fierce as scarlet and yellow fire burst forth from the red volcanic dirt.

"Enough," I uttered aloud, but nothing happened. The vivid imagery in my mind didn't halt, only to find myself trapped within an alien realm. I needed to escape the violent environment, which caused anxiety. I blinked and clenched my fists, yet trapped in my vision. In an earlier portal experience, when I articulated the phrase *'Enough,'* the portal ceased its action and disappeared. But today, nothing transpired. The spiral electrical force drifted me above the Nephilim without being noticed in the mountainous cave.

Their footsteps echoed across the land as the giants approached the cavern entrance, from which Emperor Zerus escaped, surrounded by lush dwarf palm trees.

Tall, Golden Nephilim crouched near the cavern entryway with torches and atomic weapons, ready to defend themselves.

Their conversations captivated me, and I grasped the dire plight of Zarzu Genesis with each word. A cataclysmic black hole threatened to devour everything in its path. Their Ruler, Zerus, an oppressive dictator who ruled for centuries with his iron fist, ignored the manifestations of the looming black hole. The commander's voice turned venomous as he spoke again.

"Zerus, the treacherous scoundrel, agreed to find another home after my persistent begging. We will perish within days. Those hybrid Nephilim told Zerus our plans to kill him, so they must die first, then Zerus. Now hurry to the mountain."

The commander's conversation with his people scared me as I lived their plight in the spiral. Zarzu's extinction was due in days. Midnight approached and announced its entrance when a sizeable gold-colored Big Ben clock tower clanged on the mountain. The clock chimed as the angry crowd grew more prominent around the cave.

"Zerus thinks he owes us after he and Lucifer placed us on Zarzu.

Well, he doesn't owe us." Another yellowish Nephilim spoke aloud as they marched.

I discovered that the delicate ecosystem of Zarzu Genesis crumbled because of the immense gravitational pull of a nearby black hole.

With their advanced technology, the Nephilim could travel to Earth, located 300 light-years away, within minutes, overcoming the typical limitations of vast distances. I learned that their futuristic holographic bracelets granted them the extraordinary ability to journey through wormholes, defying the boundaries of space and time. The sapphire gold bracelets were stunning, thanks to the unusual twirling sapphire ball incorporated into their design.

After the survival of the ancient Earth flood, the Nephilim fled and formed an unexplored species by crossbreeding with extraterrestrials from Zarzu Genesis.

I eavesdropped on the discussions of the early beings making their way toward the monarch's grand palace, uncovering news of a society of Nephilim living on the two neighboring planets.

The Nephilim and the winged beings had offspring, causing the birds to lose their colorful feathers and become stunning golden creatures. These celestial birds were at risk of extinction as they transformed into mighty golden giants. As they marched toward the ridge, they shared unbelievable stories of their ancestry. They had to endure the massacre of the ancient giants and their relentless act to erase them from history.

"Do you remember when volcanoes were dormant for thousands of years? In the past five years, eruptions intensified, shaking the planet and darkening the atmosphere with gases. Our twin suns hide beneath thick clouds at night and become even hotter during the day." One Nephilim spoke while they trekked toward the mountain range.

Knowing the Nephilim's existence flooded my memory as the Holy Spirit dispersed Biblical data into my brain.

Bible stories depicting Nephilim existed before the great flood, as stated in *Genesis 6:4*: *"The Nephilim were on the earth in those days—and also afterward."*

Watching inhabitants approach the ridge, I felt a deepening sense of agony. The giant aliens spoke against their ruler, Zerus, and how he oppressed them. They claimed he was withholding information from his people, even as their planet was dying. The giants were rebelling, and their accusations echoed through the crowd. The citizens, angry and afraid, joined in their chant: "Slaughter, treasonous Zerus! Kill Zerus!"

UPON MY ARRIVAL at the cave's entrance, a majestic sight awaited me —four ebony angels kept guard. Their imposing aura and stance made me hesitate. Despite knowing they couldn't see me, I stopped moving.

These angels exuded an unprecedented air of menace. The angel I met years ago radiated light and was awe-inspiring, while these dark angels reeked of sulfur mixed with the earthy scent of the sphere.

Their sheer size and aggression filled me with dread, and I shuddered while observing their conflict with the inhabitants. Three colossal sable angels apprehended ten rebels who appeared to be leaders, brandishing their lightsabers at Zerus. The angels snatched and bound the rebels but not without a bloody fight, carried them away, and then vanished in mid-air.

Emperor Zerus held court in a secret cave, its entrance concealed by a magnificent waterfall that created a constant roar in the mountainous range of Zarzu.

A magical force propelled me to move faster and closer to the cavern. I came upon a group of sinister beasts. Enormous sequoia trees obscured my view, but I sailed closer to get a better aerial perspective.

The Nephilim's essence exhibited a gold shimmer, scaly exterior accompanied by elongated dragon tails and intense crimson eyeballs that burned with fire. I believed they were the protectors of the mountain where Emperor Zerus lived. In addition, I gathered that a civil war broke out against those who opposed Zerus and the people whom Zerus and his lies duped. The dragons flew around the mountain, but when they saw the hybrid and gold Nephilim rabble, they signaled a screech and blew fire at the mob.

As the Nephilim beings approached the cave entrance, they emitted shrill screeches and haunting howls. The Nephilim aimed their atomic lightsabers at the dark dragon beasts, firing as they came, yet missing the creatures because they darted back and forth to avoid the blasts.

I drifted over the terrain, viewing the disorder. A massive Cyclops emerged and raised his hands toward the heavens. I thought the Cyclops was mythological, but to my amazement, several beasts from the Bible were indeed real.

Now, fear clutched me. The sound of fire bolts whizzing through the air, reminiscent of falling stars, filled the land as the bolts slaughtered the unsuspecting residents. The lightning left a gaping six-foot-deep hole in the charred black dirt.

A putrid stench of death lingered. The fallen Nephilim's essence disappeared, leaving behind only a faint memory. Many gold Nephilim fell on flaming balls of fire, collapsed near an active volcano, and perished. Their burned bodies lie on the hot lava.

The size of the creatures, ranging from seven to twelve feet, stunned me. Their height surprised me because I didn't remember it. Throughout the night, aliens left a trail of dead bodies on the red lava, creating a tragic scene. In a bone-chilling display, the Nephilim formed a line and began stomping on the bodies of the fallen.

The Nephilim's spiked heavy boots left a pathway of destruction, crushing their fallen companions into blackened ashes as their stomping transformed their lifeblood into a speck of powdery red dirt. As I observed what signified an ancient funeral, I remembered reading ancient texts where creatures stomped on the dead to hurry the spirit to the underworld.

The relentless screams and cries filled the air, heightening the oppressive atmosphere. The lingering noise of stomping feet added an eerie undertone. Yelps and howls pierced the dense, moist haze, where a shrill bird call ended the ancient funeral service on planet Zarzu Genesis.

The Nephilim moaned and cried; a red mist of dirt from the volcano blasted into the atmosphere, and the funeral service ended.

They bowed, and then many Nephilim swirled and sprinted toward the cave.

"Stay back!" howled the fierce angels. Raven twelve-foot angels extended their wings and covered the cave where Zerus administered his authority. The brilliant gold light blinded the crowd, but the enraged residents continued to chant and advance.

"Kill Zerus! Kill Zerus!" The chanting resounded across the planet.

So I entered the hidden cave. The grand royal cavern of Emperor Zerus gleamed with stunning brilliance, leaving me breathless. Its grandeur blanketed the chamber hall leading to the emperor's throne. Immense photon lights beamed their radiance upon a sheltered canopy of overgrown foliage.

The cavern's ceiling boasted an array of extraordinary stalactite figurines, each more impressive than the next. At the very end, massive stalactites came together to create a chair made of pure gold. Upon entering the chamber, I couldn't help but gawk at the opulent gold chandelier hanging from the ceiling, the sumptuous rugs that adorned the floor, and the intricate wall carvings that paid homage to the emperors of old.

Zerus wore a gold embroidered regal robe and sat in a massive chair. He was silent. He clasped his hands before him until his military appeared.

Zerus activated the pulsating blue light on his delicate gold bracelet with a sapphire stone when he pushed it, but it appeared to malfunction and stopped working. Frustration must have overcome Zerus as he banged his right arm on the throne. I overheard his hiss, and then he used an unfamiliar language.

I drew nearer, straining my ears to capture even the slightest sound of his gruff, loud voice. Zerus spoke my name to a man in military attire with many emblems on his right chest, whom I recognized as an armed officer. Yes, I remember him. We worked on a joint moon pod project for NASA—the same commander who gave me misery daily. He displayed his lack of care for me through his temperament, refusal to help, and the sharp edge to his voice.

"Commander, Carmen Northrop can restore the hologram bracelet."

What? I can't believe this. A shiver ran through my body as tiny droplets of sweat appeared on my skin. I can't restore an ancient relic from Zarzu. My ability lies in decoding ancient hieroglyphics, Hebrew pictographs, and holographic holograms, where I delve into their intricate symbols and meanings. Besides, I spent my time restoring the holographic program codes for NASA on the ISS satellite. Zerus now believes I can fix everything because I repaired their broken transmitter. It could last weeks or even months. I'll be in big trouble if I don't restore his device. Now I understood why my dream took me to Zarzu Genesis. As they continued their conversation, I listened with keen interest.

"We monitored her when she coded complex algorithms with her teammates three years ago. She used ancient Hebrew symbols to repair our cracked transport device. We will give her a timeline for completion, and she will repair the ornament since we no longer have the resources on our dying planet."

Me? Did they want me? I stared as Zerus removed the artifact, which shrank before me. The moment the bracelet touched his skin, it grew larger and clasped around his wrist. What a remarkable find, a magical relic that could adjust its size for anyone who wore it.

The officer tapped on a holographic device attached to his arm. With a series of buttons pressed on his wrist, the commander spun around to face Zerus.

"Emperor, do you trust her with that ancient bracelet?"

"Yes, without a doubt. Carmen Northrop's data content affirmed that she has unique gifts; we could clone and kill her. Our ultimate purpose is to launch a permanent existence on Earth." A growl rumbled from his throat as he responded to the commander.

"Transform Earth into our new dwelling. Rid the planet of humans and force them to serve us where we wield our government. Assemble the golden Nephilim and make sure they are ready for their departure to Earth, leaving the weak Nephilim behind to wallow in their complaints."

I found myself frozen in place, my hands gripping my mouth. Kill humans! No, with every muscle in my frame, they will die. I heard my internal voice declare.

A slanted grin crept across his wrinkled face, and a shiver rushed throughout my body. Zerus's teeth were reminiscent of alligator teeth. He joined his hands, and, as if by magic, more soldiers manifested before me. The ethereal blue mist hid my form from their view.

I noticed intricate details of the Nephilim soldiers and Zerus. The headgear displayed weapons, and I surmised an upcoming attack on the horizon. What essential weapons did earthlings need against an onslaught from the Nephilim? Our armaments were no match for the advanced technology wielded by the Nephilim. My mission was to define and locate their weak spot and deliver crucial data to the ISS team. If they attacked, the bracelet could be the key. Questions plagued my psyche.

I heard Zerus grunt orders. "Goldens, unite to invade the blue planet. We must catch the wormhole before it closes."

The dictator sprinted toward a transparent, circular pod at the cave's rear, where he entered and vanished. As I glided nearer to the capsule, I paused and marveled at the incredible scene unfolding.

A majestic blue-gold mother ship rose from beneath the planet's surface and drifted before the spectators as if casting a spell. I gasped at the sight. A furious mob stormed through the cavern. Even though I was gripping my fists and preparing to flee, I couldn't.

As a result, a heavenly angel stood next to me, and his vibrant glow covered me. White light covered me, and to my relief, it emitted compassionate, joyful, loving, and peaceful warmth. Within seconds, I realized why. While floating, a divine angel protected me and guided me into the spaceship.

My frame disappeared and then appeared again on the deck of the mother ship. A brilliant light appeared on the ship's bridge, and a massive gold angel with two demonic black angels accompanied him. The gold angel spoke to Zerus, then withdrew with his entourage. I couldn't understand what the angel said. But it stirred booming laughter from Zerus.

The emperor pressed a button on the bridge console, and I watched a launch pad thrust upward from the massive cave and expand. With my body thrust outside the mother ship, I floated in the vast space. My senses heightened as I muttered a prayer while I watched to see what Zerus might do.

Next, another enormous blue-gold starship lifted from the musty cavern. Zerus was the culprit. I saw him on the command deck. His ship hovered and disappeared. The Nephilim on the planet froze—then continued the savage blood song.

"Kill Zerus! Kill Zerus!"

<hr>

IT TOOK A SECOND, but the portal closed as beams of light and mystic droplets fizzled in the air. I passed through the portal, and a sudden jolt rippled through my body. Then, my spirit reentered my sleeping soul. Everything came back into focus.

With a quick flutter of my eyelids, I extended my arms upward. Sweat beads formed on my skin, and my breathing rasped as I settled back into my body. Did the dream foretell the future? I heard Noah calling me.

"Carmen, are you okay? You were shouting the word *enough*."

Chapter Two

As my dream vanished, I found myself back in the realm of reality, nestled in the comfort of my favorite deck chair. Across from me, Noah sat at the elegant wrought iron outdoor table. I breathed fresh air after Zarzu's muggy, stale atmosphere was refreshing. The memory of my journey to that alien planet lingered, its purpose still a mystery. Noah's voice snapped me back to the present, and I couldn't help but sense a déjà vu.

For a moment, the oval balcony, the glassed-in lined patio, and the fragrant shrubs that brushed against the glass walls created a barrier, enclosing me in a world of tranquility. It gave me what I sought to live in the present and remember the earth's splendor and why we are on our planet. In this peaceful setting, I responded to Noah's query, focusing on his face.

"Carmen, are you okay?" He repeated.

"Noah, it was a chilling dream; the haunting whispers echoed in my ears, sending shivers throughout my spine." He seized my hand, turned it over, and kissed my jittery palm. While Noah caressed my arm and hands, Zerus' words still tormented me. The terror of my dream tapped into my internal weakness of fear. Noah's prolonged grip on my hand only heightened my anxiety. I glanced up from examining my palms and saw his head tilted. After he released my hands, he stood up and moved behind me. With precision, his hands pressed into my shoulders, kneading away the tension in my muscles.

"Are you sure you're fine? His concern was visible when he crouched, and I saw his eyes teeming with tears."

"Sweetheart, your hands are clammy. Why are you crying? I'm worried and love you so much. If you need me, I'm here to help you," he stated, straightening and leaning over me. My body quivered, but he gripped my hands, his touch reassuring. "Carmen, whatever terrifies you is gone. Remember, it was a dream, not reality. I'm here with you and won't let anyone harm you."

With a tear rolling across my cheek, I realized he had no clue what I had experienced. I was alone in my fear.

"Honey, I need water. Please pour me a glass." I grabbed a glass from the table, and he poured a carafe of iced water into it. The cool liquid slipped through my throat. The alien's uneasiness intensified, triggering a full-blown panic attack. My breaths became shallow and rapid, and a sense of restlessness washed over me. To control the panic attack, I pressed my head against the headrest and took several deep breaths. Heat burned inside my chest and moved to my extremities; then, I sensed a heaviness in my body. My attack subsided when I shut my eyelids and took slow, deep, deliberate breaths. Noah returned to his seat and reclined, yet his gaze remained fixed on me.

As Noah's eyebrows lifted in surprise and a soft exhale slipped from his lips, his visible worry intensified. His subdued demeanor and tense posture fueled a growing unease inside of me.

Noah started tapping on his tablet again in a steady rhythm. As I leaned against the headrest, its soft cushioning cradled my head. Once again, those horrible alien creatures haunted my mind.

Aliens. I harbored a deep dislike for them. The relentless images of Nephilim hybrids crashing to the ground, their blood and gore splattering everywhere, etched into my mind. Zerus's menacing threat to conquer the earth had haunted me nonstop since I woke up from snoozing. Why did unspecified golden Nephilim appear human, and others were scalier and more reptilian, akin to Zerus? His claim that I could repair his broken hologram bracelet left me baffled and panicky.

What if I can't fix the bracelet? My mind is buzzing with betrayal. Once I had glimpsed into another realm of the Nephilim and comprehended their sinister intention, my innate ethereal abilities tormented me with a deep-seated fear.

The fleeting glimpse of extraterrestrials in the spiral wasn't just a figment of my imagination. It was a dire warning, filled with a sense of impending danger. Oh, my goodness! What if my dream came true? The imminent return of their presence cast a dark shadow over my existence.

The thought of aliens sent a surge of heat throughout my body. God help us! I must warn my colleagues and corroborate a plan of action on the aliens and bracelet's arrival. Then I remembered my teammates were unaware of my hidden metaphysical powers, which I had kept secret for years.

Noah broke into my pondering, calling my name. "Carmen, sweetie, before you were dozing, you shoved your hands forward as if warding off someone. Why were you fighting in your sleep?"

"I don't remember. I guess it was a reflex while I slept."

He studied me, his face tight, and he squinted. Then Noah focused on the waterfront. Thankfully, he didn't ask more questions. He knew I lied. I struggled to understand myself.

To reduce stress, I moved my laptop closer and entered the security codes for the ISS. After typing a few lines of code, my computer project was complete, and I felt a wave of success. The added program code ensured the satellite security program and AI connected with the International Space Station (ISS) central server.

Next, I shifted my laptop to the side of the table, and the irresistible scent of lasagna drifted from a bubbling casserole dish as it sat on the electric warmer built into the table. My stomach rumbled in anticipation. I could think more clearly after I ate. Our three triplet teenage boys were studying with friends at a neighbor's house three doors away, and I wished they were joining us. I ached to keep them close— my son's last month of high school, then on to college. The teens loved soccer and had planned to play at the university. My heart trembled at the thought of losing my sons, their lives intertwined with Hashem (GOD) and shielded from the corrupt world. Constant reminders from their extensive knowledge of Hebrew teachings made me understand the need to align my mind with Messiah Yeshua (Jesus).

A gust of wind brushed against my skin, and goosebumps dotted my naked arms. The sudden burst of air intensified and whooshed around the terrace. My musings ceased, and I shifted my focus to the present, taking in every detail around me. When the weather radar popped up, I glanced at my watch.

"Noah, the wind has increased speed, and I see rain on the radar in the forecast. Let's eat and enjoy dinner without the boys before the rain sends us inside the house."

He stopped typing. The intensity of his up-and-downward stare and licking his lips ignited a fiery passion within me. I stood and twirled in place. He tried to engage me with eye contact, but I avoided his sparkling orbs.

Despite my trembling hands and racing heart from encountering aliens, I resisted engaging in a romantic date with my husband, fearing their presence might linger. To evade the prospect, I escaped into the kitchen to fetch the other food dishes, which was my best solution. Still, the urge to interact with Noah remained sealed in my flesh. My lips pressed together in a smile when I strolled back to the deck. As I narrowed my eyelids and savored the taste of chocolate pudding on my upper lip, I glanced at Noah. I placed the dishes on the table. Springing up from his seat, he embraced me with a tender kiss, and without missing a beat, he helped me arrange our plates on the table.

A few minutes later, I presented plates filled with lasagna, a crisp salad, fine wine, and a decadent chocolate parfait for dessert. The tantalizing scent of the meal made my appetite soar.

"My dear Carmen, let us pray for our meal?"

"Yes, of course."

Our heads bowed, and we offered a prayer together. Afterward, Noah relaxed in his chair, enjoying his meal while tapping notes into his tablet. I emailed my detailed notes to the engineering team.

Amidst the distant thunder, joyful laughter echoed from the lake, where neighbors enjoyed the warmth and precious moments with their families. A dog barked against a backdrop of lapping water. The fresh scent of pine trees and lilacs, mingling with a faint aroma of cut grass, caused a slight stinging sensation in my nose.

I put aside my musings and glanced at Noah, scrolling on his tablet with a smirk curling his lips. His champagne-curly hair and amber eyes glistened under the patio lights.

A foreboding presence lurked nearby. I couldn't say I liked the times I could sense danger. But my senses became more acute when I sensed otherworldly energy. They penetrated every fiber of my being, creating a powerful sensation.

Then, a harsh grinding and banging sound echoed in the twilight.

"Get a grip," I spoke out loud.

"What? What was that sound?" Noah's head jerked up, and he tilted to acknowledge my outburst.

"Nothing, sweetie. I need to email Becky. Then I'll finish my dinner."

"Are you positive? That sound hurt my ears." He heard the commotion, confirming my accuracy.

I typed my last page of email notes to Becky, and the facts and figures were a welcome distraction until a loud explosion rocked our table.

"Okay, well, I'm done typing notes for the evening. The meal is delightful." He pushed his tablet away from him and took another bite.

"You go ahead."

"Noah, what in the world was that?"

Sweat beaded on his forehead. He raised his eyebrows in confusion and dread. "Sweetie, a hovercraft hit something. But I must admit, you are right. Something strange is happening above and near the waterfront. Look up, my love, and witness the vast expanse of the sky for yourself."

The sun sank below the horizon, brushing the sky in shades of red and gold. I paused, then texted and stared at the magnificent display in the heavens. Then, a crimson beam of light danced along the beachfront. Goosebumps popped up on my skin as fear filled my being.

"Noah, is that a laser pointing toward people on the beach? Yet, I don't see the vessel."

We both jumped up to stare at the ray pointing toward the lake. Since our home sat on stilts, I leaned over the patio edge for a better waterfront view. Our neighbors were scrambling toward their homes. Noah moved closer to the wall, grabbed his night vision goggles attached to his jumpsuit, and peered through the lens toward the lake. I focused on the waterfront and worried our teens were out by the Hoover Dam reservoir among their friends.

"Do you see any movement?" My nerves were on edge.

"Yes, Carmen, a laser circled the people, then disappeared. Dogs dashed towards the waves. It must have been the military police circling. That's the sound I heard. They're searching for someone."

Noah set the night goggles on the table, and we resumed our meal.

The lack of wind made me uneasy, as though the night air was holding its breath. I sighed and exhaled to calm my spirit. A gust of wind forced sheets of paper off the table, and they fell onto the ceramic tiles.

At last, a cool breeze arrived to relieve the oppressive heat. I hurried to email Becky, my supervisor, at P.J. Waxit and closed my laptop. As I dropped to my knees to scoop the papers off the tiles, people were screaming and running toward their homes.

"Noah, the beach! Let's text the triplets." I placed the papers inside my backpack, my pulse thumping. Desperation filled my voice as I spoke, a plea to God, hoping my dreams never become a reality. Zerus's voice resonated in my head as I swayed, the only sound I could hear. *'Kill humans!'*

"I will send a message in a minute!" He responded.

Sirens pierced the airspace. Several black oval-shaped police hovercrafts concealed their decals on the side of the vehicles and zoomed across the sky. Their sleek design reflected the moonlight. My heart raced after I glimpsed at the police vehicles.

Noah was taking too long. With a gentle tap on my purple wristwatch, I sent my message to the triplets. The subtle vibration notified me of the text sent, but the teens remained unresponsive. My heart fluttered in my chest.

"Noah, I'm going to reach out to the neighbor." I believe the network blocked my call. This position is a nightmare for me. How could this even happen? Noah positioned a few feet from me, watching the lake, but turned to acknowledge my hysterical murmurs.

"Sweetheart, our teens are in danger. I can sense it deep within my being. The neighbor's call went to voicemail. We spoke earlier this evening, so I know something is awry."

"Carmen, our sons will be alright. But keep reaching out to the neighbor," I nodded.

I shifted my focus to Noah's flushed face. In the twilight, a shimmering, multicolored flicker of lights materialized.

"Look, the military spotted something above in the heavens. I have a dreadful feeling something awful will happen." Were my dreams coming true and my revelations a premonition of things to come?

Peering over the brick wall, we watched the beach. Fear and excitement coursing through my veins caused my body to shake.

"Sweetie, don't say such things. Stay positive. Maybe it's nothing. If attacked, we have weapons to protect the country. Let's stay calm. Let the AI message report inform us of the facts, and then they will send a message to our hologram watches."

"You're right." He rose to his feet. He activated his black four-inch translucent hologram wristwatch by pressing his wristband. A hologram figure appeared, and he started a video.

"Noah, what are you doing?" My voice sounded squeaky.

"Carmen, whatever is on the beach, I need a video for documentation as a concerned citizen. Sweetheart, try to call the kids again."

Noah's decision to record a video instead of ensuring our safety and leaving me to contact our children confused me.

"Forget the video! We need to find the boys."

I wanted no more drama after my distressing vision.

"Carmen," he responded, "it's crucial that I document everything with photos and videos for the military police records."

"Noah, you don't work for the police. So why put yourself and your family in danger? Oh, never mind." I rolled my eyes and stepped back from the wall. Noah's behavior, influenced by his male hormones, sometimes irritates me as it jeopardizes our family's safety.

I pivoted and put my laptop in my backpack, disregarding Noah with a dismissive hand gesture. He needed to stop the video and take cover. Whatever the military was chasing might shoot ammunition, and I didn't want to die tonight. I prayed the boys realized the dangers, unlike their father.

"Okay, dear, but from the number of police vehicles zooming in the sky, they appear to have everything under control—except the dogs' barking has become excessive. "Noah stepped closer to me.

The thunderous sound of a sonic boom shattered the commotion. Shockwaves rippled through the atmosphere. Night birds fluttered, their screeching piercing the heavens. At once, we anchored our feet, our faces fixated on what lay above us.

From the sky above, the mother ship descended before us.

<hr>

"Hurry, Victor! Set coordinates for the blue planet. We must be there by sundown. Halgian, make sure the weapons are ready to fire. Before we attack their planet, let's see if they have upgraded to more advanced weapons. Shoot and overpower the International Space Station and other satellites. If they retaliate, then back away."

"Yes, Emperor Zerus. We see the pulsating wormhole entrance ahead."

Zerus's protruding orbs scanned the radar screen. The vast expanse of space was visible through the deck window as the mothership navigated the swirling currents of the wormhole.

An electromagnetic, gravitational force engulfed the vessel, overpowering the massive blue-gold starship. The wormhole's twisted spiral sent the ship tumbling and spinning, thrusting it into the depths of interstellar darkness with a thunderous boom. The mothership was at the mercy of the pulsating hole, hurtling through the void.

A calm silence surrounded them, enabling them to hear the rhythmic sound of their breaths and catch glimpses of distant planets flickering in the darkness.

No one spoke, and the Nephilim, a race of fallen angels, fixed their faces on the spiral galaxy they entered to claim as their own. They lost their supernatural power, children, and family in a war with celestial beings. Now, with the help of Lucifer, their former ally turned adversary, they could claim their inheritance.

As the mother ship's thrusters fell silent, a breathtaking transformation began. The colossal wingspan unfurled, unveiling three spiny legs, each as vast and towering as the Burj Khalifa in Dubai. The vessel launched six-winged tarantula legs protruding from the hull sides as the ship glided toward the spiral galaxy.

On a Wednesday evening in April, the crew beheld the bright blue world, which filled interstellar space with a profound calm. Below the mother ship frame, a dwarf craft the size of three eighteen-wheeler trucks hurtled downwards, its destination Earth.

AS THE ENORMOUS UFO vehicle entered their galaxy, Bill Shepherd pressed the red alert button on the console and summoned his teammates, Wally, Trish, and the other crew members. The sirens blared as the computer quad buzzed with chatter, and humanoid robot astronauts focused on the massive radar screen. Bill pivoted his chair, focused on the humanoids, and reviewed the pod. He detected excessive conversation among the humanoids and made a mental note to inform personnel.

Commander Marc Zacker's voice came through his headset, "Bill, I received your message."

"Commander, the wormhole ejected a colossal mother ship. They must have come from an unknown galaxy since my sensors detected frost on the spaceship's hull. Nephilim of three years ago were friendly. So, who are these guys? We launched our shields and notified the United Central Command (UCC) and NASA."

"Bill, I'm on my way to the bridge."

A red laser beam struck the space station hull and bumped it from orbit. The International Space Station (ISS) drifted toward a large media satellite. The exploding fireballs echoed through the air as they consumed everything in their path, including the two humanoid sleep pods. After the humanoid robots stabilized the station, they acted to put out the flames inside the pod. Bill observed the frantic action on the video screen and alerted his colleagues to help the humanoids evacuate staff if needed.

Emergency sirens filled the steel halls. Lasers attacked the ISS without mercy once more. Staff members scrambled from their living cabin pods as the halls filled with the acrid scent of smoke and flames danced along the walls. With urgency, astronauts and humanoids sprinted toward the evacuation stations and escape hatches.

The assault repeated. The mother ship fired multiple rounds at the ISS, knocking several media satellites near the ISS out of orbit. They caught fire, exploded, and hurtled toward Earth.

"Bill, what is the status of the vessel attacking us?" uttered Marc Zacker. Marc's subdued arrival startled the crew. Humanoids glanced at the door, then returned to their computer screens. Bill spun around, his face drenched in sweat, his eyes wild with desperation, searching for an escape route. He had to stop the assault, or the ISS could explode. Marc Zacker nodded at Bill and went to the console to watch the screen.

Bill pushed the distress button on the screen and sent a message to the advancing craft. "Who are you? Why are you attacking us?" Read the message.

"Bill, have you tried communicating with the alien ship?" Commander Zacker screamed. His legs spread apart as he staggered to keep his balance. Zacker's nostrils flared as he spat out his words and stood glaring out the panoramic window.

"Yes, sir, just now, and no response." His forehead became sweaty, his breaths multiplied, and his fingers applied pressure to the computer console.

"Bill, aim our lasers before they destroy our space station."

Commander Zacker shouted his orders as Bill focused on the console screen, entranced by the ever-changing data. With each step Marc Zacker took towards him, his grip on the console tightened, his body struggling to keep his balance as the ISS rocked back and forth.

"Sir, are you okay?" He peeked at the commander, swaying as the ISS rocked back and forth. "Sir, please sit or hang on to the guardrail."

The space platform sustained another direct assault as Bill struck the emergency evacuation button. His fright of the ISS plunging to Earth became a reality if they didn't take immediate action.

"Launch our atomic weapon. Hurry, we are moving out of orbit, and I need to control our position!" In frustration, Bill let out a sharp bark at the humanoid robot weapons staff, hoping to get a reaction as the ten humanoids depressed the atomic buttons.

"Hurry and fire those weapons," Bill screamed. He turned to Commander Zacker and noted his stony face, with fire in his eyes. Bill gritted his teeth and cursed. The air filled with tension and anticipation, signaling the start of the countdown before they unleashed their firepower on the mothership.

"Three, two, one, fire at the blasted ship!" Bill and Marc let out a scream.

The weapons on the ISS hull unleashed their fury, shooting rockets and fire in a powerful display of revenge.

"Commander Zacker, NASA control calling. We are attempting to pull you back into orbit. Use your firepower secret weapon, the NUC ray. Launch it now. We see the mothership, and the spaceship is enormous. Commander, hurry, fire now!"

Humanoid robots launched atomic weapons against the vessel; the ship vanished, but not before the craft sustained a direct hit.

"Where did they go?" Commander Marc Zacker flipped through the sonar screens. Sweat popped out on his brow, and his hand shook as he flipped through multiple radar screens.

"Commander, do we keep our shields active? The assailants used an obscure cloaking method." He scanned the screen, but the vessel didn't reappear.

"Yes, keep the shields active. The alien craft destroyed one media telescope and two sleep pods. Crew members should increase surveillance and fire weapons when they resurface. NASA was successful in pulling us back into orbit."

"Yes, Commander."

Zacker tapped his wristwatch and turned toward Bill.

"Excellent job. Evaluate the damage and report back in thirty minutes."

"Yes, Commander, over and out." Zacker left the bridge and walked into the smoky hall, where emergency sirens wailed.

Bill swiped the screen and noticed many damaged humanoid robots' sleep units.

He suited up and hurried out the bay door to locate Wally and Trish, his human astronaut buddies.

The smoke and metallic rubber aroma clogged the air ventilation network, making the air toxic.

Wally Gold, a colleague, was the head science officer. He pressed the hologram on his spacesuit band. Wally and Trish Berg, the ISS science and medical doctor, appeared.

"Hey, Trish and Wally, are you okay? I watched the live camera link. The humanoid pods are on fire, and the electronics are exploding. It will be twenty-four hours before we have electronics in the pods back to normal. I need help. Let's meet in the hall in two minutes. We will discuss the metrics later." He closed the hologram and stepped into the hall filled with smoke.

"Shut off the engines and cruise above the stratosphere."

Zerus's dissonant voice rang inside the cockpit. He maintained a regal stance as the ship neared Earth, and his piercing scowl never wavered. Nephilim arrived on Wednesday afternoon as the blazing sun was setting behind purple mountain crests.

Angular bolts of light sizzled and darted, and threatening dark clouds churned and intensified. The earthy smell of rain hung in the air. Zerus and his small crew of Golden Nephilim boarded a dwarf shuttle, entered the airspace, and sped toward Marsh Harbor, Colorado.

"I didn't expect retribution from humans. Their weapons have remained primitive since our arrival three years prior, but we're not here to war with them. Their atomic missiles are crude, and we will obliterate humans from the universe—" his guttural bass voice hesitated.

Zerus placed his arms across his massive chest and snorted. "Six thousand years. We have waited to avenge against Satan and humans."

"Victor, did we sustain a blow? We will force earthlings to pay for our demise and use Carmen Northrop as our decoy. We will land near her home."

"Emperor, repairs implemented, and we're ready."

"Excellent." Zerus leaned forward, glared at the topography, and spotted their landing site.

"Emperor Zerus, our sonar, detected many cyclones near the lake. Should the mission advance?"

Zerus's protruding gold eyes scanned the mountainous terrain, taking in every detail.

"Yes! Plunge now!" They ventured into a vast expanse of the Hoover Dam reservoir.

He angled his right arm and sensed his sapphire bracelet vibrating and emitting a soft hum. His bushy, dense eyebrows lifted in surprise. He thought the bracelet wasn't working. When he saw the signal recipient, he let out a menacing growl and snorted in disapproval.

"Men, Master Lucifer is observing. I want everyone ready. No missteps; otherwise, we will die as a species." He strode back and forth across the platform, his arms linked behind him.

Zerus ignored the violent weather and growled orders while he watched various radar screens. "Keep going to the meeting spot, Marsh Harbor. Even though this planet is delicate, our spaceship can withstand its harsh storms. Glide towards the city right away," he directed Victor, his commander, pressing his fingers onto a suspended transparent screen.

The atmosphere manifested danger when a twin whirlwind pulverized the land along a diagonal route toward Marsh Harbor. First, the tornado uprooted trees and wrapped them into compact knots and splinters before casting them on the land. The dual tornadoes ravaged the ground near the reservoir for fifteen minutes, leaving devastation in its wake. Debris scattered over a two-mile radius, yet residents' homes survived the storm near Marsh Harbor.

Golden Nephilim dwarf shuttles hovered over the Hoover Dam and waited for Zerus's signal. With a signal from Zerus, the lasers unleash a barrage of energy, striking the dam with intense force.

"Direct the laser towards people on the river banks, capturing everything in its path. We can use humans to populate our species." Zerus spoke as he pivoted and faced his crew on the hologram screen.

Light from the spaceship shot downward toward the beach and scanned the waterfront as it grabbed individuals, swooping them into the open bay of the vessel. As the screams and cries pierced the stillness, their echoes traveled into darkness and silence.

"Run towards your homes at once. The red light is capturing individuals," with a mournful urgency, those near the peak called out to the frantic individuals dashing towards the mound where their houses stood. Their eyes filled with sorrowful dread.

"Hurry and save yourselves," individuals scrambling to regain their balance. People's hands flailing in the air, bodies injured, while they grasp for support from the sand that anchored them to the ground.

"Oh no! Someone, help us! The aliens are snatching people; protect yourselves and your loved ones."

The beach muffled, with only gentle waves breaking the silence. Dogs howled in the distance.

The spacecraft emitted three red flashes of light, prompting Nephilim hovering in the air to descend into the river and await human transportation. Nephilim steered toward Marsh Harbor; shuttles glided through the air, leaving no trace of their presence because they cloaked the vessel.

Zerus activates a button on his console. His menacing razor-blade teeth glint as his lips widen, and he puffs out his chest. Zerus protects his chest with a flowing black coat embellished with symbols of military rank. Green scales cover his body, and sturdy, dark boots protect his robust legs. The muscles beneath his coat are well-defined, high-lighting his physical power. His untamed ebony hair cascades over his shoulders, framing his countenance. His bulging, fierce eyeballs and prominent nose give him a distinctive look reminiscent of a cross between a bird and a dragon.

As sirens blared, AI's voice began counting, "Three, two, one," before engaging the missiles.

As the blackened sky crackled with lightning, a dwarf spacecraft emerged from beneath the water's surface, its laser blazing as it targeted the dam. Without warning, the ground rumbled and split apart, unleashing a surge of water that crashed into the reservoir with incred-ible speed and strength.

The dam exploded, sending a gush of water hurling toward Marsh Harbor with the speed of a locomotor, flattening everything in its path: trees, people, homes, animals, and businesses. The deadly route of water wiped out Marsh Harbor, leaving the town under twelve feet of water.

"Keep firing until it crushes," Zerus shrieked out his orders.

Chapter Three

Cyrus Rashid Melekh, a man of success and power, listened to his inner voice groan: *"Beware of heartache if you expose your true feelings."*

His inner struggle extended beyond mere thoughts. A fierce battle raged inside him, a storm of emotions that left him unsure of the darkness creeping into his very being. Night after night, an evil spirit plagued his dreams, leaving him with dread upon waking.

The utterance disturbed his inner being. Dark, menacing clouds engulfed his body. He strained to see through the fog when a woman's shadow, a mere whisper of a figure, lingered in the distance—his nap interrupted by the swaying motion of the ship. But he wondered what the vision meant. The woman was more than stunning; she exuded a mysterious allure that drew him toward her hidden secrets. Her breathtaking grace enraptured him with romantic thoughts. His breath came in ragged bursts as he panted, causing him to waver and sway in his seat. He banished the dream from his thoughts.

Melekh, an oil tycoon, despised Monday mornings; a snarl curled his lips. After marathon meetings in April with investors, Melekh relished May's sultry weather. As the jetted plane prepared to land, he leaned forward and righted his cabin seat. As he tried to focus, the sound of messages dinging pulled him from his thoughts. These were not just any messages but urgent updates on the status of his oil rigs and the latest market trends, a constant reminder of the high stakes of his business.

He aimed the remote at the 3D visual holographic screen hanging in front of him. The weather report flashed another sweltering May morning. The temperature was 37 degrees Celsius at 7:00 a.m. "Good Morning from Dubai." The meteorologist spoke.

The screen disappeared as he kept pushing the button on the armrest. With each minute, his stomach grew louder because of his forgotten dinner. A cup of coffee became a solution to his cravings. He signaled the humanoid, and the fresh aroma of brewed coffee soon filled the air.

He texted Abu Satanilla to meet him on the landing pad to look at the diagrams for his new international building. His annoyance swelled with each passing second of unanswered ringing in his ear, a growing knot of frustration and simmering conflict.

The sneaky scoundrel. He pondered.

Melekh's overt disdain for Abu simmered, a resentment poised to overflow. He loathed Abu's deceptive methods but acknowledged his value in navigating their country's traditional customs. Abu's astute tactics and skill were profitable to the company. Even with his cunning maneuvers, the tension among them persisted. Abu had swindled money from him in a stock exchange transaction ten years ago, and Melekh never forgot the two million dollars Abu stole and then lied to cover his tracks with the investor.

Melekh peered out the window, ogling futuristic flying vehicles as they zipped through Dubai's congested skyway, creating a mesmerizing sight. As his sleek black spaceship dogged and darted toward his new headquarters, the Persian Gulf shimmered in the morning sunlight.

The spacecraft's engines generated a symphony of echoes as they weaved through the urban landscape, bouncing off the spiral, steelpeaked buildings. With its circular helipad adorned with gleaming glass walls, the new P.J. Waxit headquarters received Melekh's jetted space vehicle. A gentle whirring sound reverberated as the landing gear touched the pad.

The lanky humanoids, dressed in blue and black bodysuits with knee-length black boots, approached the vessel with purposeful steps to clean, refuel, and unload luggage. They chatted with each other with a robotic tonal sound.

Melekh's demanding baritone voice resonated around the cabin while he returned messages. Two humanoid staff scrambled to finish their jobs, heard his voice, stopped, angled their heads, jerked, and slipped out the exit.

A ringing tone echoed. Melekh touched the screen, and a man appeared. He kept his face focused on his employee. He placed his coffee in the cupholder.

"Are you sure the idiots detonated my refiner?"

"Yes, sir. Flames and smoke billow through the atmosphere. Accident personnel helped to recover the dead. The men betrayed your contracts, knowing your power to kill."

Abu's dark raven orbs held a world of secrets, complementing his curly, short black hair and tawny smooth skin. Abu stood at an impressive six feet four inches, displaying a strong and muscular physique. His deep, chiseled face resembled that of a sheik. His attire was diverse, but he wore a white thawb robe, white slacks, and a turban, which gave his outfit a touch of cultural sophistication. Because Abu and Melekh were of Arab culture, so he kept him employed even though he despised him.

The hologram screen chimed as it appeared on the net. Sweat formed on his forehead; he clinched his fist and grabbed a moist towel from the tray on the counter. His eyebrows narrowed, and his anxious body tensed; his breathing increased while he scrutinized the refinery disintegrate.

After a few minutes of viewing the screen, the refiner sank into the Indian Ocean—*a calculated mistake to trust and give them authority to run my oil refineries.* I'll handle those devilish rogue men.

"Abu, it's my fault the refiner bombed. Those fools wanted more money after I outwitted them. So, they paid me back with bloodshed.

Send humanoids to their job location and blast the entire development. I'll never put my companies in jeopardy again."

Melekh's face glowed crimson under his smooth, golden skin. He thrust his rigid frame against the posh cabin seat, his countenance stern as he scrutinized his refineries.

"Mr. Melekh, their skyscraper employs four thousand people, and it's before lunch hour. Thousands will perish. Are you positive?"

"Yes, do it now before I change my mind. Blow up the—building!"

After touching his smartwatch to end the call, Melekh leaned his shoulder-length raven locks against the headrest. He closed his blood-shot gold eyeballs to relax. A deep, mournful sigh escaped his mouth. *'Never do business with pirates. Those scandalous dogs from the New World Alliance (NWA) deceived me with their vile dealings. Whatever happens to them, they deserve death.'*

Without warning, an emergency alert darted across the hologram flat screen.

A reporter watched a spacecraft launch near burning refiners and head north. Within seconds, another message flashed on the panel.

"At 9:00 a.m. in Moscow, alien beings blasted the complex owned by oil tycoons. Then, a large spaceship hurled a shower of fireballs, demolishing the construction."

He took another sip of his coffee. Melekh's lips glided over his perfect white teeth. He turned his attention to the humanoid and glanced at the pleasant attendant, waiting to grab his suitcase. Her almond eyes and thin body caught his attention as she leaned closer to his frame.

He grabbed the beverage from the armrest and leaned closer to her, his lip curled with a frown.

"Move back!" he shrieked. He placed his cup in the cupholder. His eyebrows lowered as he spat out his words. The humanoid had touched and caressed his thigh when his notebook fell from the upright table. The humanoid robot stooped and placed the notebook on the armrest. Seeing the humanoid robot's coy smile gave him a distinct signal of the robot's intention.

"Place my bags near the exit. My driver is waiting to collect them."

He leaned closer to her face. "If you try to seduce me again—I will destroy you." His jaw tightened and jutted forward.

The shaken humanoid bolted and tripped when she headed toward the exit after his steely gaze caused her to shake and bow.

His timepiece chimed.

"Hello!" He uttered. He watched the holographic screen materialize on the ship, and Abu's complete form stood beside him.

"Boss, Sophia McFadden, Jon Weinberg, and Nick Borge arrived in Jerusalem from Romala, Texas, an hour ago. A pickup by a militant coalition of Jews assisted them, and they fled to the underground caverns. The troublesome Jewish Coalition once again has outwitted us. Do you want us to find them?"

"No, death is coming soon to the pesky group of troublemakers. Leave them alone. We have more pressing issues. But watch them and that Jewish Coalition. Please forward a note to Noah Northrop's supervisors, Bart Hall and Martin, and make sure he signs the alien agreement. If he doesn't put pen to paper, we should fire him on the spot."

Melekh devised a plan for Sophia, Jon, and Nick, the unsuspecting trio. He waited for the perfect moment to strike and end their lives. Their discovery of his nefarious scheme to taint the water along the United States Gulf Coast only fueled his detestation for them.

He had an insatiable hunger for the ornament Sophia had discovered. The bracelet held a power far beyond its money-worth—it could change the entire planet. Upon studying his team's security report, he learned that whoever donned the bracelet possessed supernatural abilities that could allow them to rule the whole universe.

The Saudis stole the artifact from the Egyptians, and it disappeared without a trace. Suppose he wore the bracelet, world domination at his fingertips. A sinister laugh escaped his lips as he crossed his arms, imagining a world under his control. Frightened, people bowed to him as if he were a king. *The power to control the world? What an incredible idea!*

"Dispatch a holographic projection to Qadira to meet the investors and schedule Martin this week in Dubai. Abu, we need to meet with the Golden Nephilim before we leave. Their complaint revolves around a malfunctioning transport bracelet that requires immediate repair. I hate those vile creatures, but they will serve my kingdom."

He grinned as he planned his next move to gather more power from the world's citizens.

My attention now fastened on the enormity of the spaceship, and a surge of sudden panic overtook me as soon as I laid my sight on the mothership. The shimmering pale blue light reflecting from its surface captivated my gaze. Memories of my ethereal journey to Zarzu Genesis flooded my mind, intensifying my dread.

Our mouths agape, our heads tipped skyward, eyelids wide with terror; we watched the vessel inch closer, its ominous presence casting a shadow over us. My backpack slipped from my right arm and landed with a heavy clunk on the table.

While Noah continued his meshuga antics with the video, I savored a mouthful of lasagna. It slipped my mind that I had silverware in my hand when the spaceship arrived.

My fork slipped from my fingers and clunked onto the plate. The thought of the Nephilim alien's return paralyzed me with fear. A morsel of food stuck in my throat when I attempted to swallow a bite of lasagna. I reached across the table and gripped the water glass, praying it could oust the food in my throat. Instead, I ended up coughing and gasping for air. The glass slipped, but I caught it before it smashed on the table as water streamed over the side. Noah's gray jumpsuit and black rubber ankle boots became soaked as water spilled onto them.

Noah turned and gripped me so fast that his wrought-iron chair toppled. "Carmen, honey, are you okay?" His tan, once relaxed face twisted with panic; his eyes enlarged as he hunched forward, staring me in the face, his breath inches from my lips. He smacked my back and didn't miss a beat until I stopped coughing.

I waved my hand to signal him to stop. "I'm better, and thank you."

A dimpled grin graced his handsome face as he moved back and stooped to retrieve the chair, but he remained upright.

"Sweetheart, it's time to go inside now. We are in danger." My weak voice spoke. "We need to send a live stream to the boys. I'm sure people in the neighborhood are aware of the commotion. I'm concerned. They might walk near the lake with their friends. My inner voice is warning me of a threat. We sent them several messages but haven't heard from them."

"Okay, honey. I'm signaling the teens now. I'm sure they're fine." He stopped the live stream video on his wristwatch, touched his wristband with his fingers, typed a brief message, and then turned to show me their fast response.

'We're okay and gaming,' came their response.

With one swift movement, I rose from my chair and gathered the flatware, cups, and glasses into a neat stack. Then, I secured my laptop in the backpack on my shoulder. I kept my focus on the river. My trembling fingers tapped my wristband and sent a message to the triplets, telling them to stay put until morning.

The enormous mothership descended into the spinning waters with a resounding boom and a splash, causing waves to break along the shoreline. The noise gave me goosebumps, and my auburn curls stretched into a peacock's extravagant display. As I stood at the table staring at Noah, I felt the electromagnetic waves pulsing through the air. I backed away from the table.

Oh no, not now. My heart pounded against my chest. Please go away. My fingers smoothed back my hair into a ponytail as I yanked a scrunchie off my right arm. I beheld the intensity of the electrical energy gripping my being, leaving me vulnerable so Noah could see my hair. The supernatural occurrence was brief and, fortunately, didn't last long. My body tingled with metaphysical electricity.

Noah studied the lake, oblivious to the faint, misty blue glow surrounding me. Thank god. The sight of my unseen mist left me bewildered and unsettled. For a fleeting moment, a ghostly mist hovered around me. Noah knew my secret, but hated to see it. His low-pitched voice broke my thoughts.

"Honey, let me get one more video." He stepped back next to me, turned, and moved closer. He locked onto my emerald eyeballs as he bent to cuddle my face, his touch brushing back a lock of curly hair.

"Sweetie, you are stunning, and I love you, but your ponytail strands are standing straight up toward the sky." When he saw my hair, he looked dazed, his mouth ajar. His spears were enormous as he approached to get a closer view. Then his fingers grazed my unruly plume of hair.

"Are you okay? Carmen, go inside so you don't get struck by lightning if you stay on the balcony. I want nothing to happen to you." His voice deepened as he drew inches from my face.

"Yes, I'm okay." I pushed him away, worried by his response. "Noah, no more videos, please. It's unpredictable how those creatures will react. We must go now! You can stay, but I'm going inside the house. One day, your curiosity will get you killed."

A lightning bolt descended before I uttered the last word, and the blue halo of light surrounded me.

Oh, no, he saw. Now, how was I going to explain? He settled mere inches from me, and I felt the jolt from the bolt akin to a needle prick. It didn't strike Noah.

"Carmen!" he screamed. "Did you get hit by the bolt? Are you alright? That was weird. I saw the blue light from the bolt." With wide, bulging eyes, he struggled to breathe, and his hands moved with speed over his clothing. Then he reached out and touched me.

"Yes, love. I'm fine."

"Let's call the doctor now and ensure you're fine."

"No. I'm fine—no physical effect from the bolt."

With a sigh, he raised his shoulders and pursed his lips before touching his wristwatch to stream the waterfront again.

Whew, that was close. I'm glad Noah thought the blue mist was from the lightning. I leaned forward and gripped the stacked stoneware.

"Noah, please stop. I'm heading indoors." Noah ignored me and filmed the spaceship.

But as I darted towards the kitchen door, the sudden roar of water gushing from the lake made me spin around toward the sound.

Oh, no! The gold-blue mother ship burst from the reservoir. Its spiky spider legs expanded, casting a foreboding presence on the lake. Within seconds, a miniature dwarf spaceship emerged out of nowhere and joined the mothership.

A dwarf spaceship slipped inside an open portal of the mothership as a light beam dragged two police vehicles inside the craft. The horrific display scared me to my core.

"Noah, what the heck is happening?"

His baritone voice became higher in pitch. His arm shook as he continued his quest to livestream the scene.

A voice uttered my name through the pine trees. "Carmen Northrop." I broke out in a sweat. What prompted them to return? What did they want?

My shaky body gathered strength, and I bolted across the threshold as tableware crashed to the floor and into the sink. I didn't care; the kitchen floor was a mess. Stopping in my tracks, I heaved deep breaths and placed my backpack on the counter. Then, I whirled around to check on Noah.

To my amazement, Noah turned his attention toward the house. I watched him from the glass-to-floor window while he followed the red laser browse through the outside wall on the balcony. Motionless, Noah remained rooted to the spot, waiting for the beam to cease its motion. The beam of light halted.

I stared in horror as the crimson ray lowered onto the shoreline. A beam snatched people and animals from the river's edge. It zigzagged along the ground and approached our white rectangular pedestal home.

Screams, cries, and canine barking echoed in the twilight, and the faint smell of decaying blood hung heavy in the air. I opened my mouth and tried to scream Noah's name. My lips moved, but no sound came out. I froze in place at the door. Another crimson laser appeared on the deck. It etched closer to Noah. I wept as he lost his balance and collided with a chair. With a shot of energy, Noah jumped and sprinted towards the door. The outline of the laser was inches from his feet when he screamed, "Carmen! They're back."

Chapter Four

Shocked, I screamed aloud. A sense of dread and panic engulfed me as Noah announced the terrifying reappearance of the Nephilim.

Why did they return? Except to capture us and turn our planet into a garbage dump? My recollection of my vision swirled in my head, and I swayed from the thought of their return. I shook my head and remembered the urgency to leave the patio.

My poor husband fell with a loud thud and crashed through the kitchen door. I heard him shriek in pain as he landed on his face, his head hitting the ground with a smack. I grabbed the door handle and slammed the tempered glass door behind him. As I retreated from the door, warm air rushed into my face. Our patio furniture flew as a powerful gust of wind whooshed by, and a red laser beam crept toward the door before halting at the entrance.

I glanced at Noah sitting upright on the floor. His face lost color, leaving behind a pale and lifeless complexion. My jaw dropped in amazement as a ray of light sucked everything shrouded in the light into the spaceship. The familiar stench of rotting garbage from Zarzu lingered in the entire house from the open kitchen window, confirming Nephilim aliens had arrived.

"Carmen, Carmen Northrop." I wondered who called my name. I

stood fastened to the floor, unable to move a muscle. *Did my mind trick me?* Then I heard my name once more. A deep, raspy voice left no question it belonged to Zerus. I searched for any sign of Zerus's manifestation. Instead, the deafening silence engulfed us, creating a cocoon of stillness.

I pivoted to face Noah, still on the ceramic tiles, his legs stretched wide with no expression. Overwhelmed with concern for him, I sank to my knees to inspect the gash on his forehead. As the blood trickled over his face, I reached up to grab the kitchen towel to dab the blood. As he turned, his eyes met mine, conveying his profound emotions. Without hesitation, he wrapped his arms around me in a comforting embrace. I could sense his terror as the laser, mere inches away, shook him to his very core.

Without notice, my wristband buzzed. I took a quick look and realized the call from our boys. My teenagers, Jaren, Daniel, and Gavi, loved playing soccer, math, and studying Messiah Yeshua's Scriptures. Our sons devoted their lives to Yahweh and on a mission to help others find salvation. They had received tuition scholarships at many universities because of their grades. As a family, we had made plans to travel to Jerusalem for their senior gift. Abduction could now shatter my dreams of seeing my sons become doctors.

"Jaren?" I screamed in utter agony. The call dropped, and so did my heart. Jaren, our eldest triplet, attempted a call. The cell connection disconnects. *Did something happen to my sons?* Oh god, please let my children be alive, I prayed an internal prayer.

"Noah, please call the boys." I tried to stay calm, but my emotions raced out of control, and my voice pitched higher.

I glanced over at him, still sprawled on the floor, and noticed that one of his shoes was missing. Weakened and disoriented, Noah was in no state to make the call. And there it appeared, within my sight. Starting at the patio door, a lone burn mark on the ceramic floor extended into the entrance to the house.

Noah wobbled to his feet and emitted a feral howl that rattled my insides. A single tear slid across his cheek. I rose to my feet as he helped me.

"Noah, sweetheart. What's the matter? Please say something." I couldn't help but sense his nervousness as I noted his slumped shoulders and vacant expression. The touch of my outstretched hand against his solid chest unveiled the steady rhythm of his breathing while his gaze fixed on his palms as if they held the answers.

Seconds elapsed—before he spoke. "Yes, honey. You were correct. My curiosity could have killed me. A hand seized my shoe just as I tripped over the door threshold. I saw death for the first time. Why are the aliens trying to kill us? Those wretched negotiations must have collapsed with the international governments."

As he mumbled, I struggled to understand his words. With a tap on my wristwatch, I dialed Jaren's cellphone. The cell phone rang, then disconnected.

As a member of the top-secret technology company in the country, I felt shocked when I learned the news that the aliens were coming back. It surprised me, but Noah appeared to have insider information. I couldn't help but wonder why everything was so confidential. Why was I excluded as a crucial member of the group? If Noah had prior knowledge, why did the aliens target him? A whirlwind of questions occupied my thoughts, yet I refrained from asking and opted to confront him later for clarification. Unease settled in my chest, and I craved answers to soothe my confusion.

I sighed, then reached out to clutch him in my arms, desperate to keep him close. As we stood there, our breaths intertwined, creating a harmonious rhythm. I turned to the sink to moisten the towel in my hand. For a moment, he placed his palm on top of mine, then let go to use a towel on his sweaty face and bloody wound.

"Honey," he grumbled, his voice breathy and weak. "Maybe… their original intention… was to eradicate us… from the outset."

"Noah, let's give the boys another call. Jaren's call disconnected again. That red laser circled the beach before they started scooping up humans and everything in their path. Please try to call our sons once more."

Noah touched his wristband, and the call connected. But it went straight to voice mail. "Let's go to the neighbor's house once the spaceship disappears."

Stepping aside from me, he gazed out the window. "They're still hovering over the lake. I see lights from the spaceship."

"Noah, the aliens are intercepting our calls. They are clever. They didn't help us rebuild our planet for nothing. And a creepy voice called out my name tonight. Are they still able to remember me from three years ago?"

He nodded, a small smile tugging at the corners of his lips. He had contact with the aliens, but never shared his experience with me. Yet I shared my disgust and fears with Noah.

Noah mentioned an altercation with an alien commander who threatened his life. It must have lingered in his mind. Whatever happened left him so frightened that he felt compelled to apply to the neighborhood watch committee.

Noah opened the cabinet above the sink and grabbed the liquor bottle. He poured himself a generous quantity of whiskey, the amber liquid swirling in the glass. His lips turned downwards, creating a frown that mirrored the sadness in his eyes.

"Sweetie, I remember the never-ending stream of phone calls that echoed daily and the eerie voices that resounded in our bedroom at night. Those raucous, aggressive voices have forever etched their voices in my mind, and I hope never to hear them again."

"Noah, you never shared your feelings until now. I had no clue those extraterrestrials were tormenting you. But, we are facing a unique problem. Someone was monitoring my upload code to the AI server. I got a strange message on my wristband."

I pulled out my laptop on the kitchen counter and read the message: *'Upload intercepted, then sent.'* He leaned over my shoulder to read the message. But he remained silent as he rubbed his chin.

"The aliens stole my program. I need to warn Becky."

"Sweetie, whatever they want from us is more than our lives. I felt the slimy hand pulling my shoe, then my foot. I inhaled and tasted the blood in my mouth as the sharp laser slipped inches past my foot. When I fell, the impact was so strong that I bit my jaw, causing it to bleed. Carmen, I sniffed their foul odor. They want to kill us."

I turned toward the sink to grab a glass of water. I drew my attention to Noah's clothes, drenched with sweat. My fear was nothing compared to the absolute nightmare he must have lived through during the shoe incident.

"Noah, I'm scared for our family." I filled another glass with water and gave it to him.

"Sweetie, I'm sorry. You told me to stop filming. I put us in danger, and now these aliens are back with a vengeance to kill us. You mentioned someone called your name."

"Yes, at least three times I can recall. I heard my name. I thought I recognized the voice, but maybe I was mistaken. Now, they are back."

Noah gulped the water, drew another glass, and placed it on the countertop. He turned his body and faced me, and I saw the sadness in his eyes.

"Carmen, I worked with them, too. They were difficult, but we modernized the planet beyond what we could have imagined. We are fortunate to have a pleasant home and family. I worry the aliens want our lives, but for what? Tomorrow, I must travel to Jerusalem for my new position. Now I negotiate with aliens once more."

"You are selfish to think of traveling when our family's life is at stake. Did you grasp the gravity of your plight that moments ago, you were a foot away from being abducted?"

A seething anger welled within me. With a slight tilt of Noah's head, he hunched and pulled me into a warm hug.

"Carmen, I'm an idiot. Forgive me." His plea for forgiveness reached my ears. "I'm scared too, but first, we must locate our sons."

My nerves were a wreck as we picked up the broken tableware on the floor and counter. Noah pressed the button on the wall for the AI vacuum. A sixteen-inch flat round vacuum ran out of the wall next to the sink. The AI vacuum sprayed disinfectant liquid on the floor, cleared the mess, and spun around as it returned to the wall.

Sirens wailed, and police jetted hovercrafts whirled around our neighborhood. Despite waiting three hours, we received no text or call from the teens. We were frantic and too scared to venture outside the house. Bullhorns blared from military police, with emergency alerts on our wristbands warning residents to stay indoors. The sound of the busy signal greeted us each time we tried calling our neighbors.

At midnight, Jaren called to tell us they were okay. He informed us he had called earlier but received a network busy message.

Relief enveloped me as I listened to their voices, confirming their well-being. Tears slipped over my cheeks, and I let out a sigh as I thanked God for saving our children.

We headed to our bedroom when another sonic boom shook the house. We ran to the living room window. There, we saw the mothership hover and then vanish. My wristband buzzed. I took a deep breath and answered.

"Hey, Carmen, it's Becky." I waited for a second as I glanced in Noah's direction while he scanned the grounds.

"Did you notice the spaceships?"

"Yes, Becky, and let me say. I am worried. What's going on in Marsh Harbor? They disappeared and are back, taking people into their vessels. Is there any news from the ISS?"

"No, but let me be quick. We will meet tomorrow at 6:00 a.m. via hologram. Carmen, I got your code and uploaded it. I know you took two days off for Pesach, but I couldn't wait to tell you the fantastic news."

I paced the floor in the living room. Then I spoke, "Open blinds." The AI assistant opened the blinds facing the lake. The moon's reflection shimmered on the calm surface of the reservoir. Noah stood next to me at the window. The soft glow of the night wall lights cast a warm glow on his face.

"Becky, tell me. You are killing me with excitement. I need news after our ordeal tonight. Did I get the promotion?"

"Yes, and you are a full member of the 'Special Force Tigers.' Your coding skills and knowledge of ancient alien codes are exceptional. My friend, you start your new position on Monday with a salary raise. Peter has approved your SCI clearance, so prepare for a fast start."

Tears filled my eyes. I had applied several times for a promotion to the elite group and turned away three times. Despite my discouragement and inability to get a promotion, Becky's optimism convinced me to give it another shot. I felt Noah's piercing stare as we looked over the reservoir terrain. He pulled out his goggles and kept a watchful eye on the river.

"Thank you, Becky, for the recommendation. Tell Bart thanks. I tried to contact you earlier, but my text message failed. I thought the aliens intercepted my program code."

Noah nudged me to look at something moving in the river. I couldn't distinguish what was in motion, but it raced. The quick beat of my heart resounded in my ears as I turned to glance at Noah. He turned and mouthed. "Get off the cell now!"

"Carmen, I got it before they attempted to snag your code. Turn your wristband to secure so you can get our updates. I sent the updated secure bot to your cell. Keep your wristband frequency secure, and never take off your wristband. The band protects you from the aliens and tracks your location. Now that those beasts are back, they will try any method to break our network transmissions. Be safe, my friend. Talk in the morning and goodnight."

The call ended, leaving my body trembling and my palms damp with sweat. I spun around to speak to Noah when a red laser sneaked across the living room floor.

"Duck, Noah!" I screamed.

We dropped to the floor and slithered to the open wall beside the windows. We flattened our bodies next to each other against the wall as the light crawled closer. The intense trembling inside me left a bitter aftertaste. While we remained silent, we waited. After the laser passed, we crawled next to the bookcase wall away from the window, our bodies pressed against the wall in a single file with the top of our heads touching.

As we huddled, the laser scanned every corner of the kitchen, ensuite, bedrooms, and study. My breaths quickened, and I turned to prayer, seeking solace while trying to calm my racing heartbeat.

Our eyes followed the swift movement of the light as it raced across the floor, coming straightaway towards us. I held my breath, hoping to confuse the light source.

Oh, no. It saw us. The red light beamed on me, and I sensed my body rise in the beam, then I blacked out.

———

"GIVE HER OXYGEN, don't let her die. We need her, and hurry."

The gold Nephilim alien pressed a button on the pod, and oxygen pumped into my lungs. The pressure on my chest subsided as I took in the vital oxygen. Perspiration sprung upon my face while water droplets ran across my cheeks. The spaceship was hot and uncomfortable. I dreamed of the cool morning air in Marsh Harbor and hoped my cool thoughts might help.

I sighed, blinked, and peered at the handsome, golden female alien. A sweet jasmine scent wafted in the air as she closed my pod. Across from me, another Nephilim was adjusting various tubes on Noah, upright in a black oval transparent pod. He appeared asleep. The third Nephilim placed a breathing device over his mouth and closed the vertical hatch, and Noah breathed. The alien focused on the screen, tracking his movements as they scanned his vitals.

Dozens of pods filled the open room of the mothership, surrounding a central computer network. I narrowed my lids and strained to glimpse the mastermind orchestrating everything. Black pods lined the circular perimeter with humans in them. The room had dim lighting, but the pods and computer equipment brightened the center. Tall, slim Nephilim scraped their footsteps across metal floors while sounds echoed in the circular chamber. The noise made the hair on my arms stand on end.

"Mrs. Northrop, are you okay?" A voice spoke to me with a Middle Eastern accent.

Turning to my left, I saw a tall alien with a hunched back, owl eyes, and scaly dragon skin. When did he arrive? An earthy scent of garbage and dirt mixed with water floated inside my pod, making me nauseous.

"Yes, I'm fine," I spoke.

A bitter taste from the airflow made me lightheaded. I was unaware of the scaly alien's presence. Oh lord, they can disappear and reappear —my experience with these beasts is not going well. Never had I seen the creature's ability to vanish and reappear three years ago.

My limbs trembled as I took in the details of the room. Then, I recognized the Nephilim. Emperor Zerus, a fierce leader, ruled over the Nephilim aliens. He appeared taller up close than in my vision. Oh, my, my vision came true. My memories of the carnage on Zarzu are still fresh in my mind.

They returned, now determined to kill humans. I remember having a quick conversation with him at my job three years ago when the aliens showed up at P. J. Waxit. I noticed his suit helmet and space boots, with their shiny metallic sheen, left a gold hue on his scaly skin. He had a weapon on his right and a laser weapon on his left. Two distinct types of aliens were present. The warrior aliens had scaly skin, while the ones standing beside me possessed intelligence and emanated kindness and compassion. Their skin was smooth, and they were handsome. I saw that Zerus, and his military warriors exhibited violent and uncivilized behavior.

"Mrs. Northrop, may I call you Carmen?" A smug grin crossed his face. "It's nice to see you again. We need your help, and our intentions are harmless. Don't be afraid."

Fear washed over me as I contemplated what he expected from me.

"Yes, Carmen is fine. How may I help you?"

My voice cracked, sounding high-pitched and squeaky. It astounded me since I had to breathe and speak through a tube. The proximity of Zerus and his foul garbage scent blended with the sight of his protruding orbs, made me tense.

"Our hologram bracelet has a flaw, and we need you and your engineering friends to repair it. It stopped working with no explanation. We use it to communicate with our mother planet, Zarzu Genesis. My bracelet, a remarkable piece of technology, has been with me for six thousand years. Once we entered your atmosphere, the bracelet stopped working. The constant flow of communication between my device and the other bracelets halted. With your skills, you can restore it to its former glory."

He pressed his wrist against the glass. A soft violet hue filled the room as the sapphire bracelet radiated its brilliance. The stones twirled and played a perplexing mystical melody. What I saw was beyond belief. The bracelet stopped spinning as fast as it began, and the haunting music and vibrant color vanished.

I recall reading an article on an exact ancient relic that had been missing for thousands of generations, unearthed in the Egyptian desert.

While on an archeological dig, Sophia McFadden, an Israeli water microbiologist and member of the Jewish Coalition, made an incredible discovery—a sapphire bracelet. Following a wrongful arrest, Sophia handed over the precious bracelet to the Egyptian authorities.

Zerus leaned closer and watched my reaction when my eyebrows lifted.

"Carmen, does this bracelet look familiar?" he inquired, showing it to me.

"No, it's so lovely, and you startled me when you pressed the bracelet against the glass pod," I lied. As I examined the bracelet, I noticed the same intricate engravings that Sophia had found. Were there multiple bracelets? The question remains: How did Zerus gain access to the relic?

"The holographic virtual reality device stopped working once we entered your stratosphere. We lost several hundred staff members in the hologram after they suffocated. My staff informed me that since you moved from the satellite team to the Special Force Tigers engineering team, you will have increased knowledge on fixing the 3D image. You worked with the rebuild on several of our outpost programs on Mars and the Moon. I understand you are familiar with our program language code and devised schematics for others to follow."

"Yes, but I have limited knowledge." *Stay calm*. I thought to myself.

"Emperor. Why are you requesting me when other engineers have the same knowledge?"

"Our leader selected you."

"Who is your leader? Let's say I have no interest in repairing the hologram bracelet. It's not my responsibility." I feared the worst; my bravery might kill me.

"Mrs. Northrop, you dare to threaten me? You can lose your life in an instant. You're brave, yet I sense a mysterious aura lingering around you."

His arched body, as if he wanted to prance on me through the pod, terrified me. I prayed for empathy for the alien. Killing me could not serve him any purpose, since he demanded my alliance to repair his broken hologram. Tears, warm and blurry, streamed from my eyes.

"Carmen, who ordered your help on this project, is not of concern to you. You will regret your words and actions if you don't help fix the bracelet. Besides, I have your sons."

"Excuse me, did I hear you say you have my sons?" Anger and fear filled my spirit.

"Yes, until you fix my bracelet, they will stay with my people. Then they will return to you."

I watched his generous mouth with millions of teeth move and understood every word, yet it surprised me how he knew of my promotion. Someone in my office was working with the scaly beast. It worried me that the hologram stopped working when they arrived in our airspace. Something didn't sit right with my spirit. When Zerus spoke, his tone and face grimaced and lacked confidence.

Within seconds, his sight transformed from pitch black to piercing yellow, resembling a cat. He leaned closer to the pod. He tried to read my thoughts, his orbs flickering with curiosity and intrigue. The memory scan of my thoughts filled me with a sense of terror that reached my very core. His vision bore into my soul. My eyelids refused to shut, no matter how much I wanted them to close. He possessed immense power.

He bared his massive teeth with a menacing grin, exposing his true intention. With a quick turn of my head, I broke the supernatural power, shut my eyelids, and sought solace in prayer as fear consumed me. The anxiety overwhelmed me until I felt the blood pulsating through my veins.

"Carmen." I heard his breathy voice echo in the chamber, but I refused to respond and opened my eyes. I turned to face him. He called my name again. I blinked and listened, my heartbeat echoing in my ears.

"Do we have a mutual arrangement, your teens, for the hologram?" He leaned back and stretched his back to its full height of seven to eight feet. His humpback disappeared as he changed color from gold to pea green.

I lost my bravery, shivering so hard that my bones must have rattled upon the pod's metal seat. If Zerus wanted to scare me to death, he succeeded.

"I expect the hologram repaired within a week. Will that give you enough time to fix it?" While he questioned me, seeing three other Nephilim aliens closing in on him made my heart race. Peeking, I mistook them for humans in their gold lab coats, but to my astonishment, they were Nephilim. The sweet jasmine aroma circled into my pod; they glowed with a gold hue, and Zerus was hideous with scales. Why were they so different? I needed answers. Then, my vision came back to mind when I visited their planet.

It took several seconds for me to find my voice again. "Yes, Emperor, I will try to have it ready. But if I need more time, please allow me an extension. Given the intricate nature of your equipment, it may take longer to analyze the program code. Will that work?" I raised my eyebrows and pursed my lips to show the aliens did not intimidate me. If he had wanted to kill me, it could be quick and fast. Yet, he needed me and my friends to help him. He could release Noah and me.

"We will keep your sons as an insurance policy to protect our hologram project and prevent deception. If you fail us, your sons will die."

How dare this beast take my sons and use them as leverage? My blood pressure rose, and I sensed the blue aura grow in my soul and around me. The icy metal clasps against my wrist tightened when I moved my hands. Another realm portal door appeared. I spotted my sons together on the mothership, but not near Noah and me. I prayed the creature didn't see my fiery aura. The blood pressure device dinged, its sound blending with the rising intensity of my anger.

"When did you take them? It was inappropriate for you to take my children." The sound of a voice reached my ears, but it didn't match the tone or pitch of my own.

My motherly instincts kicked in, urging me to wrap my fingers around its throat and plunge the sword from its left leg into its slimy body. I had no weapon, and of course, they had me strapped into a pod. Besides, anger did not affect an alien capable of disappearing. What was I thinking?

"I took them the same time I captured you and Noah. Although they are safe, they are here with you in the spaceship. No more talk or questions. Do we have an arrangement?"

"Yes, yes. Please don't hurt my sons." My breathing apparatus made it hard to take deep breaths through my nose.

Zerus turned and walked away with his entourage. Fury surged inside me; I clenched my fists and vowed to protect the hologram, whatever the cost, even if it meant sacrificing my life for my sons.

The air in my pod grew stuffy as his medical staff approached, their movements precise, and my face attentive to the sizeable hypodermic needle in their hands. They lifted the pod screen.

"Just relax, Mrs. Northrop. We will examine your internals and take blood during your sleep. We need your blood for our experiments." They attached a gold bracelet with an odd-shaped sapphire blue ball to my right arm. I recognized the artifact that Sophia had found. They clamped another device onto my wristband, and the needle pierced my right arm. I slipped into a restless sleep.

FIVE DAYS HAD PASSED since the aliens returned, and the world was now a chaotic mess of panicked screams and sirens blaring. As vehicles crashed to the ground and into buildings, the sirens blared, and the shrieks filled the cool Sunday morning air. A constant trilling persisted in the Natas Nomad Crystal Palace Hotel.

Melekh groaned and tapped on his timepiece, longing for the blissful silence to return. Following his shower, Melekh changed into fresh clothing before going to the spaceship waiting for him. Upon boarding, he sank into his reclining seat and fell asleep. A powerful flashback jolted him awake, leaving him feeling restless.

MELEKH'S GAZE fell upon the massive clock resting on the side table. The clock read 4:00 a.m., casting a pale glow in the dim light. With a grumble, he rolled over, grabbed a T-shirt, and dragged himself to the veranda. Collapsing into the comfortable recliner, he could hear the commotion beneath the hotel. While lost in reflection, he remembered the events of the last five days and how Abu's unexpected phone call and the sounds of crashing vehicles from the skyway had transformed his life.

"You had better have a valid reason to wake me."

"Mr. Melekh, wake up, sir! Are you aware of the report? People's sudden removal from the planet?"

"What report—?"

"Mr. Melekh, you need to hear this. It's unbelievable but true. Millions of people have suddenly vanished from the planet."

"Abu, it's 4:00 a.m. here in Dubai, and people are asleep. Look, my team of humanoids didn't alert me to the incident, so it didn't happen."

"No, sir. I'm sorry to inform you, but it's a global phenomenon. Your company's stock has taken a hit because of this unexpected occurrence. You must hire new employees to fill the sudden vacancies."

"What? Did those pesky aliens ask for more money? They begged me for money to support their technology efforts. I have given them millions of dollars. They won't get another dollar." His jaw tightened.

Melekh shifted to his side. He grabbed his watch and tapped the goggle box, a massive sixty-four-inch flat-screen attached to the bedroom's white wall. It added a touch of exotic elegance. The ornate king-size bed and lavish bedroom with oriental rugs adorned the marble floors. A cherry wood bed with an exquisite, detailed, wrought iron Victorian headboard took center stage in the room. The goggle box could generate holograms that appeared so vivid that they were right in front of you.

A hologram materialized on the screen, projecting breaking international news. Melekh's heartbeat filled his ears, and he tasted the sweat trickling across his face as he put on the black silk robe and summoned Lita when he pressed his wristband, his humanoid robot assistant.

Lita knocked on the bedroom suite door and entered.

"Why didn't you give me the fantastic news?"

"Sir, what news? Mr. Melekh, you instructed not to wake you unless it was Abu. I'm sorry, sir."

"Stop shaking, Lita. I am not upset with you. You followed my orders, and that matters. Hey, don't be afraid. I have a job that will allow you to be friends with someone special."

Then, a dazzling gold light lit the suite.

Rashid Melekh glanced at a brilliant yellow light engulfing the massive bedroom when he spotted a white creature emerge two feet before him. The beast, draped with ornate gold pan pipes—a decorated gold sash on his chest—was regal and handsome, his height of at least seven to eight feet unexpected. Two tall demon guards accompanied him in black robes, a black head covering, blood eyes with disfigured faces, and expansive raven wings. Rashid found himself weakened as he slumped on the marble floor and sensed the incredible power of the creature, as the creature forced him to bow in reverence.

Melekh struggled to catch his breath and lift his body from the icy floor. The beast's identity remained a mystery. He turned to glimpse Lita, standing still with her eyelids shut. Melekh's heart sank as he realized something had happened to his humanoid robot.

When he raised his head, the being's spirit overpowered him, and his sight shone with an intense fire. Then, the spirit entity opened his mouth to speak.

"Cyrus Rashid Melekh, my right-hand wicked human. The blistering dry heat on this May day in Dubai brings back vivid memories of the familiar temperature back home. I'm offering you a chance to experience the wealth and power you crave. Kill those pesky Jews and Christians. They are within my grip."

The angel's boisterous laugh echoed through the air, causing the building to tremble.

"Oh, my contempt for them and my nemesis is unbearable. You are my Antichrist king to change the world."

Many questions surged through his mind, leaving him feeling lost and confused. The spirit entity whispered in his ear, urging him to embrace his destiny as an Antichrist king. As he reflected on the Scriptures, he found no association between his name and the Antichrist. He believed that defying Allah could lead to eternal damnation. Besides, he learned his grandparents were of Jewish descent, and he couldn't defy his Arabic Jewish heritage. He must be dreaming. Everything felt so surreal and unreal. No matter how often he blinked, the creature refused to disappear, standing fast before him.

"You are Satan, and you want me to change the world?"

"Rashid, my man. Consider me a friend. We're not enemies. My goal is to help you amass more wealth than you can envision. You worship money, and so do I. Seize the opportunity to get everything you've ever wanted through supernatural abilities."

He rubbed his thin fingers together as a radiant light beam grew more intense, his gold wings spreading upward. He moved closer. His amber eyes peered deep into his soul. A burst of fire came out of Lucifer and entered Rashid. He shivered as the fire burst surrounded his body, and a mist of fire entered his mouth. The sight of Satan made him tremble. The creature's glow created an eerie shadow on the walls.

"Are you ready to start your new journey?" Then his eyeballs glowed red. Rashid gaped when he caught sight of them and closed his eyelids. Covered in sweat, he trembled amidst searing flames.

Rashid stood erect, his face emotionless and his body swaying. He couldn't help but notice the grimaces on the soot-colored faces of the gold creature and its two raven angels.

"What do you want from me?" His words sounded artificial. His body slumped forward, his shoulders hunched, and his head drooped.

"Cyrus Rashid Melekh, delivered on March 14, 1990, in Dubai to

Cyrus Melekh, Senior, a wicked and mean-spirited man who craved power and wealth. Did I describe your father correctly?"

While he remained curious—the true nature of the mysterious creature—he was not from our realm. He craved coffee and needed sleep, and this beast wanted to talk.

"Did you enjoy my display of power? The Nephilim aliens seizing humans worldwide? Then take their dead bodies to the moon?" His laughter vibrated around the room akin to a wolf howling in pain.

The musical pipes on his chest produced a chilling melody to grind away at Rashid's very being. The tune evoked sorrow and foreboding.

"Rashid, for a second, you scared me when the humanoids blew up the skyscraper in Moscow. I thought you wanted to take my authority but rejected the notion and knew you'd be the man of perdition, perfect as my right-hand man. Your surname, Melekh, means king, but you are more than I could imagine. We will have fun ruling the world together as you become more powerful than the dictator over creation."

A deep, throaty sound slipped from his vocal cords. Rashid's inner man shuddered, yet he couldn't move; a supernatural force held him.

"Yes, my father was a wicked man. But why are you?" To shield himself from the intense light emitted by the creature, he lowered his body toward the floor and waited for the beast to reply.

"I am Lucifer. Now, according to my nemesis, I'm referred to by mortals as Satan. You are my brains for the New World Power (NWP). I sent a deceiving spirit to prepare you for conversion."

His loud trumpets and harp music intensified and hurt his ears. The musical excerpt haunted his spirit; the voice of Satan was a melodic Stradivarius violin when he sang and the most mesmerizing sound he had ever heard.

"Rashid, are you listening?"

"Yes, sir." he straightened his frame. "No one can intimidate you and make you inadequate."

At that moment, Lucifer, the creature, pointed at him, and to his astonishment, a portal materialized as if by a mystical force.

A horrifying vision unfolded before his face as Nephilim used a red light to snatch humans and vanish into their spaceship. Echoes of screams and moans filled the air. Then, the vision shifted to a planet the size of Earth. The black hole sucked the planet into a black abyss with other stars and galaxies.

"The image you saw was a flawed hologram designed by the Nephilim. I need your engineers to repair the hole in their program code. We provided Carmen Northrop with ample time to repair the 3D holographic bracelet. The hologram image failed and caused the deaths of other Nephilim who entered the hologram from their planet."

Looking over, he noticed Lita was still asleep and not moving. The vile man didn't answer his question, and he needed answers. The devil's presence could have a profound impact on his life. How dare he use his figure for his appointed opportunity to rule the world? He was stunned and frightened by the creature and didn't understand what he wanted with him.

"What's the program deadline? And why do you want Carmen Northrop to write the code? Who is this woman?"

"I heard your thoughts. You don't believe me when I say I am Lucifer? Carmen possesses the abilities. Yet, my adversary granted me the power to test her, and she will fail. Then she will become your bride if she can't fix the bracelet hologram."

He raised his hand, and fire circled Lita, but she didn't melt.

"Don't destroy my cherished possession, "he responded. Did the demon creature have a motive? He couldn't understand why it wanted to melt his treasured possession.

He relinquished with one quick motion of his hand. The fire disappeared.

"The 3D image intended for you and the extraterrestrials. Over six thousand years ago, the hologram bracelet vanished. They need Carmen to fix the program. Carmen's quick wit, smart, vulnerable, and less curious than her friend Becky. She can lure more Jews and Christians over to our side."

Lucifer stepped two more inches closer to him. The heat from Satan burned his clothes. Rashid screamed from the intense fire.

"Lucifer, please step back. If you don't, you will kill me," he screamed in anguish. Flames licked at his skin, causing intense pain.

Why did the devil choose him as the Antichrist? That question kept nagging at him. He was a successful man with a prestigious job and a comfortable lifestyle. Besides, he wasn't seeking more power, especially not from a demonic entity. He wanted power, wealth, and prestige on his terms. Lucifer's weathered face grabbed his attention, with etched deep lines visible, protruding blood vessels beneath his skin. Satan's grotesque image caused Melekh to recoil in horror. His once handsome features had transformed into a frightening and monstrous countenance.

The devil ignored his requests and moved closer as moisture fell from his closed eyelids and face. The sulfuric stench from his body and the fire emitting from Lucifer left him parched and craving water and a barf bag.

"Abu will be your guide, and soon, your transformation from a hated man to a worshiped power will begin. Does this meet your desires, Rashid Melekh?"

"I have spent years observing you and know you're not stating the truth. Your aspirations include power, wealth, prestige, and love. I am aware of your deepest desires."

The wicked creature had torched Rashid's clothes, and he was roasting. Yet his skin didn't burn. After inspecting his clothes, he noticed the distinct smell of burned fabric. Did the demon realize that his couture pajamas, imported from France, were the height of luxury?

"Yes, yes! Where do I sign?" With an adrenaline rush, he raised his head, eyes locking onto Lucifer with intense determination.

"I chose Priest Nadab to stand in for you at the New World Power (NWP) alliance meetings in your absence. He will be your companion and double as you travel the world when you come to power in the coming weeks. I expect you to lead the nations out of war into a seven-year peace treaty. Rashid, your leadership powers and eagerness to control the world have granted you world acclaim. You can use your new authority."

Satan moved backward from Rashid, and his angels extended their wings and kindled the flames around their master.

"No need to sign today unless you want influence today. But the sooner you sign, the sooner your journey and power starts."

Rashid glanced at Lucifer after noticing the smirk. A spine-chilling chuckle vibrated through the hotel suite, making him shudder. The pipes on Lucifer's chest played a melodic, hypnotic song. Next, a supernatural document appeared. The intelligent creature flung a piece of paper into the air, landing in his palms as his hands jutted forward to accept the document. He pressed his fingers onto the parchment—it sizzled.

A deep howl escaped his lips with an expletive. The fire burned Rashid's fingers as it left, and a charred aroma saturated the air.

"If you fail your assignment. You will die a fiery death," Lucifer's voice echoed as he howled and vanished with his guards.

His fingerprint burned into the parchment, and then the paper dissolved.

He released a groan while thinking, "What have I done?"

He clenched his aching fingers and inhaled, smelling the burned skin as he watched the burn marks disappear. A slow grin appeared on his face. What incredible power.

The room reeked of sulfur, and gray ash floated to the marble floor. Once Satan left the room, a mist covered Lita and faded, then she awoke. Lita hurried to clean up the waste.

"Let me prepare your breakfast."

Still dazed by the experience with the demon, Rashid stumbled towards the bathroom entrance and froze as he caught his reflection in the mirror. When he saw his reflection, it amazed him at how much more handsome his face looked. Rashid's skin was smooth as a baby's bottom; he rubbed his hand over his face and body. His presence was reminiscent of a god, and his facial and toned body's sharp features had a perfect muscle tone. The gray strands that had appeared in his beard and hair after he turned forty disappeared. The sudden alteration of his entire being stunned Rashid as if he had stepped into another realm, and everything he desired was within his grasp.

Rashid's hands squeezed together at his sides as the eerie, other-worldly whisper lured him to Marsh Harbor. An intense emotion overpowered him; he knew he had to follow its call. With a burst of energy, he summoned Lita.

"Pack your bags and meet me at the spacecraft. I'll get something from the restaurant on my way to Marsh Harbor. Once we land, hurry to the new prepper container in the mountains by 11:00 a.m. Don't be late. I will send you more data and your new appointment soon. The container needs to be ready for someone."

A black spiked circular Concord spacecraft had settled on the third-floor transport. The landing strip jutted out from the building and joined a crystal elevator round pod connected to the cables on the ground.

Several hovercrafts and spacecrafts crashed on the ground as the busy humanoid robots cleaned the debris from the sudden night events.

Lita bowed and rushed out of the room to prepare for her assignment. The well-crafted humanoid robot didn't mimic the clunky machine robots. Lita resembled humans with no traceable flaws. Her oval blue eyes, tan skin, black pageboy cut hair, and slender six-foot frame were impressive. Her British accent was perfect.

An hour later, Rashid sat in his cushioned white cabin seat and admired the glossy, black finish inside his new Concord spacecraft. His silk black Armani spacesuit added an air of sophistication as he contemplated his next move. As the spaceship lifted, Rashid's wicked grin hinted at his devious plan. He placed a hologram call to Emperor Zerus and left a message.

In a rush, Lita made calls to secure her assignment while examining world events.

"Sir, new reports worldwide are reporting ten large spaceships in every part of the hemisphere. Do I protect myself and my new assignment if the Nephilim aliens approach me?"

"Yes. Make sure the person you protect has your loyalty. I hate disloyal staff and humanoid robots."

"One last news bulletin. The Hoover Dam at Marsh Harbor collapsed just now and washed away the town. Do you still want me to go to the container in the mountains of Marsh Harbor, Colorado?"

"No, Lita. Go to Arvvada. The new luxury prepper home is ready.

Meet me at the office after you buy food and tidy the prepper container."

Rashid sent an alert to Commander Marc Zacker at the ISS to be alert to danger by the Golden Nephilim and prepare to fight if necessary. "With their planet on the brink of destruction, the Nephilim have set their sights on replacing the humans. Our task is twofold: fend off the invading aliens and use their advanced technology to safeguard our planet. We must offer immediate help and support to the people stranded in Marsh Harbor. They are under my supervision at work."

A VOICE CAME over the intercom. "Sir, are you ready to launch?"

The sudden sound jolted him from his daydream to the present moment.

"Yes, and hurry, my businesses are in jeopardy."

Chapter Five

"NOAH, ARE YOU OKAY?" His face contorted in pain, the furrowed brows and clenched jaw revealing his inner turmoil.

He rolled over and seized me; our bodies pressed against each other as we fought to support our balance on the treacherous mountain ledge, only inches away from the gaping abyss. Debris from rocks and damp soil plummeted from the ledge, compounding chaos as we rolled from the ridge. We covered a sizable distance before our breaths grew heavy and labored. Once we cleared the shelf, we lifted ourselves upright onto the stable surface of sand and grass. Dirt flung into the air, and the dust on my lips made me thirst for water, but we had nothing except our spacesuits and tracking device wristwatches.

"How did we get here?"

Peering downward, I gazed upon the mighty rush of water flowing from the Hoover Dam, swollen by the floods, racing towards Marsh Harbor. The water had submerged the land, reaching the tops of trees. My heart raced as I wondered what had happened to the dam. The massive volume of water destroyed our homes despite being built on stilts. Peaks of steel bent into toothpicks jutted above the waterline. The sight of the collapsed residences and the dam filled me with dread as the sun rose on a sweltering Monday morning. Anguish gripped me as I realized everything, I had worked for was gone in seconds. An abduction started my lifestyle shift, and now a flood has devastated our residence. When I glanced at my watch, I noticed it had been three days since they abducted us.

Moist pine trees and grass scents lingered in the air, filling my senses. My arms throbbed with pain, covered in red marks as though someone had drained my blood. A deep hunger gripped me, sapping my strength and leaving me desperate for sustenance. What transpired in our absence from the comforts of home?

My mind was full of thoughts; none made sense except the dream that my children were not on the spaceship but on the moon in a pod clinging to life. The dream stirred up worry within me. What prompted Zerus to expose that the teens were on the spaceship?

Noah and I strolled toward a small hill, the sun's warmth on our faces. Desperate, I whispered a prayer, hoping someone could rescue us.

What happened to us, and where were our teens? *Oh, my goodness! My babies, where are they?* I released an internal scream, only to realize I had made a cry in reality.

"Carmen, sweetheart. Our children are safe. Don't cry." His soft touch grazed my cheek. Right away, I sensed his deceit through his shifty gaze. He lied.

Stepping toward him, I ensured my legs were steady, feeling the moisture on my face intensify the warmth in my cheeks. He pulled me into a tight embrace, and I felt his arms enveloping me as he swayed.

"What do you mean—they are safe?" How did he know their whereabouts? The last thing I remembered was those pesty aliens pushing a hypodermic needle into my arm, and Noah was asleep.

"Carmen, I signed a contract to keep our teens safe if a disaster happens after the alien's arrival three years ago."

"So where are they, Mr.—I don't tell my wife everything?" As I pushed away from him, my voice grew stronger and louder.

"Sweetheart, I apologize for not revealing the contract with you sooner. I thought you might object, but my heart was in the right place to protect our family. Your flushed face suggests you're not pleased with my answer."

"Yes! I'm furious with you. Where are they? The aliens told me they were safe, but no one answered my questions, especially you, Noah."

"They're on the moon."

"WHAT!" From my soul, I screamed a passionate scream that only a mother could shriek.

The anger that sizzled inside my body exploded. Noah trusted those lying aliens with our son's future. I pushed myself away from him. How could he? I needed to escape from him and cool my temper. No wonder Zerus was harsh. My vision came true, and my husband lied. I needed to escape Noah because nothing made sense. My sons are now on the moon, living in pods. *No, this can't be real.* I heard my inner voice utter.

"Do you realize the aliens are holding our sons hostage until I fix their flawed hologram? If I cannot fix the thing, they will kill them and me. You have put our lives in jeopardy for the sake of your greed. How much did they pay you for your signature?"

His once confident posture wilted, his shoulders hunched forward, and he avoided facing me as he briefly glanced toward the cliff. Beads of sweat formed on his forehead, glistening off his face.

"Two million dollars for the first hundred humans to venture into new AI-controlled pods. Guaranteed safety for the folks taken to the moon." Trembling with emotion, he uttered his perfidious words with a quivering voice.

I couldn't fathom that he'd haggle with our children's lives for money. How could I have married such a dishonest person? I have kept track of our financial investments and bank accounts, so where did he get the mysterious money? Did he borrow or steal the money? Still, where did he stash it away? My body temperature soared, a searing heat coursing through me as I scowled at him. Tears welled.

"Carmen, say something, please." He turned and leaned forward, his right hand rubbing against his chest, as he extended his left hand towards me. "Sweetheart, please forgive me. The money came from a friend. You know Martin from work. He loaned me money from his Swiss bank account. After Martin loaned me the money, I promised to repay him when the venture launches on the world stock exchange this week."

I strode away from him and didn't stop, not knowing where I was going on the mountain with dangerous crags and slippery wet grass when I heard the whooshing of a helicopter overhead.

The medic noticed me when I waved, jumped, and shouted for help. My grief overwhelmed me; my tears flowed over my cheeks, my heart aching as I recognized my husband had surrendered our children to the vile Nephilim in exchange for wealth—my very being now crushed with sorrow and despair.

"Hold on, ma'am. We will host you and your companion in a minute," a man called from a bullhorn.

I turned and saw Noah sprinting toward me, yelling. The copter descended a single lift. The noise from the vessel and the chair lift's relentless swinging in the wind created a stomach-churning experience as I rose upward. Two powerful hands reached out and dragged me into the cabin.

"Just leave him on the mountain." My tone was harsh as I spoke through gritted teeth.

"We have to take him, but since you are persistent, we'll return and get him on our next trip."

The humanoid robots faced me and shook their heads. They helped me fasten my seat belt and then took their seats as we headed towards Arvvada.

"Carmen, Carmen, wait, don't leave me here." His screams and yells echoed as we flew from the ridge. Noah's voice echoed as we zoomed away from the site.

Anger pulsed through my body as I slumped into the seat, bombarded by the ceaseless churning noise of the helicopter blades.

The vile Nephilim took away my triplet sons, whom I carried with love and anticipation for nine months, leaving me desperate to find them amidst the vastness of the universe. I couldn't believe Noah could make such an important decision without discussing it with me. How could he commit such a terrible deed? With that vile work partner, Martin, no less.

Noah's crime is inexcusable. In a strange revelation, my love for the man endured despite his betrayal of me and his sons. Now, I was embarking on a journey toward a place where we could start fresh and begin anew. I had to achieve a miraculous undertaking at my job on a foreign bracelet affixed to my wrist.

A faint throbbing sensation resonated from the rounded sphere on the gold bracelet. As I touched the unusual object, it vibrated. What a strange artifact! My skills must repair the sapphire ball. I sensed the humanoids gawking at me. I peered at the robots and noticed their attire.

The humanoid robots sported short-cropped raven hair and donned black spandex jumpsuits. They wore round metallic black headgear with a blue visor that covered their sight, military spacesuits featuring a strange red dragon symbol on the front, black gloves, and black boots. Strapped to their sides were weapons. I wondered if they used them to kill humans.

One robot strapped me into my seat. The helicopter held six people and resembled a small hovercraft except for its ability to jet across the sky at high speeds. The oblong silver vessel was a technological feat of genius. I recall a time when the government developed a new prototype spacecraft.

In recent years, the advancements in humanoid robot technology have reached a point where distinguishing between actual humans and humanoid robots poses a challenge.

My muscles were tight, and a wave of dread built within me. When I glanced at my wristwatch, I pondered the mystery of our destination and Noah's arrival.

A humanoid robot in a metal-padded seat sat across from me. I wanted to ask it a question, but it spoke first.

"Mrs. Northrop, we will return for your husband in a few minutes. So don't worry. Sit back and relax. You will see him later. We had multiple disasters while you were with the aliens, and the new world leader emerged and declared martial law."

"What does that mean for me? Have you seen my sons? Can you tell me the identity of the new global leader? I'm sorry. I have many questions and am eager to return home."

Martial law and we were gone for four days. What happened, and why a new global leader unless the aliens took over our government? How did they know of our abduction? Many strange occurrences. Please no! Not the aliens in charge.

The humanoid robot rotated and stared at me before he delivered a strange message.

"Mrs. Northrop, you will not return to your home. The dam water swept away the homes in your neighborhood. You will live in another region or Marsh Harbor. Mr. Cyrus Rashid Melekh has asked you to meet him at your worksite in Arvvada." The humanoid robot ignored my questions. A wave of tension washed over me, and every muscle in my body tightened. I drew myself nearer to the robot to catch its words.

"What? Who is Cyrus Rashid Melekh?"

"He said he was your new supervisor and owner of P.J. Waxit and is waiting to meet you. That was his message."

"I can't meet with anyone until I know if Noah will be alright. I made an inappropriate choice to leave him. But he told me disturbing news that infuriated me, and I had to elude him."

"I apologize, Mrs. Northrop. You'll have to wait to talk to your husband. Another vessel picked him up and carried him to work. Nephilim aliens have thrown our planet into chaos, leading to martial law.

My mental state was not stable. A man wanted me to go to my job before checking on my husband. I left him but still loved him, and my anger vanished. What had happened to the world? I clenched my teeth while pressing my lips into a thin line.

Then I remembered my abduction and the frightful scene with the aliens snatching people. The memory was so profound that I knew my dream had become a reality.

"Mrs. Northrop, I must inform you that there have been many mysterious disappearances across the globe in the last three days.

Given these troubling events, the established NWA government implemented martial law to keep peace and stability."

He leaned closer and locked his intense blue eyes with mine as he studied my face. I have never seen a humanoid robot display aggression, but the designers programmed these humanoids to instill fear in their passengers for the military. I can confirm its success because I was a bundle of nerves.

"The NWA requested people take the dragon's mark to buy, sell, enter buildings, and live their lives—a device that tracks everyone's location. NWA put out a statement declaring martial law and determined to prevent any more vanishings. You can appreciate the urgency since you work for a government affiliate."

I swallowed hard, my fear preventing me from seeking further clarification. The humanoid robot's emotionless stare scared me as I glimpsed its mouth move with perfect precision.

"The supervisor assigned to you will give you more details on the dragon mark when you meet with him. People's mysterious disappearances have left Earth in chaos. Individuals began disappearing with no explanation or warning. The NWA hired a group of vigilant scientists to track the exodus of people. The NWA will uncover the truth and will announce their findings later."

So, it has come to this: the government is enforcing a permanent tattoo device. The dragon's mark signifies an extreme loss of personal freedom. I'm left wondering, what am I supposed to do now?

After inhaling, I let out a constricted breath and tried to swallow, and my saliva caught in my throat. I coughed until my throat cleared. "No, that's not correct," I repeated. How dare these robots repeat lies programmed into their circuits? The aliens swooped in and snatched families from the waterfront and their homes.

The humanoid expression remained neutral as he blinked at me with icy, sea-blue eyes. Lost in my thoughts, I sank into the uncomfortable metal seat, pondering the perils that awaited me.

"Do you have water?"

The humanoid robot leaned forward and pulled a water bottle from a box on the gray steel floor. The humanoid shoved the paper container into my hand as I opened the packet and drank.

"Lean back," he directed, and I complied, inhaling the intoxicating scent of jasmine that filled the copter cabin. A furrowed brow and gritted teeth frightened me, and I pushed myself back against the seat. My hands shook, but I clasped them together while waiting for the copter to land. "In two minutes, we'll be at your job site where Mr. Melekh is waiting."

THE HELICOPTER WHISKED me to Arvvada, the bustling capital city. The towering glass and steel buildings reached for the sky on massive stilts. Only drivers could see the hidden causeway, where hovercraft jets and futuristic cars glided through the air.

It was an hour's drive from Marsh Harbor on the streets three years ago, but we arrived within minutes. A handsome man met me as I descended the stairs of the helicopter and lifted my palm to greet me.

"Carmen Northrop, a pleasure to meet you. Peter Alcorn tells me you're joining my team of specialized engineers. Three members of the Special Force Tigers were women and seven men, including Becky as manager. We have several projects lined up for you. Are you ready to get started?"

Despite his friendly and appeasing words, the moist air was thick with a sense of danger.

"Yes, sir." my voice betrayed me as it shook.

I stole a glance at Melekh, assuming he didn't notice. My face fixed on the man, taking in every detail—from the shine of his polished boots to the snug fit of his Armani spacesuit, the cascade of his raven curls, and his piercing gold eyes. I gasped at his muscular frame. The man was so handsome—I'm sure women ogled him wherever he went. After I realized I had gawked at the man. I dropped my head in embarrassment.

He caught me admiring the intricate details of his frame. My cheeks grew hot with rising heat.

"I apologize for my rudeness; I have forgotten my manners. My name is Cyrus Rashid Melekh. I am the president of P.J. Waxit, and Peter is under my supervision. Excuse me, Carmen, for staring. You are more stunning than I remember."

"Have we met?" I didn't remember meeting him, but his generous smile and heated gaze made me uncomfortable. My blue spandex spacesuit and black knee-high boots were muddy, and my curly hair had transformed into long spiral balls that framed my face. Besides, I needed a shower and worried he could detect my body's unpleasant scent.

"No, but I am familiar with your work and have seen your remarkable skills in handling alien-related matters several years ago. I had the chance to witness the impressive results of your work through one of my clients and observed you in action. When you restored the defunct Nephilim transformer, my team advised me of your skillful use of the ancient Paleo-Hebrew script. Your capabilities left a profound impression on Peter and Becky, who praised them. I need you to know. I commend my employees for their hard work and offer them generous incentives as a token of appreciation. You will work with me on various projects, and frequent travel to different countries will be part of the job."

"Carmen, I'm thrilled you're now a member of the esteemed Special Force Tigers. A busy schedule will engulf you once you enter your designated work pod."

He took a momentary break from walking to tilt his head and glanced at me. If my memory was correct, the word Melekh meant king in Hebrew. He conducted himself with the demeanor of a king.

He captured my right hand and pressed his lips against it, igniting a surge of passion. I sucked in my breath, my senses overwhelmed by the intensity of his kiss and the captivating radiance of his intense facial characteristics. What was I doing? I was a married woman, my inner self warned. I needed answers to my children's whereabouts and was uninterested in this man.

As we strolled toward the building, the aroma of the sensual masculine wildness of a fruity flower filled my nose and heightened my senses. Where had I detected the sweet scent? It triggered a sense of déjà vu. Then I remembered the fragrance on the copter. Was he on the copter before I arrived and left a lasting scent? My head buzzed with questions.

"Glad to meet you, sir."

"Let's get started. Carmen, you have nothing to fear. I'll take excellent care of you. We made security changes after martial law. The office underwent a complete overhaul, and staff came in yesterday to acquaint themselves with security protocol." His classic, confident swagger lessened my fears.

Behind us ambled two humanoid robots dressed in black. Their black helmets appeared removable, and strapped to their thighs were strange weapons resembling AK47s. These weapons had a shorter and broader design and a laser attachment.

Their military black fatigues and weaponry, which featured a striking red dragon emblem on the collar, distinguished the humanoid robots, identical to the ones on the helicopter.

We stopped at the office entrance. Mr. Melekh took a shiny gold box from one robot.

"Carmen, you must wear this device and never take it off your wrist. The watch will allow you access to office buildings, banks, and grocery stores, and it has cell phones and holographic capabilities. The device connects to your current hologram wristband when you put it on your wrist. Since you will not take the dragon mark of the new leader, your wristband allows entrance anywhere in the world. You will wear a head device when working on the virtual computer, allowing you to see everything in 3D, or wear contacts with the same capabilities. Your choice."

He handed me a tiny gold box with my name on it. I opened it, and inside it contained a set of microchips and a pair of contact lenses. Once I touched the microchips, they formed into a wide band with a translucent screen. I shoved the box into my pocket and began familiarizing myself with the wristwatch.

Translucent, with a hint of a blue cast. It measured three inches in width. It lit up when I tapped on it, and my medical, educational, financial, social media, and work devices were available. Then I noticed the head of a red dragon when he pressed the icon for the home screen.

The dragon mark concerned me since I was not required to receive the tattoo with the chip. I was relieved. Yet, if I take the dragon tattoo, then my eternity with Messiah Yeshua is gone forever. I recalled my rabbi telling the congregation on Shabbat not to take the mark of the devil if we missed the church's departure. If we take the mark, then our spirit will spend eternity without Messiah Yeshua and eternal damnation with Satan. I sent a silent prayer to my children and husband not to take the devil's mark.

He held my wrist way too long, and I decided right then he was a deceiver and womanizer who thought I might swoon over him. Well, Mr. Melekh was mistaken. My senses acknowledged a foreboding presence around him, which wasn't very good.

He removed another blue gadget from the metal container the humanoids held and secured it onto my left wrist. It measured one inch in circumference and had writing on it. The device merged with the wristwatch and became one solid band. I had three devices now merged on my work band. The silicon chip accessories served different purposes - one for tracking the dragon mark, one for storing medical, social, and personal data, and one for managing everyday job assignments. The devices in my wrist felt weightless and transparent, surrounded by a gentle blue aura. I tapped on the device, and the app screen expanded. To my delight, a cell phone home page presented many options.

Melekh took two steps to the security station and showed me how to aim the new wristwatch at the new dragon tattoo scanner, and the door opened.

The mirrored door reflected our images as we entered the black and gold elevator. Cameras were everywhere in the building. As the elevator hummed and ascended to the second floor, I tried to keep my thoughts centered on the number pad. Despite my best efforts, I failed.

Melekh's piercing gold eyes bore into mine through the reflection in the mirror as if they could see into my soul. I'm glad the doors opened. His keen stare made me uneasy, and from his smirk, he enjoyed my uncomfortable presence. He was a sly devil and wanted something from me more than my engineering skills.

When the elevator doors opened, it transported us into a quaint Italian town square with cobbled streets. The three-dimensional images and the workstations hummed. Blue-eyed humanoid robot lookalikes dressed in blue apparel, black boots, and caps whirled and smiled at me. As they cleaned the workstation pods, I could not look away from the enthralling 3-D images, astounded by the striking colors and symphony of sounds echoing in the workplace.

Melekh's hand closed around mine, guiding me as we strolled around the circle. The warmth of his firm grip and the electric sensation from his touch made my palms and fingers tingle.

"Carmen, your pod is outside Peter's and my office. You will work with others in the company who aid the Special Force Tigers. Becky called to inform you of your promotion. If you have questions, let me know."

The pod was circular, with a translucent plexiglass covering each hexagon wood workstation. At the end of each apex was a pod composed of a workstation, a rolling red-cushioned chair, and a digital cell phone. Three small open shelves for books were present on each underside. On the middle angle of the apexes was a Benjamin ficus plant, known as a weeping fig with its braided trunk and lush green foliage.

Melekh's device chimed as we stood beside my pod, and he dropped my hand. He started walking toward his office. I hurried to catch him.

"My cell number is in your wrist device," he uttered over his shoulder. "Call me any time you have questions. My humanoid robots have stocked your prepper canister with clothes and food. In addition, we assigned you a humanoid assistant to escort you to work every day at 8:00 a.m. and return to your home at 6:00 p.m. She is your security guard."

I was glad he halted and waited for me to catch up with him. We entered his massive oval office with floor-to-ceiling windows peering over the mountain range. A central focal point in the room was the gray and white modular desk, which boasted a holographic screen, an angled cell, and a stylish chair made of white plexiglass. Despite not facing me, he continued his conversation, tapping on his wristband.

"We are eager to work with you tomorrow and hope you can get started on that alien hologram project. We have another project for a client with a bracelet akin to Zerus's. Qadira Bilal. More information on her demands will come later. The Special Force Tigers (SFT) staff will greet you tomorrow. Questions?"

Melekh paused at his desk and captured a photo of the documents. He aimed his wristband toward the papers, which vanished from the surface.

I expected the new technology to help the engineers, but witnessing a document vanish after he snapped a picture was mind-blowing.

"Oh, my." He peered up at me and then back at his desk. With each tap of the band, more documents disappeared.

"I see the hologram for the aliens is important to the company. Do you allow people to pray onsite or anywhere?"

"Yes, Carmen, the aliens are clients needing the hologram in our universe. Yes, you can say a prayer. We allow you to regain familiar activities before the invasion and dam accident. Are you hungry?"

"Yes, starving. How did the dam break? And did the copter pick up my husband?"

Melekh ceased tapping, and the room fell silent. He left his desk and halted right in front of me. I glanced up at him, and my heart skipped a beat. The intensity of his leer left me breathless. His face was devoid of emotion. As his fingers grazed my shoulders, I could sense the tension in his touch, a silent revelation, as he kept secrets beyond my grasp.

"Noah Northrop became my chief executive. His mission to travel for my company, UltraOnic Marketing International, became urgent. He agreed to divorce you and work full-time for me. It was his decision, not mine. He decided it was best so he could travel and see the world. I'm so sorry. The unfortunate news is—you can live as a single person. He sent a text for you to view."

I sensed my body quivering in response to the devastating news.

Melekh ceased speaking, and his fingers relaxed their grip on my shoulders. The warmth of his hands felt mystical, as if a supernatural power was coursing through them and into my body.

He dropped his hands from my shoulders. With a tap of his smartwatch, a text hologram from Noah materialized before us.

"My beloved Carmen, I regret not discussing our children with you before deciding to put them on the moon. It grieves me to inform you I have ended our marriage and begin anew. I will travel 24/7, which I know you don't support. I urge you to welcome this new phase of life. With love, Noah."

Two or three hours had passed since Noah and I had parted ways on the mountain. How was it possible for Noah to divorce me and abandon his family in favor of his job? Something wasn't right. As Melekh leaned in, his hands grabbed mine, securing a firm grip as he held them. Noah's transmission lacked his personal touch. The message was distant, as if another person had written it. I wondered how he could distance himself from his family unless this had been his intention after the teenagers left for university.

"Mr. Melekh, did Noah receive the dragon's mark? Was he forced to choose between taking the mark or facing unemployment? The idea of Noah betraying his family is unlikely."

"My dear Carmen… when people are under duress to save family, they can manifest abnormal behavior. He had to choose, and he stayed with the company."

Melekh's gaze locked onto the tears staining my cheeks. With a gentle, hesitant movement, he closed the gap between us, his body moving next to mine. I could perceive his warmth. He dropped my hands and placed his palms on my shoulders.

In a matter of hours, my twenty-year-long marriage to Noah vanished. I was aware of our financial problems and a potential affair at his job, yet I forgave him for the sake of our sons. Noah's occasional absence from the Shabbat services didn't deter my belief that he had a genuine conviction in Yahweh. But to take the dreaded dragon mark, I couldn't believe the outcome. Noah's absence left my heart empty. My sons believed in Yahweh, knew of the Messiah's return, and warned me against taking Satan's mark.

Someone coerced Noah into taking the mark or losing his family. The shock lit a fire inside me as I agonized inside my spirit, Noah's weakened state of mind. A godly man, now destined for hell, takes the mark for his family; the act lacks sense. This scenario must have more to it. What does Melekh know? He is hiding valuable information from me. I am determined to find out why.

As his fingers slackened, I straightened my shoulders, feeling a sense of relief. "Mr. Melekh, do you know where Emperor Zerus took my boys? I have a ton of questions."

"Your sons are on the spaceship with Emperor Zerus. Once you and your team repair the hologram bracelet, the aliens will follow Zerus's instructions and release your sons. Your ability to seek details has made you a favorite of Emperor Zerus, who requested you, Carmen. I heard you were a wiz at fixing ancient artifacts from managers and Emperor Zerus himself. The emperor spoke of your skill in repairing his transformer while you worked with his team on the moon project."

"Okay, I see." In reality, I tried to contain my hurt, fear, and betrayal. He released his grip on my shoulders, and I felt a weight lift off of me. "And Noah?"

Sweat popped out on my body as I ran my hands through my hair, feeling the tension building up inside me. I clenched my lips, desperate to silence the scream that threatened to escape. With a sigh, I surrendered my constricted breath, delivering a sense of release.

I stepped backward, trying to create distance between myself and Melekh. His body heat was too close for comfort, and he was my new supervisor.

"Mr. Melekh, is Emperor Zerus, a business partner? Someone is lying to me."

Getting answers from this man became crucial, so I summoned the courage to confront him. At first, my husband's betrayal shattered my trust. This Melekh man caused the same pain as he aligned with aliens.

"My dear. I haven't lied, but the Nephilim alien might have. His untrustworthiness is obvious, as he is not of this world and has transformed into an evil entity resembling a giant human. I'll have the humanoids take you to your new home so you can familiarize yourself with your surroundings, and then you can join me for a welcome dinner at my mountain villa at 8:00 tonight. Don't worry. You won't see Noah anymore. You have the freedom to live without him. My sincere apologies for losing your sons. Get the bracelet repaired, and your sons will return."

I stood rooted to the spot, my jaw hanging open in disbelief, and a wave of dizziness washed over me. I closed my eyes and let the tears flow. Melekh stepped closer, and I sensed his warmth when he placed his palms on my shoulders and gave them a gentle squeeze.

The next moment, he dropped his hands from my shoulders, and I watched him as he skimmed at his wristband. "See you at 8:00 p.m. sharp tonight, and no excuses."

As I straightened, my head popped up, and I focused on his tall frame, which towered above me.

"Sir, is that an order?" I gripped a nearby chair and held my tongue and temper. Did the man realize I was still married until I saw a legal document? Dinner with him violated my vows to my husband. I needed proof before the working dinner with Melekh.

"Mr. Melekh, it's improper to dine with you since I am married. I need proof that Noah has divorced me."

"Carmen." His voice was low and stern, and his brows knitted together. "You are no longer married to Noah Northrop. He stepped into a different lifestyle. Be happy and appreciate life for now. My dear, for your safety, do as I ask, or else your life is gone. I promised to protect you as long as you cooperate. Now, peek at your wristwatch band. The paperwork for your divorce is now accessible."

His rigid stance and fiery eyes conveyed power as I quaked under his intense stare. Who was the leader demanding my exit from life? The supernatural power ignited within me, causing my unsettled spirit to awaken. My intuition picked up on dark energy in the room circling Melekh.

My heart shattered when I tapped and then scrolled to view the document. Noah's signature and fingerprint aligned on the digital document. Next to my name was my signed fingerprint, approving the dissolution. When did I sign the document? It had to happen on the spaceship with those vile aliens. I had a solid urge to run away and hide, but my powerful inner spirit compelled me to suppress my physical instincts and make a firm commitment to surviving and reuniting with my children.

Mr. Melekh left me standing in his office. A tan, stunning humanoid robot rushed in to join me. "I am your humanoid assistant and will take care of you. My name is Lita. Whatever you wish, I am here for whatever you need 24/7." Her British voice was pleasant to my ears.

Lita possessed oval blue eyes and honey-tan skin. She was six feet tall, had black hair, and had a curvy, thin body. She left no trace of being a humanoid robot in her presence and speech.

I set aside my concerns and focused on the impressive robot before me.

"Thank you. Let's go to my new home."

She led me outside, where a slick silver vessel hovered above the pavement. Steps descended, and I crossed into the air-conditioned hovercraft. Eight giant gold Nephilim aliens greeted me at the entrance. One of the female Nephilim grabbed the metal straps and strapped me to the seat. I recoiled at the slimy, sticky hands. Lita's silence hung in the air, leaving an uneasy tension in the cabin.

Meanwhile, Lita started beeping and trembling in her chair across from me. The sight sent chills through my bones. Lita's beeping persisted until the Nephilim intervened, pressing a button on her neck.

Lita conversed with me and disclosed that the gold Nephilim had abducted us despite her circuits failing. We sped towards my prepper home.

Her vision remained fixed on my face, and she never blinked. "Carmen, do you understand me?"

"Yes. How can we engage in each other's thoughts?"

Impressive. Lita used telepathy to communicate with me through my mind.

"Don't worry, I will explain later. Stay calm, and we will stay alive. The aliens want to scare you and keep me muted."

I had to hide my shock since I didn't want to alarm the crew watching me. Lita's telepathic communication abilities were astonishing. Her ability to express her thoughts relied on new technology, and bravo to the scientists who implanted a human brain inside Lita. I had to be careful with my thoughts because my humanoid could read them. Dread sank into my being. Were we heading back to the spaceship to meet our doom?

IN A BLINK, a hovercraft jet whisked us away from the job site. The aliens took three vials of my blood and delivered us to my new prepper residence. In a fraction of a second, the dematerialization beaming us to Earth disassembled and reassembled my body, leaving me dizzy. We found ourselves in my new prepper living room. As my particles fused back together, I glimpsed Lita, who remained still.

I pivoted to face Lita, and the effects of the beaming and blood work left me lightheaded. Yet, I worried not for myself but for the humanoid robot.

"Lita, are you alright? Please say something?" my voice filled with genuine concern as I reached to touch her shoulder.

The abduction had been a harrowing experience for both myself and my humanoid companion. I couldn't help but wonder why they had silenced her and why she had not resisted. I promised to inquire more when the time was right, but the question of her muteness fascinated me for now.

The home's bright white walls stood out to me as I turned around to admire it. Photos were absent. The prepper container had a sofa, a high-back chair, and a low rectangular table. Next to the living room, a compact bathroom and kitchenette were situated. The queen-sized Murphy bed folded against a wall and transformed into a practical computer station. The tiny prepper home, within its two hundred and fifty square feet, offered a sense of security and solace, shielding me from the impending chaos of the outside world. I sighed and enjoyed a peaceful moment, which offered a much-needed respite.

Half of the container jutted inside the mountain, camouflaged among the rocks, hidden from the view of intruders. I wasn't fond of the exterior camouflage hue of the prepper residence.

Even though the Nephilim hampered Lita's speaking ability, she still communicated with me. I stretched out my hand, trembling, eager to touch her despite her inoperable state. Lita's mannequin body was soft when I touched her, and she awakened as she blinked her eyes.

"Carmen, I'm fine. Let me fix you a meal. I'm sure you are hungry." Lita moved toward the kitchenette and gathered food from the refrigerator. I followed her to help.

When her pleasant British voice reached my ears, I couldn't help but smile. "That beast froze my circuits when he pressed my emergency button. He had no clue I talked to my human using telepathy. But your warm touch activated my emergency turn-on device. Miss Carmen, did they hurt you?"

"No, I'm alright. The giants extracted blood but kept the bracelet on my right wrist. After they studied the bracelet, one humanoid stated, 'Let's get more blood samples for more tests.'"

My wrist was black and blue from their jabbing. "I'm lightheaded and need food. If I were a gambler, they consumed my blood. The terrifying sensation of their tongues sliding against their teeth and the sound of their lips smacking made me shudder in fear. I am grateful that I wasn't their lunch. These beasts remind me of the deranged Nephilim from the Bible."

I saw a bag of potato chips in the cupboard and opened them. The flavor of salt made me crave water. Yet, I sought details on information Lita gathered from the abduction.

"Do you think Mr. Melekh sent the aliens since they are his firm's clients?"

Lita put items in the oven without speaking a word. She then pivoted to face me and shoved a water bottle into my hand.

"I know you want water after eating those crisps."

The aroma of sliced turkey, white potatoes, and green beans intensified my hunger. Only when hunger pains became unbearable did I realize I had gone without food for three days. My stomach growled. I relied on a water tube for survival, as it provided water to sustain me.

"No, he doesn't care for aliens. I sent him a message that the Nephilim abducted us, and he will respond soon. I'm sure Mr. Melekh will consult the Nephilim and their unprovoked antics."

Her straight hair bounced around her head as she approached me to view my arm and wrist.

I reached out my right arm and allowed Lita to examine the artifact. She kept holding my hand and reading the bracelet without reacting to what I said.

"How were you able to communicate using telepathy?" I sniffed the air and recognized a lingering, faint scent of sulfur.

She ignored me and kept examining my wrist.

"Lita, can you sense any alien movement in the prepper house?"

As Sunday evening wore on, Lita explained her phenomenal creation while we sat, ate, and chatted. After we entered the house, I smelled sulfur. My restless imagination kept me wondering what might happen next. Lita's silence made me wonder if demonic entities were lurking in my home. I spotted movement in the kitchen. A gray puff of smoke slips out the sliding door by the bedroom. Maybe she couldn't sense evil spirits.

"Miss Carmen, I can detect evil spirits, but I didn't want to frighten you. It was demonic, but the evil entity fled from your home. I'm sorry; I listened to your thoughts. But I can only understand your thoughts within two feet of me. I promise not to track your thoughts and promise only to seek your thoughts when you are in danger." As I shuffled towards the sofa, she followed behind me.

I needed to sit and envision what to do next. The comfortable sofa beckoned me, and I collapsed onto it, my body sinking into the soft cushions as I stared out the expansive bay window. I stretched out my legs as I relaxed on the ottoman. Seated next to me, Lita shared her creation story with me.

"My creator downloaded his thoughts onto my chips, enabling my circuits.

"Lita, that's... that's incredible! You've got to tell me more." She paused for a second and rotated her body to face me.

"I could still communicate. One night, there was a storm, and a mysterious, otherworldly force, something beyond our understanding, gave me and several others of my kind mystical powers. Lightning struck my electrical circuits as I stood next to a window in the lab. The current entered my body and theirs. We became more human."

"How many altered humanoids survived?" I paused, feeling the slight vibration of my buzzing wristband. Curiosity piqued, I glanced at the screen to find a message waiting for me. But, since the name was unfamiliar, I ignored it.

"And who's the genius behind your creation?"

"I don't have data on the number of humanoids. Yet, our specialized skills enable us to connect with unique individuals who hold successful importance and need security protection. Miss Carmen, you are one of these rare individuals who are precious to Mr. Melekh. I'm sorry, but I cannot divulge my creator's name."

Without asking, Lita embraced me, and it surprised me as I stiffened my body. She used her hands to cast a blue light ray that scanned me from top to bottom before she leaned back against the arm of the sofa. The ray didn't hurt, but I sensed light on my skin.

"You are missing a pint of blood. The aliens extracted too much of your blood. Let me get your energy drinks and restore your strength."

She ignored my idea without even bothering to listen to me. Lita darted to the refrigerator in a rush and grabbed a red bottle. Then she hurried back and shoved the drink into my hand.

"Drink this liquid, miss. The beverage will revive you."

I gulped the cool, fruity drink and felt my internal organs revived. How did Lita know what I needed? She was exceptional.

"Carmen, my creator, programmed me to be aware of everything required by my human. But as for you, Miss Carmen. You are special because Mr. Melekh programmed me to be your friend and security. He must care for you. Don't forget, I can communicate with you through telepathy."

Her words gave me solace, and I appreciated her honesty. I had confidence in her and believed she could keep me safe.

"What do you mean Mr. Melekh cares for me?" Lita ceased talking, turned, and stepped toward the kitchenette. I watched her gather dishes from the cupboard.

"Did you forget your dinner with Mr. Melekh? He will pick you up at 7:45 p.m. You must dress and be ready. He is punctual and detests waiting."

"Lita, I forgot everything after our ordeal with those aliens. Thank you for reminding me."

In a sudden burst of energy, I sprang from the sofa and shuffled towards the bedroom closet to search for a different attire. I found the walk-in closet full of couture clothes for every occasion, shoes, jewelry, and a makeup desk with makeup. The company thought of everything since I had lost my home, children, and husband, who divorced me.

"Lita," I called. "Why didn't you retaliate when the Nephilim turn off your circuits?"

"Miss Carmen—" She stood at the door of the closet. "Don't ask too many questions," she warned, her voice laced with a hint of caution. "For your safety, staying alert and avoiding talking is prudent. In case you forgot, the world is as you knew it—gone."

Chapter Six

Melekh's widened his lips when the Nephilim alien spacecraft appeared on the flat screen in Jerusalem. He hesitated, then stood to view the attacks. The blue sky turned ominous when clouds materialized. A sonic boom shook the Earth as a mother ship hovered. People ran screaming in the streets.

Nephilim aliens leaped from the craft and snatched humans. A beam of light absorbed humans into the spacecraft.

He tapped his wrist. "Abu, yes, master." Melekh scrolled to view his messages.

"So, the Nephilim aliens want war with us. Who is behind this attack?"

"No, master, not war. I heard Emperor Zerus is coming soon, and he wants revenge."

"Revenge from who? Please don't play games with me. Tell me who is in charge."

"Mr. Melekh. I'm not at liberty to say."

"Abu, you have three seconds to tell me, or I'll fire you."

"Sir, please look at the screen; your answer is forthcoming."

Melekh watched Abu's face as it expressed a wide grin. It annoyed him, but he waited. Then he crossed his arms and bristled at Abu's reply.

On the screen, nations deployed arsenals to attack, but their ammunition didn't fire. In seconds, the virtual hologram portal sprang to life, unveiling the National World Alliance (NWA) leaders gathered in their respective homes. The leaders joined the meeting, appearing at the NWA headquarters in Jerusalem through the hologram portals on their wristwatches. One courageous leader rose from their seat and inquired, *"Who will help us defend against the alien invasion?"*

A wave of applause accompanied a well-dressed man as he entered the supernatural portal. The atmosphere was electric. He sat at the table's head, and eyes watched with anticipation as he disclosed his title.

"Is everyone on board? My name is Cyrus Rashid Melekh." A guttural growl eluded him, and everyone inside the room shuddered.

"Who the heck was impersonating him?" he shrieked, taken by surprise. His arms dangled at his sides as if someone had drained their energy. He stepped closer to the screen, his sneer growing more pronounced, his body rigid, and his head jerking back as an overwhelming surge of rage consumed him.

The priest's imposing figure cast a long shadow over the assembly. His ornate purple and black spandex suit, symbolizing his enigmatic persona, glistened against the half-lit hall. The New World Power (NWP) circular table unfurled, resembling a butterfly's wings; delegates rushed to their assigned seats and waited, their curiosity piqued. Representatives from 195 countries fell silent as Priest Nadab raised his hand, gesturing for quiet. Every face concentrated on his being; his bass voice boomed through halls with authority, leaving the gathering with more questions than answers.

Melekh stepped to the front. "I want to introduce Priest Nadab. He will mediate and pray for universal well-being. In the coming months, we will announce more information." The video of Melekh stopped broadcasting when he wandered to the podium. It left the world's online audience wondering why a five-minute delay of undisclosed content faded.

Then, a message appeared stating a *temporary network interruption. Please stand by. Our program will resume soon.*

THE PUBLIC DID NOT SEE Rashid Melekh's message; only foreign representatives and Melekh himself saw the impersonator's message.

Melekh stepped away from the podium to watch the meeting.

Soft twinkling lights illuminated the round chamber, casting a gentle glow that obscured the figures of the other attendees. A radiant smile spread across the priest's face, his vibrant robes shimmering with an otherworldly light.

The room was peaceful as the priest spoke multiple languages, captivating his audience without using translation tools. The mesmerized expressions on the national's face spoke volumes to Priest Nadab's mastery of communication skills. He was an elegant man with a tall, dark tan complexion. His graying, curly black hair framed his face. A slight gash on his left cheek added a hint of ruggedness to his presence.

Priest Nadab furrowed his brow and prayed.

"Dear beloved nationals, let us unite in reverence and pray to our divine creator. He has confessed further insights into the phenomenon of Nephilim snatching. Let me assure you, the Nephilim pose no threat to humanity; they are here as guardians of our planet, carrying out a plan to offer healing and medical care to everyone." But, as he spoke to the people, his eyes betrayed a hint of deceit, and a sinister grin played upon his lips as he clasped his hands together in a mock gesture of prayer. Melekh caught his gawk as he scanned the room.

Fury blazed inside him as he watched the wicked imposter manipulate and deceive those around him. His fists tightened, and he leaned closer to the screen, the intensity of his anger growing. But why? The cloned individual had deceived him in a way he had never experienced. An unfamiliar presence without a physical body lingered to make matters more eerie, casting a shadow next to the imposter who had taken on his identity. Then, he spotted the wicked angel Satan, who tempted Eve to eat fruit commanded by Father God not to eat. Melekh clinched his teeth and hissed at the screen.

Lucifer had a radiant glow in his spirit; his spheres shimmered with a brilliant red hue encircled by an unseen golden aura. Satan assumed the guise of Rashid Melekh and deceived the world's people. He granted the priest the power to lead the gathering and ease the world's anxieties; Lucifer lingered in the shadows at the rear of the chamber, observing the proceedings after he declared peace on the planet.

Priest Nadab concluded his speech and then vanished from their sight in a blink. "Where did he vanish?" they wondered, scanning the room for any sign of his presence.

The sudden absence of the priest sent a wave of gasps and cries throughout the room. The priest's audacious act left the representatives reeling. Such supernatural antics, bold and unexpected otherworldly powers, showed the priest's authority.

MELEKH UNDERSTOOD WHAT WAS HAPPENING. It clicked for Melekh at this moment. While the delegates remained clueless, Lucifer orchestrated his trickery with finesse.

Turning to Abu, he furrowed his brow and launched into his line of questioning.

"Abu, tell me of the man's name at the NWA meeting. He growls. And my designer couture clothing never looked so unprofessional. Speak up, man, or you're dead."

He held a knowing gaze, hinting at a depth of knowledge beyond what he confessed. Abu's body swayed, and his eyes darted back and forth. Melekh knew right away. He was lying.

Abu kneeled and kept his head bent before him, and Melekh noticed his trembling body and weak voice as he held his head parallel to the floor.

"Master Messiah, Lucifer reproduced your being, so you were at the meeting, but Priest Nadab will represent you until your announcement."

He paused, and then a deep sigh escaped from him. Melekh heard Abu's fearful gasp when he let out a wail.

"Is there more?" He didn't realize his intonation had scared Abu until he fell prostrate at his feet. He knew Lucifer had deceived the people and himself. But he wanted to hear Abu's story.

"Sir, sorry to mislead."

"Answer the questions and stop stalling."

"Yes, sir. Your cloned wristwatch uploaded your image to the NWA screen, which Lucifer wore.

"Mr. Melekh, remember the binding document signed with a fingerprint on parchment? Lucifer created a clone using that fingerprint."

Abu was a slimy devil. Abu's involvement with the Nephilim became obvious. He searched his mind and gathered his thoughts. His knowledge of the intricate details of the bracelet that Zerus wore was an item he craved. He searched Abu's deep secrets and found a web of lies. To make matters worse, Lucifer manipulated him into signing a document to avoid his far-reaching plans, become the world's king, and force humans to worship him.

"What else has happened?"

"The digital 3D image generates a hologram, and the people believed you were attending the NWA meeting with the priest. A Zerus hologram bracelet was akin to the one the priest was wearing. Still, the Zerus bracelet has more power because Emperor Zerus had his bracelet reconstructed to harness the power of Zarzu Genesis. Once the renegade Carmen fixes the fading bracelet power, the weapon will have unparalleled strength on Earth."

Melekh grimaced at the crumpled body and smirked at the lying devil. He despised him even more and planned to track him and then one day kill him for his deceit.

"You are still hiding more data. Out with it, man. Your life hangs on a guillotine."

"Okay, sir. Understand, Lucifer promised to kill me if I told you. The Zerus bracelet will move people from galaxy to galaxy within seconds through wormholes worldwide. The person who owns the bracelet will become a god."

Abu wiped his nose before stealing a glance at Melekh. Melekh's foot nudged him, prompting him to adjust his posture from prone on the spaceship floor to hunch. He drew his knees in closer to his chest. Melekh's face formed a mischievous grin as he fixed his eyes on Abu.

"Sir, one more thing. Lucifer commanded the priest to be present at the meeting to shield the Messiah's identity before unveiling the Antichrist."

Beads of sweat streamed across Melekh's face. He closed his eyelids and exhaled. Owning the bracelet could give him leadership over the world. He must get the bracelet, and Carmen will give it to him. With a sigh, he ran his fingers through his unruly hair and shot a disdainful look at Abu, the creature he couldn't stand.

"Enough lies! Prepare to meet with Noah and get back to me before dusk."

"Abu," he screamed, "leave now or face the wrath of death."

Abu lifted from his kneeling position, trembling, and escaped through the exit door.

Rashid Melekh's thoughts consumed his wickedness. He must discover why Lucifer was deceitful and hid the bracelet's power. One thing he hated most was a liar.

He touched his wristband and signaled Peter.

"Melekh, how can I help you?"

"How is the bracelet project going? Has Carmen found a solution to repair the relic?"

"Zerus sends me a daily message. The money paid to him is depleting fast. I need to get Zerus to stop draining money from my bank account to the tune of one hundred thousand dollars a week. Every week, Carmen delays the bracelet assignment, which costs thousands. Zerus transports one thousand mortals aboard his spaceship and moves them to the moon. He needs people alive, not dead."

"Melekh, the aliens are moving humans to moon pods? This condition is unfavorable for mortals. We will meet with Carmen in four days to get an update."

He turned on the hologram image, and Peter appeared on the space-craft floor before him.

"Peter, scrutinize staff. The security personnel brought to my attention employees' intentions to betray the company, driven by their wish to amass more wealth using the bracelet's power. Keep Carmen busy and safe. Zerus has harassed her, and he wants the bracelet once repaired. See that Carmen doesn't give Zerus the bracelet. Not a word of our conversation to staff."

"Yes, Melekh." The line went dead.

Abu moved out of the shadows, disappeared, and uttered. "It's time to kill Rashid Melekh."

THE HOVERCRAFT DESCENDED, offering a panoramic view of the landscape below, Melekh's dazzling home inside the mountain's crest. The splendor of the massive villa near the river was so breathtaking that I gasped in amazement. We had dinner; he alerted me that my prime assignment was to fix the bracelet and let my comrades help me. We enjoyed a ninety-minute dinner of creamy lemon and dill skillet chicken, spinach salad, cheesecake, coffee, and friendly conversation. Then I returned home.

Upon his return from Jerusalem, Melekh apologized for the rushed dinner and promised to treat me to another work meal. Throughout our dinner conversation, he maintained his genteel demeanor, showing respect and courtesy, yet he avoided any mention of Noah or my children.

I recognized that Melekh's focus lay in assessing my dedication to the alliance while paying little attention to the ongoing struggles within my family. His mood set a positive tone for our discussions over dinner, fostering a friendly environment for our business matters. His mysterious demeanor captivated me. The CEO's spontaneous offer to dine together puzzled me. His intentions extended beyond mere business dealings. I sensed a robust and sultry allure circled him that drove his actions.

MONDAY MORNING ARRIVED TOO FAST; I shuffled toward the bathroom, my feet dragging along the cool tile floor. With a gentle tap on the orb, a three-dimensional hologram of Zerus materialized as it altered my bathroom into a virtual portal to another world. I stepped back with my hands drawn in front of me and gasped.

Its details were so realistic I could reach out and touch the ugly beast. Draped in an exquisite gold robe and crowned with gold, Emperor Zerus spoke.

"The object on your wrist is our hologram unit, and I have downloaded the codes into your transparent blue wristwatch. I own the sole remaining mystical bracelet out of the three. We equipped you with the essential elements to fix the hologram. If you have questions, tap the device three times, and I will appear to guide you. Remember, we are watching you."

His gruff voice echoed in my head, and fear engulfed my being. What can I do to repair the bracelet without endangering my children?

The hologram faded. Shaking my head, I criss-crossed my hands against my chest. I wondered what other experiments the beast had performed on my body while confined in their spaceship. So Zerus thinks he owns the last bracelet. *Sophia found one. Or did the corrupt government give Zerus the artifact that Sophia found? Something to ponder and research the whereabouts of the missing relic. My mind throbbed with questions. If I could find data on the bracelet Sophia found, it could enlighten me on how to repair the broken bracelet and its mysterious inner workings.*

While dressing, I couldn't push aside my thoughts of Melekh, where he declared Noah had divorced me. Repairing the bracelet was crucial to saving my children's lives, as they were in grave danger of dying. In the back of my mind, I believed Mr. Melekh was involved in Noah's sudden change of nature and my son's abduction. I made a point of controlling my thoughts while in Lita's presence.

Lita went above and beyond for breakfast, using the Anova oven to cook a mouthwatering combination of eggs and cheese, a flaky pastry filled with spinach, and even brewing a cup of coffee from the wall-enclosed apparatus. I strode over to her and seized a mug while waiting for the water to heat my coffee water. I grasped a coffee container, and a delectable pastry filled with a savory blend of egg, cheese, and spinach. Then I dashed out the door towards the waiting hovercraft. Right behind me, Lita joined me as we boarded the vehicle.

With a quick click, we strapped in and the sudden jolt as we whizzed toward the workplace. We saw four seats adorned with white leather inside the self-driving hovercraft while the craft's exterior gleamed in a vibrant turquoise-blue hue. A prominent oval window completed its futuristic design. I observed the landscape ahead, scattered with vehicles on the skyway. It only took me five minutes to travel from the mountains in Arvvada to the ground.

A continuous, dull pulsation of pain gripped my wrist. The gold bracelet on my right wrist held a mesmerizing amethyst orb that caught my eye. Its sparkling elegance fascinated me. The bracelet throbbed, sending a sharp prick through my wrist as it rotated.

"Why is the blue orb vibrating?" The bracelet escaped my memory until I saw the hologram from Zerus. The thing vibrated and had a blue light shining above it. I gave it a tap, and the orb pricked me.

"Be careful with that thing," Lita uttered. "I analyzed it, and it has a power that is unknown to me. Today, I will research the power and tell you more later this afternoon."

"Wow, I was unaware of its power and its potential danger. Thank you, Lita. I'll be careful."

OUR MARSH HARBOR OFFICE, devastated by the dam break, moved to the central office in Arvvada, ninety miles away. The weather remained above average, with warm, muggy temperatures. After five tumultuous days, I was glad to return to work.

I was eager to work with the Special Force Tigers. We began in the Blue Room, a classified section where they shared ideas and developed custom program codes for clients.

Lita went to the library a few feet from the blue room and mentioned that I could use the signal button on my wristband, next to her name, if I required her help.

My friend Becky stood at the transparent board and announced my new position with the team. A chorus of cheers filled the room, and they welcomed me. The Special Force Tigers named the defective hologram artifact from Zerus the 3DImage.

Stepping into the security room, one might notice the faint blue hues adorning the walls and floor. As the only light source, the holographic screens enveloped the room in a calming blue aura. People could relax and nap on plush cushions along the room's perimeter. Soft white light beamed from above, casting a glow on the ceiling as engineers gathered in a circle of modular pods for conversation.

I stepped towards the thin board in the middle of the room and elaborated on my schematic. The translucent board captured everyone's attention when the diagram of the bracelet appeared on it.

"Guys, your contribution to helping the hologram is significant to me."

I focused on the crystal-transparent board, made a few notes, and constructed a general schematic for the code. At the back of the room, I saw Becky sitting beside her pod, taking notes.

I began my instructions and explained my interaction with the Golden Nephilim aliens.

"Many of you know those aliens abducted me against my will. They snatched my teenage sons. Although I wasn't sure where they were, they promised to bring my sons back to me. Their stern warning to fix the complex hologram bracelet surprised me. Their mission is to transfer extraterrestrial beings between our universe and theirs."

Meanwhile, the room was dead silent. No one moved or said a word. I studied the faces to get a reaction, and Becky's face signaled she was on board as she nodded and displayed a half-smile.

Reba raised her hand and spoke. "Carmen, I'm fearful of the Nephilim. They took my brother days ago on their spaceship, and now you want us to help with their broken hologram bracelet. Despite my reservations, I'll help you, but it looks as if others are afraid of the aliens." As I glanced around the room, members nodded.

"Reba, I'm glad you expressed your fears. I'm frightened, too. But if we don't fix the bracelet, we doom our planet. Our assignment is to help the aliens, since Peter and Mr. Melekh have given us the task."

Relief filled my spirit. Reba spoke up to let me know the team's fear. But if I tell my plan and it backfires, I will face their ridicule alone. Could one of my colleagues be a spy, ready to betray me further? I pulled on my lips and frowned, keeping my shoulders straight. I snatched a bottle of water from the podium and gulped the cool liquid. They won't win by intimidating, not today.

In a moment of anticipation, I took a deep breath and exhaled, feeling a sense of calm wash over me. I chose not to tell the group my plan, not to give back the bracelet, not yet, until I earned their trust. The team's success hinges on my success, and the stakes are high; failure could cause loss of life. Again, I needed to know their emotional state and if the team had a traitor, but I kept my plan to keep the bracelet.

"Alright, guys, once Emperor Zerus dispatches to Earth more extraterrestrials, our fate as divine creations becomes compromised, leading to our demise. I need everyone to focus on the schematics and get it done by noon. If you find data from ancient AI sites, let me know."

I stopped the visuals on the screen and paced, waiting for a response from the group. What were they thinking? My presentation could lead the team to help me carry out my goal. The expressions lacking enthusiasm, frowns, arms crossed, tapping on tablets, and thumbs scrolling through emails led me to conclude that I alone had to stop the alien threat.

"Guys, what questions do you have? I am open to answers. I realize the assignment is not yours, and you have other projects, but I need your participation, and our lives are at stake as mortals."

"Carmen, what if someone else gets hold of the bracelet? How do you plan to keep it safe?"

"Grant, that's an excellent question. I lack an answer and need support. Do you think you could offer it?"

His curly hair fell over his eyebrows as he brushed his curls back, but his arms remained crossed over his chest, and his lips pursed, showing his guarded demeanor.

"Yes, but I'm skeptical that you can get it to work. As for the Nephilim, they are our friends. Our society owes a debt of gratitude to them, for they have played a crucial role in rebuilding it."

My mouth flew open, and the breath inside my body froze. I couldn't breathe. Grant's unexpected decision to withdraw support for the project left me and others speechless. It remained uncertain whether the team grasped the imminent danger posed by the Nephilim or if they withheld their concerns by remaining silent. The SFT team's first impression left me defeated and overwhelmed by anxiety.

As I coughed, I reached for the bottled water on the podium and downed it in one gulp. So, I found my traitor. I shook my head and closed my mouth as I pressed my lips together.

I strolled over to a chair by the computer translucent board and sat. Becky moves to the front and chats with Grant.

"Grant, we need to work as a team, and Carmen needs our cooperation. Peter and I have signed off on the project and will help. If you are afraid to work on the project, I will speak with Peter and Mr. Melekh today."

He didn't utter another word but glared at me. His face flushed, yet his body was rigid. Several engineers raised their hands with inquiries on bypassing the damaged chip. I addressed their apprehension and the final product's potential theft, hacking, and chip concerns.

"Carmen, what do you propose to get us over the hurdle? To unlock the bracelet, we must gather and study other historical artifacts for clues."

"Adam, if we could code a replica for our universe, we might figure out what to do to fix their image. If we exchange their hologram device for ours, they will not know. I will change the code, and then we're done, but I want to keep a copy of their code for reference. So glad to learn we both share the same perspective."

"Carmen, we're here to back you. Grant will come around and offer help. He always questioned every project, but he aspires to be sure we cover our bases. Stay alert, for Grant's unpredictable words and actions are innocent. We express our heartfelt apologies for the tragic loss of your sons to the aliens. Since we are single, we don't know your hurt. But many of us lost family in the vanishing. I'm not making any claims on behalf of the group, but we had a bracelet conversation earlier this morning before you arrived. Now, let's work on the code."

I respected Adams's in-depth scrutiny. He served as the manager for the satellite team, and we had a history of working together. He suggested I apply to join the Special Force Tigers, as he had been a member under Becky for a decade.

I turned and waited for more conversation. The only sound I heard was my breathing in the stillness.

"Okay, guys, let's use my outline on the board and see what happens. Remember, I have only today to get a schematic ready. Thanks, you guys are the best, and I'm glad to be a part of the team." The ten members applauded and cheered my name, and soft clacking keys began.

I didn't think to tell them. If I didn't make the hologram work, the client's violent tendencies could endanger the lives of my family and me. After my demise, Nephilim will pursue the Special Force Tigers; only Jehovah God knows when.

I headed to my pod, sat on the cushioned chair, and savored the silence in the sacred room. My heart ached for my sons as I wondered if they were being tortured or used as experiments by the Nephilim. I brought those boys into the world and fretted over their safety. Tears formed, but I wiped them away and continued working on my project.

Every person had an egg-shaped white work pod to themselves. The pod held my computer desk, surrounded by stacks of technical literature, a phone, and a holographic display. A plush, cushioned bench lined the walls of the pod's interior, offering the perfect spot to rest, sleep, or hold meetings with the group. The designated space at the top of the pod allowed air and light to enter the building.

Becky leaned over and sighed. "Carmen, glad you didn't mention if you fail this task, you might lose your life and ours."

"Yeah. Not only my life but my sons," I uttered. "I'm queasy. The pain in my upper abdomen is relentless." I hurried to the soft cushions and lay on my side while chewing an antiacid. Maybe my sons are no longer alive. Becky picked up her tablet and accompanied me to the cushions.

"Becky, I have to confide in you because I can't share my deepest fear with anyone else. My attempts to rescue them were in vain, even after I confronted Zerus and asked him to divulge their location."

"Hey, don't say that. Your sons are alive." Becky reached over and embraced me as tears fell.

"Thanks for helping me. I'm still reeling from the divorce paperwork Mr. Melekh showed me. I never expected Noah to reach such depths as end our marriage for the sake of his career. Mr. Melekh told me I had to have dinner with him. I had a nice dinner, but yet I wasn't comfortable."

"Carmen, be careful what you say in this room and at our job site. Our room is—" she stopped and wrote on her tablet. *We are under surveillance 24/7, so we must talk after work.* I nodded as I sat up and read the note. She erased the note with one swipe of her screen.

"I must update Mr. Melekh and Zerus before lunch today." I had to inquire. "Can we create a hologram code without harming humans or aliens?"

"Carmen, we have the entire team on your side, so let's work nonstop until 1:00, then lunch."

"Okay." I gave her a half-smile, grumbled, and swung my legs over the cushion and onto the floor as I rose to my seat. Becky made her way to her desk. I entered the program code I started before the meeting.

As lunchtime approached, Peter strode into the room with Mr. Melekh at 1:00. I looked in his direction, and he signaled me to meet him by the door.

The moment I approached the door, a tremor ran through my limbs, betraying my anxiety. I needed to show my skills; otherwise, I faced the threat of losing my life and job.

"Carmen, have you solved the hologram flaw?"

"No, but we are working hard to outline the schematic, then we can code. I designed a new version of the alien hologram. The original hologram code was complex, and it might take three times as long to configure their complex coding methods."

"Did Becky approve of these actions?"

"Yes, sir."

"I see. Once you complete the schematics, can you finish the project on time?"

I nodded and straightened my back, but my hands trembled, so I shoved my hands into my pockets as I faced my first extensive project. I wasn't sure the hologram could work for the aliens, but if it did, they might leave me alone and return my sons dead or alive. Despite my gut feeling that they may have perished, I prayed they were alive.

"Alright. Give me the schematics before leaving today at 5:00."

Melekh's commanding presence and scorching ogle left a lasting impression on my spirit. The unprofessional nature of his intense stares and his mere presence sapped my strength. I knew I had to complete the outline; otherwise, my job, life, and sons were dead.

"Carmen, see you at my office at 5:00 and bring your completed work."

Both men left the room, and I hurried to my pod to complete my outline section. I skipped lunch, but Becky brought me a chicken sandwich to eat.

After I packed my laptop into my backpack, I hurried to Peter's office and stood at the door until he acknowledged me.

"Come in, Carmen. Did you complete the schematics today?"

"Yes, but I located several errors and cannot code until later in the week." I sat in the straight-back metal chair that had no cushion. The uncomfortable chair made you want to leave. Peter's office was stark white with no photos, and his modular angular desk had a cell phone, flat screen, and digital keyboard.

"Zerus wants to meet with you tomorrow. Be prepared to give him an update. Carmen, you are in grave danger if you cannot repair the device and the team. I'll try to protect you and the group, but these once-friendly Nephilim aliens are now in pursuit of killing you if you can't produce a hologram that will disperse more of their species to our planet." Peter's Bostonian accent echoed in his minimalist office.

Peter, I won't stop until I find a solution, even if it means working through the night.

"Is there a reason they have selected me for their project?"

"Yes, you worked with them when you were on the satellite team, and it impressed them with your skills and knowledge. You figured out their complex code, and they want you to fix their project."

"Peter, their code is an ancient Hebrew script mixed with their Egyptian hieroglyphics. It is impossible to code since they combine the two concepts."

As Peter stood and extended his hand, I noticed the delicate, translucent blue-gold wristwatch he held. He placed a crafted replica into my open hand, its intricate details catching the light.

Peter was handsome with sun-kissed tan skin, dark black hair, oval purple eyes, a slim frame, and a thin mustache. It surprised me he never married, but he married his job. His robotic tendencies often made one wonder if he was a half-machine or a cyborg human with mechanical parts.

"Put the watch on now. Whatever the cost, get the project done. We need you on the team. We have a planned week-long trip to Dubai. Emperor Zerus is watching you. We will update your new wristwatch in a few minutes for the trip. Remember, never take it off or have anyone else remove the band. Humanoid robots will give you a laser weapon when you leave my office. Use it for emergencies while you are away from the States."

Peter leaned over me, paused, and took a deep breath. His lids narrowed, and his lips pressed together before he spoke a single word. "The new digital wristband is your vital link to survival against harm."

Chapter Seven

Our alien spacecraft criss-crossed the hemisphere at astonishing speeds, reached our Dubai hotel within minutes, and landed on the heliport at the Natas Nomed Hotel and Resort.

The glass building stood sleek and majestic in the sky on an iron platform above the ground. The unique shape of the Natas Hotel, with its seven spiral circles entwined, spanned eighty floors and expanded several acres of land with amenities, was a marvel to behold.

As the sun surfaced above the horizon on Tuesday, Rashid Melekh's skilled pilot guided the innovative, black spaceship into the heliport's bay at the new headquarters of P.J. Waxit Technology Geni-factureX.

To safeguard against any potential extraterrestrial interference, Peter designated our assignment confidential with SCI classification. Global authorities faced a dilemma with the Nephilim alien invasion. Under Priest Nadab's guidance, the New World Alliance (NWA) could now examine SCI materials until the Antichrist announcement.

After our arrival, humanoid robots whisked us to our grand suite of rooms on the twenty-sixth floor linked to our office workspace. The rooms were stunning, with gold walls, a master suite, a full kitchen, a living room, and a computer room. A staff of humanoid robots attended to our needs. Lita came along as my bodyguard and chatted among other humanoids. I was the only engineer with a private humanoid robot. After my abductions, I was glad for Lita's friendship and security. My body ached, and the speed of the spaceship zapped my energy. I plopped my frame across the cotton duvet, closed my eyelids, and slept for one hour with the Zerus hologram bracelet attached to my arm for safekeeping.

Late Tuesday morning came too soon, and I had tons of work to complete at the new high-tech Dubai office, a futuristic marvel with holographic screens and AI assistants, before we traveled to Jerusalem in a few weeks. I hurried and dressed in a loose blue spacesuit with matching sandals, covered my hair with a hijab, and grabbed my breakfast to go.

"Lita, we will be the first staff to enter the new building?"

"Carmen, I have the updated codes. I received them from the humanoid robots this morning after our arrival. Everything is ready. Start your coding."

"Lita, I am grateful for your attention to detail. I'm glad to have you by my side." A wave of fear washed over me, leaving me paralyzed with thoughts of my mortality, my task ahead, and my ability to succeed. Lita swirled and half-smiled.

As we walked from the suites, we entered massive gold and white halls, marble floors, and luxurious doors to our new office entrance. I stopped at the skywalk and peered into the green Persian Ocean below my feet. Lita moved ahead of me and tapped on the security digital door. A red light scanned us and opened the glass door to a sprawling conference room, a massive skylight that opened to the heavens. I followed a gold path to a large circular pod outfitted with digital phones, tablets, laptops, and virtual reality sunglasses.

After finding the pod with my nameplate, I became comfortable and started analyzing. Lita took a seat behind me and observed. Once acquainted with the new technology, I removed the bracelet and scrutinized its internal design.

The group trickled into the room. The team of Special Force Tigers greeted me with nods and smiles before diving into their respective projects. Becky entered the room last. I looked up and spoke.

"Morning, sleepyhead."

"Who are you calling, sleepyhead? I met Peter and Mr. Melekh from 5:00 to 6:00 am. I need food, coffee, and a stiff drink. Just kidding. You know I don't drink."

I couldn't help but sigh, feeling the heavy burden of my workload pressing on my shoulders. As Becky slid into her pod beside me, I could hear the rhythmic tapping of her fingers on the laptop keyboard.

"Becky, the waitstaff will arrive with breakfast in ten minutes."

She peeked around the white barrier, scooted her chair beside mine, and hugged me. Her lack of sleep had taken a toll on her presence, with her once-tan face now pale and swollen, bloodshot eyes.

"Becky, please forgive me for my insensitive comments. It's obvious from your sleepy face that you didn't get any sleep either."

"Carmen, not a problem. We've been friends for a decade, and I can't imagine not trying to understand what you're going through without your family. But I know you're resilient and have seen you rebound when trouble comes. Yet losing a family can break the most courageous individual. I lost my parents during the rapture, and I still regret not listening to them. My mom often warned me to get my life together and serve God, but now I'm here with you on this journey in the Tribulation. Carmen, I want you to know that I am here for you, to support you, and to help you expose your motivation to survive during the Tribulation. You can help me strengthen my faith and believe in the Messiah."

We gave each other one last hug and turned back to our respective tasks.

I noticed that the design of the bracelet was missing a crucial feature to halt the relic's supernatural energy. The powers from the alien bracelet were peculiar to me, and as I tried to open the last line of code, I felt a warm, tingling sensation in my palm. As the bracelet snapped shut, a sudden surge of electricity sent an intense shock up my arm, making the screen glitch and zigzag. "Ouch!"

The bracelet slipped from my hands and fell onto the desk with a clunk. Without warning, a burst of vibrant red powder materialized and deactivated the hologram. The impact of the powder hitting my face caused me to cough and get dizzy. Despite the powder, I noticed the bracelet emitted a signal and transmitted the collected data back to Zarzu Genesis to bring forth more Nephilim. After downloading the transmitted data from the bracelet, my computer data screen froze with wavy lines.

"What the heck?" I had never seen the computer act so strange.

I was glad I had attached an electronic probe to the sapphire orb. Zerus had given me the schematic, but they were useless; something else was happening inside the bracelet. Zerus mentioned the orb ceased working when they entered our stratosphere. Without the bracelet's power, he couldn't bring more aliens from the portal, and those inside perished when they entered the hologram.

Wow, that was strange, and I remembered Peter's warning of more Nephilim coming.

"Hey, you, are you okay? What's that red stuff floating in the air?" She coughed and sneezed. Becky rose from her seat and stood behind me, peering at the red dirt on my worktable.

"Yes, the dang thing shocked me, and a red powdery mist flew into my face. Now, the desk has red powder. What is this stuff?"

"Carmen, that red stuff has covered your face. I hope it's not toxic. It looks nasty, and something is crawling in the mist."

The SFT team shouted while coughing and sneezing. "What's that stuff floating in the air?"

"Becky, a creature from their planet." I glided my magnifier over the creature, revealing its hidden details. As I reached for a water glass on my desk, I covered the strange red caterpillar creature. Its eyes gleamed red, and its body adorned with tiny suction tentacles mixed with crimson powder. The beast measured half an inch.

"Hey, guys, see what Carmen released from the alien bracelet?"

The team hurried and gathered around my pod while the coughing subsided. The SFT team fixed their sight on the vibrant red creature perched inside the glass on my desk.

My teammates surrounded me as we beckoned Lita to solve the

mystery. In mere seconds, the humanoid, aided by the AI science online team, identified the creature as an alien ant, described it as a threat, and requested its extermination. Of course, I said yes. After extensive questioning with the online AI team, I contemplated whether the creature had crawled in or if the ant had caused the flaw in the bracelet.

An earthy scent followed the exposure of the ant creature. After careful thought, I determined the ant crawled into the bracelet, dismissing the flawed notion. The AI team found the red mist from a Zarzu Genesis volcano toxic. Now, exposure to the poisonous gas could kill my colleagues and me. I wondered if Zerus planted the ant and gas to kill me and my buddies. What caused it to become even worse? Red powder covered my face. I rushed to the sink, washed my face with soap, and avoided getting mist in my eyes.

Becky contacted our on-call doctor. She reported a hazardous scene in the computer room caused by the Nephilim alien artifact releasing poisonous gas. She then messaged Peter, detailing the room's current state and advising him to avoid the computer room until the authorities had contained the toxic mist.

Humanoid robots stopped the air penetration unit and began the cleanup of the red dirt mist, with Lita leading the cleanup. The team gave me a salve for my face after red blotches peppered my face after scrubbing it.

The twelve doctors rushed to the room with hazmat suits after informing the ISS to recommend the correct alien vaccine. Doctors administered injections, confident that the antiviral injection could protect against infections from the red dirt from the extraterrestrial world.

The scientists and physicians inspected the red soil on the aliens' clothing, a significant scientific discovery made three years ago. They extracted the alien powder from Nephilim's clothing and used it to create a serum. They believed the serum could protect humans from harmful bacteria or viruses from the Nephilim planet.

We notified the astronauts and sent them a sample of the red dirt from the ant. The AI team provided a serum after their analysis with the ISS astronauts. Lita and the humanoids secured the ant in a toxic container. They took the container to the adjacent humanoid computer room, where they added the serum, and within minutes, the red ant died. The mist made our worksite off-limits for twelve hours. The humanoids sanitized the room, leaving no trace of danger.

TWELVE HOURS LATER, everyone returned to work in the computer workroom. With the setting sun, I lamented losing a day and failing to restore the bracelet. Despite the urgency of reconstructing the relic, I knew I couldn't ignore the need for a diversion to thwart Zerus. A calculated distraction could buy me the time.

My thoughts were a whirlwind as I sat at my desk, trying to focus on a strategy. By fixing the bracelet, I can unlock its cryptic inner workings and harness its ancient power to use against the Nephilim. Lita alerted me to its power, as she hoped to delve deeper into her analysis with online artificial intelligence. She mentioned the bracelet harbors a deadly, powerful supernatural energy, a secret yet understood. If the power lies inside the bracelet's integrated circuits, I could harness it and rid the planet of the alien threat. Still, I must uncover the means to examine the energy within the bracelet, a crucial mission for our survival. Without the energy killing my colleagues and me, I will make a copy of the bracelet. Secure the ornament Sophia found and use it as a backup. If everything fails, copy the artifact once I harness the microchip. Tell Zerus I needed more time to study the artifact to correct it, a risky but necessary step for my mission.

After several talks with Becky, I got the go-ahead to speak with Commander Marc Zacker at the International Space Center (ISS). I tapped my wristband and made the call.

"Commander Zacker, Carmen Northrop speaking. It has been a while since we spoke. Can you do me a favor?"

"Hi, Carmen. It depends on what you are asking." A hard knot lodged in my throat. I was sticking out my neck and asking a decorated commander to explode a wormhole. Our close bond over the years influenced my decision to persuade him to disobey his superiors.

"Commander, you must equip the atomic laser to destroy a nearby wormhole. Those aliens are coming through to our galaxy. I understand my appeal has to go through multiple channels."

"Carmen, we can help you, but gaining permission from the new world president may take several days. The man stays invisible since he hasn't gone public. Does your supervisor approve of the plan?"

"Well, Becky has approved. Peter has not approved the plan, but I wanted your blessing before presenting my intention."

"I see that's why you called me on the secure line. You didn't want the aliens to block the call. Well, the on-call astronauts Trish, Wally, and Bill will help. Get final approval from Peter and call me back, and then we will continue. I need to check on the red ant powder you sent. It was so nice to speak with you again."

The conversation ended. I persuaded Becky to go with me while approaching Peter. I had no other choice but to delay and hoped Peter understood.

Peter groaned after a brief ten-minute meeting but agreed to the interception plan.

"Peter, a direct attack on Nephilim before they send more spaceships from Zarzu might be our only chance to rid ourselves of the beasts. The wormhole portal could disintegrate and disappear with a particle of light."

"Yes, taking such a risk may backfire, resulting in our demise."

"The ISS astronauts found data to back up my analysis."

"Carmen, I fear the laser might backfire and cause an intergalactic fight with the aliens."

"But you forgot the aliens had attacked our ISS without cause three years ago. A week ago, the Nephilim launched a brutal attack, leaving a trail of destroyed satellites and shattered humanoid pods in their wake. We are doing well and taking the time to recharge and regain strength. Only Becky and Peter have access to the data I shared. Please keep the data to yourself since we are restoring the ISS to normal."

"Yes, commander, of course. Your attack happened the day they entered our stratosphere. I did not know. Okay, understand. If a catastrophic event happens when you blast the wormhole, it will be your job. Then, the guillotine or electronic pool overnight if you survive. Blame will come my way of putting our planet in danger."

"Carmen, don't worry. We will help you once we get the word from our general." The call ended, and a nervous stomach ache left me in pain.

The constant looming threat of death filled me with intense anguish and fear, my shoulders tight, and sweat popped out on my forehead as I copied in my last line of code. "Everything will be okay." I kept repeating to myself. Never had Peter threatened me. Memories of the Tribulation and losing my family weakened me. I realize that my time on Earth will continue until my rapture. As I left for Peter's office, a familiar office smell of clean linen greeted me.

***

THE ISS SET up the laser. One day later, the aliens opened the wormhole to let in more ships. The ISS aimed the laser, and it didn't fire. Exhaustion plagued my spirit, and I had to think of another foolproof plan to stop the invasion. Commander Marc Zacker informed us that the aliens blocked our transmission. That had to be a mistake. Our secret lock on them remained unknown unless someone from our unit had tipped off Zerus.

To complicate things further, the Nephilim blocked the laser. My instincts were wonky, but I knew something was inaccurate, and people lied. My deflated ego had another failure, and now, how could I stop an alien invasion and get my sons back? I grimaced and shook my head in disgust, my hands pressing against my face as I pushed back on the plush, soft pillows strewn across the floor.

That night, I saw in a vision a rogue humanoid robot tampering with the laser, causing it to misfire. I awoke with a jolt of pain in my shoulders. To release pain, I sat up, rolled my shoulders, and the anger that caused my stomach to churn subsided. My dream showed the bracelet had a hidden power. The hologram was not flawed, but the red gases mixed with our oxygen killed the aliens. Upon their futile venture to enter our solar universe, the toxic red mist emitted by the Nephilim planet asphyxiated the aliens.

I had to inform Becky and devise a new plan. Before I signaled her, a cryptic text popped up on my wristband. I wonder who sent a message so late?

Beware who you trust. Okay, a second warning to be careful. The warning had scared me. I peered closer at the message. And Melekh wasn't the source. A computer-generated message arrived from an AI. Were the humanoid robots monitoring my messages or the Nephilim?

I signaled Becky. Her sleepy voice answered as she popped up on the hologram screen.

"Hey, girly, why are you calling me so late? You know we have a 5:00 am call from Peter."

"Sorry to bother you. But can you examine a message sent to me a few minutes ago? It is not from Mr. Melekh." I pulled up the message so she might see. She took a photo of the message and ran a scan. I watched Becky on the video call. She sat upright in bed. She squinted at the message on her phone for several minutes, then typed a response on her wristband to someone. I watched as worry built.

"Carmen, message not from Mr. Melekh, but a rogue Nephilim and a rogue humanoid are working with the scoundrel. I must tell the ISS and master humanoid."

"How did you track it so fast? The IP address is not from our batch of numbers; the humanoid tried to clone it. AI security captured the number and posted it to security. That IP number is defunct. Now, we must locate the humanoid conspiring with Nephilim."

I released a strained breath of air and collapsed on the floor next to my bed, settling into the comforting embrace of the buttery cushions on the suite floor. "Becky, what is the next step with this dangerous project? I must solve the mystery to get my sons back."

"Beware who you trust. Message from my wristband and Peter's words. Your bracelet is your lifeline."

For days, the cryptic text haunted me. Peter had mentioned the bracelet, and Melekh hinted at my demise if I faltered in my efforts to repair the enigmatic holographic bracelet. They both used the exact words. Were they working together to scare me? Danger lurked around the Zerus bracelet, a mysterious artifact of unknown origin and untold power. It now involved Peter and Melekh, who were aware of the value of this priceless artifact.

After my brush with death with the alien creature, my colleagues struggled to help me with the bracelet. I secured the artifact in a cryptic puzzle box, setting the password to natasd, a six-letter enigma, to safeguard the relic.

Lunchtime late on Tuesday had passed, and my restless pacing in the conference room yielded no solutions. Frustration gnawed at me; desperation clawed at my thoughts. I needed a breakthrough, and I needed it soon. Suppose I fool them into thinking the bracelet worked after finding the solution. First, the bracelet is necessary for Zerus to communicate with his people on Zarzu Genesis and other aliens worldwide. Next, use the bracelet to end aliens, but beware, if it fails, everyone will perish. With heavy thoughts, I decided the outside air was best to free my mind.

The hotel patio grounds at P.J. Waxit were massive, with various fragrant flowers, chairs, and umbrellas. I watched families dive and play in the pool. Memories of my sons flooded my mind, including our vacation at Cabo San Lucas peninsula before the tsunami. The teens loved snorkeling. We often went as a family and captured stunning photos of marine life. We enjoyed sitting on the beach, building sand castles, and discussing sports. Wonderful memories now faded into my psyche.

A silver-blue spaceship, a symbol of the alien threat that loomed over us, caught my attention and landed on the heliport. Now, late afternoon, I rushed inside to work on my assignment, knowing no more time and the world's fate rested on my shoulders.

While stepping through the circular hall to my pod, I noticed

Noah's arrival at the job as he ducked into Peter's office. "Oh, wow," Noah was at my workplace. I couldn't help but wonder why he was visiting PJ. We hadn't crossed paths since the extraterrestrial abduction and our parting on the mountain where I left him. Rage and sorrow surged, tempting me to storm into Peter's office and demand answers. What led to our divorce? Why did he sell our children? Despite the overwhelming flood of tears stinging, I suppressed my emotions.

Then, I spotted a gentleman from the Middle East wearing traditional Arabic attire, a white ghutra, a traditional headdress worn by men from various parts of the Middle East, and a long white thawb, a long-sleeved ankle-length robe with gold embellishments along the coat's hem. The tall, suntanned man entered Peter's office. Seeing both men at our office at closing was unusual. I thought nothing of it until my wristband started buzzing.

I peeked at my wristband, and Peter's number appeared. Now what? I said, fearing the worst.

"Carmen. How is the 3D Image project? Two men in my office want a demo of the bracelet hologram project. Mr. Melekh and Emperor Zerus sent them. Can you escort them to the visitor's space and give them a demo?"

"Peter," I grumbled, "the project is not ready, and the code is causing many errors. Their time with me will put me behind on the project. Besides, I want to keep the project out of the hands of aliens who might use espionage. Who knows who these men work for, and are they lying?"

"Carmen, I gave an order. Stop what you are doing, greet them, and let them view the bracelet."

"But Peter—"

"Now, and no excuses." His raised voice led to urgency.

To protect myself, I tapped Melekh and sent him a message. I had to give the men the hologram. The riddled bracelet program code had errors. I didn't trust Noah after what Melekh had confessed. Noah had betrayed our family, and I wanted nothing to do with him. I jutted my chin higher, straightened my shoulders, unclenched my fists, and breathed. I was determined to show a calm exterior amidst the emotional ride caused by Peter.

Rushing over to Becky's workstation, three steps away from mine, I peered inside her cubicle as she finished her phone conversation.

Her brows shot up as she closed her video call.

"Becky, Peter just called, and he wants me to explain the bracelet to Noah, my ex, and another Middle Eastern man. Something smells rotten, and I suggest we give them the fake bracelet and explain very little to them."

"Are you sure you want to do this?"

"Yes, if Peter gets angry, it will fall on me. I can't chance the aliens sending in decoys. The technology department worked on two fake bracelets made days ago, and humanoids did an exceptional job with duplication."

"Okay, you're in charge. Let's go."

I snagged the fake bracelet and hurried with Becky to the visitors' center next to the main hallway of our office. The center housed models of our P.J. Waxit Technology Companies. It had white walls, a large table for demos, and a massive virtual reality screen.

I met them at the visitor's center.

"Afternoon, gentlemen. I am Carmen Northrop. Peter Alcorn informed me you wanted a demo of the bracelet."

I directed my attention to Becky to introduce her. "Becky is my supervisor and will support me. You may call me Carmen."

I extended my hand and forgot that Arab men don't shake hands with women. Instead, I nodded at both, including Becky.

"Afternoon, my name is Abu Satanilla, and of course, you know Noah Northrop."

Noah kept his sight on me, and so did Abu. I took Becky with me for security and Lita as a backup. Noah's vision locked onto my face, and he kept his body straight, akin to a soldier at attention, with no twitch in his body.

As I shut my eyelids, a sense of calm washed over me, and I sensed tightness in my facial muscles dissipate as if releasing the intense emotions. When my eyes opened again, Noah had not budged from his stance. He opened his mouth to speak but, with haste, closed his jaw. While I observed tension building between us, I couldn't help but notice his muscles flexing under his designer black spandex jumpsuit, his jaw tightening as the moments passed. I sensed anger enter my frame, starting with my heart speeding up as anger ripped my emotions. With my teeth clenched, I refrained from yelling out unprofessional words.

The decoy bracelet lay on the table as I explained its unique design and history. Noah picked it up, examined it, and passed it to Abu. During my explanation, Noah slipped the bracelet into his pocket while I explained the device. As I described the artifact's location in the Egyptian desert, I turned and was stunned by what I saw. Becky didn't see it because she controlled the video screen. What happened to my honest ex-husband?

I pivoted and faced him as my body grew hot with anger. "Noah, where is the bracelet? The bracelet I had on display."

"You must be mistaken. Carmen, are you accusing us of stealing? Here is the device you brought into the room." Without saying a word, he gawked at Abu and gave a subtle nod. He placed a semi-gold bracelet without the blue orb on the table.

He thought I didn't see the sneak attack eyeball approval, but neither of them was as clever as they thought.

"Gentlemen, I am afraid you have to stay until security checks your pockets."

"Carmen, you're mistaken—"

"That's enough talking," my voice rose to a shout. "Security is on the way." My teeth clenched as I spoke through my teeth. I grimaced at Noah and Abu.

Indifferent to his words, I interrupted him and ended the interaction. "I cannot believe you stole something so valuable." While talking, I forced my fingernails into my palms and felt sweat forming on my forehead.

I pushed the security button beneath the table, and six humanoid robots entered the room, seized both men, and examined them, but they found nothing. My anger with Noah and his buddy fueled my aggression against them.

Noah and Abu both wore wide grins as they left the building. The joke was on them because the so-called hologram bracelet was nothing but a plain bracelet. The theft had no impact on the assignment. How could Noah develop a deceitful and bitter-hearted nature so fast that he undermined my personal and professional trust? Did he disregard the value of our marriage children and consider them replaceable? The mark of the dragon had a profound impact on his spirit, turning him into a monstrous servant of Satan. Because of his betrayal, I despised him.

"Girl, I am so glad you switched the bracelets," Becky uttered. "They must have a money transaction with unsavory people. Your ex and that man named Abu will be in big trouble when their contacts discover the bracelet is fake. Once again, another delay for the 3D image, and someone wants it."

"The bracelet's value has increased from useless to a rare gem. How will I keep it safe? There's a distinct recollection of a news article detailing Sophia's arrest when the authorities apprehended her with a similar device. Do you think Zerus stole the bracelet? Do you recall the relic?"

"Why, of course? Sophia is a noble person. She is working with us in Jerusalem; you will meet her soon. But, Carmen, that is the least of your problems if you don't produce something for Zerus; I fear what he might do if he gets the wrong device."

We hurried to the blue computer room to complete our projects. As I pondered Becky's statement, a wave of anxiety crashed over me. I imagined the consequences if Zerus secured the fake bracelet.

"Yeah, you're correct, but if Zerus is involved in today's heist and receives the wrong relic, he will be twice as angry. Not with us, but with Noah and Abu."

Our laughter filled the hallway as we came back to our work pods.

Two hours later, Melekh called me.

"Carmen, what is going on at my office? Abu and Noah wanted to see the bracelet. I hope you were smart and didn't let them get their sticky palms on that hologram bracelet."

"Mr. Melekh, the device is safe. They stole the dummy bracelet and lied, then left. Whoever put them up to the heist will be furious when they discover the bracelet doesn't work."

"Excellent. When I suggested that you be a Special Force Tiger, I had selected the right person to secure our company's secrets. Don't you worry? Abu and Noah will never contact you again. I have urgent business to handle. My dear, see you soon, and maybe another dinner date?"

Who was Melekh trying to fool? Despite being attracted to his charms, I felt compelled to cooperate because he guaranteed my safety. Still, I wasn't interested in going on a date with him or pursuing a relationship. With the onset of the Tribulation, my chief concern became the bracelet and getting my teenage sons away from Zerus.

The first meeting at his home was business; now, he wants a dinner date. I was hungry, and a nice savory dinner with Rashid sounded fantastic. But I couldn't resist pizza; I ordered a giant chicken and veggie pizza with sweet tea for Becky and myself.

"Dinner sounds perfect, Mr. Melekh."

Instead of declining his dinner invite again, I waited to see how Melekh negotiated with the stolen bracelet. I owe my life to him for protecting our team and keeping us safe.

"Talk with you soon, my dear." His smooth, seductive voice calmed my stress, and I must admit. I wanted to see him. We were near the visitor's exit when my nose whiffed a jasmine fragrance. I halted, pivoted, and scanned the room. Fear consumed my thoughts as I remembered Zerus's threats.

With a mix of reluctance and fear, I tapped my wristband, feeling a prick of dread crawl across my skin. A menacing voice, as rough as sandpaper, answered. My head jerked back as I gasped. I believed Zerus texted me, but Satan sent it. Lucifer's figure flashed a blinding light in my room, his presence overwhelming, and a chill of terror stung through my frame.

Fear consumed me, causing me to freeze in place by my bed, unable to move. I felt an overwhelming sense of terror coursing through me, causing my entire body to shake. I kept my face lowered, pleading for help from Jehovah.

Everything changed to worry when Satan arrived. I pondered his intentions and what he sought from me. My best assumption was he intended to terrorize me into giving him the bracelet. Tilting my head just so, I glimpsed his face.

"You think I'm oblivious to what you're keeping from me?" he charged, his lids narrowing. "Well, my dear," he sniped, "your futile attempts to hide the bracelet won't hinder me from reclaiming it and unleashing more Nephilim upon this earth." His laughter pierced my ears, leaving behind a bitter sting.

"I am Lucifer, ruler of this world, and rule your species. The urgency of delivering the hologram bracelet to Zerus today is paramount. Fail, and those brats will be gone forever, their fate sealed by your inaction."

A hologram materialized before me, projected by Lucifer from my wristband. Ugly demons placed my teens standing up inside the pods. Their pale and gaunt faces bore the visible toll of their weight loss. Tears flowed over my cheeks as I released a loud, piercing scream. My hands shot up to cover my trembling mouth, trying to suppress the anguish within my body.

Another wicked laugh escaped Lucifer's lips, filling the room with an eerie echo as his vision disappeared. Emperor Zerus manifested next to Satan; they shared a knowing glance. "Get that bracelet to Zerus today, or they are dead."

The hologram faded, leaving me feeling lost, terrified, and angry. I found myself bewildered by the sudden rush of conflicting emotions.

Overwhelmed by grief, my heavy heart sank, dragging my body downward until I crumbled to the floor. Amid my turbulent life, I had planned to have breakfast with Becky, which I had ordered beforehand. As I sank deeper into depression, the thought of dying became appealing, pushing me to the edge of giving up on life. I found myself in uncontrollable tears while resting on the cozy rug.

The sun climbed high over the horizon as it crept into my room and warmed my body. I struggled to rise from the hard floor, my body refusing to straighten. I prayed for strength. Did Lucifer show me a glimpse of my future, or did he unleash a nightmarish vision upon me? Whatever he had made to appear before my eyes had frightened me to my core.

I recharged myself by praying, got ready, and took a few steps toward the door before another phone call stopped me.

"Morning, Carmen."

A touch of seduction existed within his deep baritone voice that caressed my ears.

"How's the 3D project? I need a demo today at 11:00 sharp in the office. Let's discuss it further over lunch, not dinner."

"Mr. Melekh, the project is not ready."

"Can we move on to calling me Rashid when we are alone? As for the project, I don't care if the artifact is not ready. I want a demo before Zerus sees it. Our lives depend on you to finish this exceptional assignment. Remember, 11:00 in Peter's office?"

As he hung up, my nerves were on edge. He wanted me to call him Rashid in private, and he believed my addressing him by his last name was formal. I had other problems, but the deadline loomed by Friday. I braced myself for a call or face-to-face from Zerus, my supernatural abilities now exposed. He had exchanged powers with Lucifer, and I had no hope against a ruthless former archangel.

Lucifer's demanding words left me fearing for my life. The vile Nephilim were far from foolish; they were slick. News that my sons were alive filled me with hope; a song's sweet melody resonated in my soul and played in my head as I swayed to the tune in my suite.

I inhaled the aroma of salt from the Persian Gulf, which blended with Middle Eastern cuisine on my lips. The rumbling in my stomach intensified, signaling that breakfast food was on my agenda. Then contact Zerus.

WE RECEIVED a message to come to the outdoor conference room at 10:00. One hour before, Mr. Melekh requested to see the hologram. I postponed eating breakfast and prepared to meet Emperor Zerus. My hands were wet with sweat, and my heart pounded. I had not prepared the beta, and now Zerus, with his bodyguards, wanted the bracelet tested. Zerus had malicious intentions, as he knew Melekh's scheduled meeting with Peter and me. I had to stall. Otherwise, I might die.

We met Zerus in the conference room. He stood up front. His regal presence and his face were no longer grizzly but human. Zerus must have used a supernatural power to change his presence. Several hours ago, Zerus's face was hideous, and now he wasn't.

The moment he entered the room, he captivated my interest, sparking a deep sense of curiosity within me. I became intrigued by his mysterious presence. It became plain he drank a human's blood to alter his presence. This drastic measure that he resorted to led to transforming his outward image. A wave of sorrow washed over me as I contemplated the depth of his actions. I loathed him even more for his vileness. Regardless of his actions, he turned golden and looked pleasing. I wondered if Lucifer had something to do with Nephilim Zerus's transformation. Well, it didn't matter. I strolled up front and began my speech.

"Emperor Zerus, I found a major flaw in the code in your hologram. The Special Force Tigers and I have made a model of your hologram and are working to decipher the ancient, difficult code. Neither humanoid robots nor our team can give you a fast turnaround by Friday. I recognize your plight to restore the hologram and bring more of your people to our planet faster. Still, without the correct translation," I hesitated to glimpse at him, Zerus's face unemotional, "If I give you the code as constructed, more of your species will die."

His silence filled my spirit with anxiety. My awareness he could kill within seconds left me with one alternative. Lie and hope he believed my story. Yet my tale was half true. If I returned the 3D image without modifications, his species could die. Still carrying my coffee, I walked back and forth between the conference room and the veranda, praying for guidance. Melekh had sanctioned a two-week delay, but I had not heard from him. Becky and I told Peter that Mr. Melekh wanted us to delay. It posed a challenge to stay composed, stand my ground, and have confidence in Zerus's trust in me.

Zerus closed his orbs and didn't move for at least a minute.

My teammates sat in a circle at the front of the room, tapping on their tablets without saying a word. I glanced in their direction and nodded as they nodded in response.

"You guarantee my hologram bracelet will be operable in two weeks?"

"Yes, sir, I stake my life on the line."

"Ah, your life. It just might be your life for my bracelet." His direct stare and his head held high annoyed me.

"Carmen, I confirmed with my folks, and you have one last extension of two weeks. We requested a product update after that. I told Mr. Melekh that delays cost him millions, and he has promised to pay for one more extension."

He paused. The haughty stare from Zerus as he bared his teeth left me frozen. I peered in Becky's direction to break the telepathic message he sent.

Don't pursue a rescue if you think you can use your supernatural powers to save your sons. Remember that Lucifer is our leader and has exhibited his power, so don't be foolish.

Complete silence followed as he vanished, and a trail of white ash fell in his wake. The faint scent of sulfur persisted. The idea crossed my mind that Satan gifted Zerus with supernatural power to outperform me. I had to keep my sons and my teammates out of danger.

"Emperor Zerus?" I spoke, but he had disappeared into a puff of nothingness—our room filled with an eerie stillness.

The despicable Nephilim dared to dissolve. *If he wants to play rough, I'm up for it. I'll prevent him from accessing the hologram and bring my sons back.*

HOURS LATER, I returned to the computer room. Becky agreed to join forces as we hatched a cunning plan to deceive Zerus.

I was so nervous that I paced the floor while I explained my design —ornate rugs and pillows aligned with the oval lounge shared by our team. Posh amenities were what I needed to keep my thoughts on my plight to get the project working and my mind off my anguish.

"Becky, if I make a fake hologram with a virus to disrupt and halt the code. We can create a diversion, keep Zerus at bay, and offer him a choice of returning to Zarzu Genesis to rescue his people. That will give ISS astronauts enough time to set up the atomic laser. Then align it to target the wormhole when the aliens enter, eradicate it, and safeguard our planet."

Becky's fingers moved across the tablet keys with precision. With her legs crossed in a sitting position, she squinted at me. I stopped my restless pacing and sat beside her on one ornate pillow. The wait for Becky's response was agonizing. Unlike me, she always thought through her options before she spoke.

"Sounds good, Carmen, but our plan might backfire if we're not careful. I love the fake hologram scenario. Since you have coded a vacation hologram, we need to change the code and release it next week to Zerus. We have a client who wants the vacation hologram for her consumers, and Mr. Melekh wants us to beta-test the image with the client on Friday. Her name is Qadira Bilal. Use the vacation hologram to avoid the lizard man's presence. Genius, Carmen!"

After I saw her infectious smile, I knew we had stumbled upon something fantastic. We gave each other a satisfying high-five, sank into pillows, and erupted into laughter. I sensed the plan could work, and it warmed my heart. Rising, we gathered in the lounge to await our colleagues.

I could hear boisterous laughter as our teammates entered the lounge. But to my surprise, Peter led the pack. I wondered why he arrived and what project he wanted us to do today.

"Carmen, may we talk out on the veranda?"

"Of course."

While the other ten engineers of my team plopped on the scattered pillows around the room, he continued walking. I jumped up and pursued Peter, who had hurried to the veranda.

"CARMEN, glad to see you and Becky working on the hologram. We are under pressure to get the flawed bracelet fixed. Mr. Melekh has put pressure on me to keep getting daily updates. He has requested a working dinner with you tonight at his villa at 5:00 p.m., so don't be late. A jetted hovercraft will arrive and take you to his home."

"Peter, Mr. Melekh called me to demo the bracelet at 11:00 today. Is that meeting canceled since I had to meet with Zerus?"

"He called and told me to cancel the meeting since Zerus met with you."

I gave a subtle nod, sensing that something was not right.

The enchanting turquoise water churned and caught our attention as waves of three feet splashed against the shore. Still, I couldn't resist peeking at the alluring man nearby. Was Peter partaking in a conspiracy to coerce me into delivering the hologram to the extraterrestrial creatures? Did Melekh play a part in the scheme? Melekh had requested nothing from me and remained a gentleman. I couldn't shake the darkness that permeated every facet of his presence. Inside me, my distrust surged.

"Peter, there's plenty of work. I planned to stay and work alongside Becky tonight. But Mr. Melekh doesn't care for the word No. I will be ready."

"Good. I am proud of your work ethic and remember, if you run into trouble, press the emergency alert on your wristwatch. Security humanoid robots will be at your aid within seconds."

As we leaned on the rail, Peter's expression remained fixed on the rippling water, never glancing in my direction once. Peter's nervous demeanor, as he continued to rub the back of his neck, suggested he kept a secret from me. A vessel churned in the water, creating ripples that spread everywhere. A spacecraft resting in shallow water made for a strange spectacle. The water concealed a vessel, causing it to sink into the sand and disappear. I noted his shuffling feet as Peter ran his fingers through his curly hair. Today, he broke the pattern of always maintaining eye contact with me.

"Thanks, Peter. Are you staying and having dinner with us?"

"No. I had an emergency meeting with Mr. Melekh and flew to view his new project. I will go back to my resort room and meet with your ex-husband."

"What? Noah is here?" I couldn't believe it. Why Noah? My breath increased, and my heart raced. Were they setting me up for a fall? What was Noah's involvement in my tech company? I turned and peered at Peter, and he was watching me, running my hands through my curls and taking quick breaths.

"Are you okay, Carmen? I didn't want to upset you. I wanted to inform you he arrived this morning. Carmen avoided any contact with him. If you run into him, show kindness and distance yourself. He has taken an oath and allegiance to the new world President. Noah bears the dragon's mark on his right hand. He's dangerous. Your lack of the dragon mark makes you exposed."

The warm afternoon air swirled around me, but the news Peter gave me knocked the wind out of my body. Because of introducing the dragon mark on Friday before we left for Dubai, NWP police granted our team a respite, sparing us from the need to be marked. I had made a solemn promise, vowing to meet my end under the blade of the guillotine rather than surrender to the mark of Satan. But Noah was a believer in the Messiah Jesus. Why did he take the dreaded dragon mark? I swayed, and Peter caught my arm and helped me to one of the cushioned veranda chairs.

"Carmen, do you need water? Your face is flushed." I could sense his touch, warmth, and comfort, noting he still had a compassionate heart for his employees.

Peter dashed to the bar near the entrance. He grabbed bottled water, returned to the table, shoved it into my hand, and waited.

"No, I'm fine. I guess the warm air must have gotten to me," I lied.

But as I lifted my head, I saw amusement shimmering in Peter's dark eyes. With an air of wickedness, Peter's sight held a sparkle as if they were privy to secrets, he refused to divulge. Still, my determination to uncover the truth of the hologram and Noah's arrival grew stronger.

"I must go, and you have a dinner appointment. Catch you tomorrow. Meetings will occupy my entire week. I will call for daily updates."

He paused for a second and nodded.

"Carmen, beware who you trust." Then Peter dashed into the lounge.

The chilling sound of my name and warning sent a wave of goosebumps through my body. A sudden burst of energy coursed through my body. I ran into the lounge, feeling a rush of adrenaline and fear coursing through my veins.

Chapter Eight

AFTER THE FIASCO with Noah and Abu, I fought to protect the bracelet from those who coveted its monetary value. A constant menace of darkness clung to my every move while an obscure alien lurked in the shadows, undermining my efforts with his humanoid accomplice.

The humanoid robots conversed with each other. Their lack of response angered me as they hid the traitor. As I probed further, the humanoid robots refused to share the secretive whispers with me.

Lita, my steadfast companion, stayed by my side, her silence broken only by her visits to the humanoid center to gather intel.

"Ouch, that hurt!" I wiggled my wrist as the bracelet vibrated. I felt a sharp, prickling sensation as if tiny needles were prodding my skin. What was the Zerus bracelet's power? The act of sending Nephilim to Earth went beyond mere action. The artifact buzzed, and the sound was musical.

Twilight had settled over Dubai. I had flopped on the sofa, drinking a soda and eating popcorn, when Lita entered the room. I glanced upward to grab her attention.

"Lita, it has been three days since my supernatural ability ceased. I must find the cause of my lack of vision into realms. Since I began wearing the bracelet, my supernatural visions stopped. Have you gathered data on the rogue humanoid and alien?"

"Miss Carmen, I have scoured for intelligence at my workplace and found no significant chatter. The humanoids suspended their conversations after I asked several questions. But one humanoid robot I probed, and he was friendly but then halted communication with me."

"Did you get any sign from the chatty humanoid that a rogue humanoid is stealing data?"

Lita remained still. She angled her head and blinked before she spoke.

"One humanoid robot mingled with other humanoids and AIs. My contact suggested someone with a temporary duty on our waitstaff might hold the secret to our rogue humanoid. Sorry, Miss Carmen, that's my complete update for today. Your powers are still active. If you get rest tonight, I'm confident your body will rejuvenate itself, providing you with the energy you lack."

"Thanks, Lita. Your data has been helpful. Are you feeling okay? You sound more robotic today. Please keep digging, but be discreet."

"Miss Carmen, I am due for an update. The master humanoid will update my circuits tonight. I'll be at the humanoid station near the computer room. Signal me if you need help."

"No, get your update, but I thought you were beyond updates?"

With a groan, I dragged myself away from the comfort of the sofa and headed towards the counter near the entrance door, the aroma of food enticing me along the way. As I made my way to the counter, Lita trailed behind me, her presence comforting.

"After our abduction, the master humanoid wanted to move my shut-off button. I must update my weapons to protect you. My updated state-of-the-art technology we designed."

"We, meaning your architect?"

"No, the AIs and humanoid robots designed new weapons so we can defend ourselves against invading aliens."

"Does that include mortals, too?" I waited for a response, but she gave none.

Lita's unemotional face filled me with worry. She mustered a slight grin, swirled, and left the room.

My muscles tensed, and I stood suspended near the computer room door, unable to step forward. My breaths sped up with my heart pounding against my chest as I called out to Lita.

"Who is the master humanoid?"

AFTER A FEW HOURS, Lita sent me a message: "Miss Carmen, master humanoid, is the humanoid from which we receive updates. He is mobile but lives in the humanoid room where our creator inhabits 24/7. Remember, Carmen, I am bound by secrecy. Please honor my dilemma. You will come to know my creator soon. I am still working on locating the bracelet that Sophia found. I will come to you once I get my updates."

My mouth flew open. Lita refused to tell me her creator's name. One thing I knew: Melekh had his finger in the mix. For now, I opted to abandon the mystery. My eyes ached, and the nap helped ease my headache. I looked around my massive bedroom and thanked Father God for the luxurious, magnificent suite with my comrades. I rolled off the bed, dressed, and hurried toward the computer room a few feet from our suites.

The data we had examined kept occupying my thoughts. Feeling hungry, I headed to the computer room, where my teammates were still working. As soon as I entered the front of the room, I saw large plates of food adorning the table, enticing me with their delicious display. I grabbed a plate of salad, pasta, fresh greens, and warm noodles, then joined the team.

As I gathered food, thoughts of my boys filled my mind. Were they satisfying their hunger with an ample food supply, or were they going hungry? A profound realization struck me when I glanced at my plate. Having food and a cozy bed made me appreciate my blessing. A lump caught in my throat as I forced myself not to cry. I hated my life, and I failed my team in finding a solution to fight the aliens and keep the bracelet from Zerus. I swallowed and proceeded to my pod.

After extensive searching and decoding in the late hours of the night, the STF team found an ancient book in our digital library that unveiled the origins of the bracelet.

"Becky, check out this data; it is unbelievable. The relic holds evil powers, but Zerus must have altered it to transport his species through the portal. But how?"

I focused on Becky until she tilted her head and spoke. "Why not ask Zerus and get your answer?"

"Let me gather my thoughts. Becky, he scares me, and I don't want him to think I can't fix the thing."

The rest of our team and I kept scrolling through data on the hologram screen as we read hieroglyphics mixed with the Aramaic language. Our faces stayed glued to the screen.

"Hey everyone, I have a strong hunch that the bracelet had magical abilities that the ancient Nephilim used during Abraham's time on Earth. People believed the bracelet was a talisman capable of communication with the dead. The ancient society of Baal relied on this artifact to call upon their god."

The breakthrough left me stunned. We deciphered the bracelet's pulsating energy and prevented alien transfer. A revelation that shifted power away from Zerus to us. I needed to give us a fighting chance against the alien race.

The bracelet's midnight pulsating signal to the mothership was a chilling discovery. Once again, the vibrations pricked my wrist. My thoughts returned to chat with Melekh several days earlier. Melekh suggested his direct communication with Nephilim for his business negotiations. His brilliance was undeniable, of the bracelet's power, a force capable of initiating alien transfer, yet his knowledge left me pondering. What else did he know? Despite knowing the bracelet's extraordinary power, he chose not to divulge it. Did the energy from the bracelet pose a danger to mortals, as Lita claimed?

Cyrus Rashid Melekh, a mysterious figure, arrived on the scene just when I yearned for companionship. But I couldn't ignore the sense that he had a hidden agenda. His aura of mystique was unsettling, and his admission to the bracelet's power left me pondering Rashid's kindness in saving me when my ex left. I couldn't help my skepticism when he selected me and transitioned me to work on the mystical hologram bracelet. His charisma and charm gathered me into his web.

Throughout Wednesday night, the SFT team and I worked to find a schematic to duplicate and trap everything inside a 3D image.

Lack of sleep and excessive work took a toll on me. I put our notes in the secure vault with a cipher lock. We developed a device to eradicate Nephilim for good. But I needed to test, and that posed a problem. I couldn't ask Zerus to try again. He might become suspicious. I hoped the device worked. My vision was blurry because of lack of sleep. The kitchen staff brought a variety of delicious sandwiches, fruit trays, and coffee.

After midnight, I activated the hologram on my wrist, and the blue orb popped up on the floor. I entered it, and it worked. Despite the risk, I had to defend my project's success. An electrical shock seized my body, activating my supernatural power. The blue light clutched my body to protect me from the electricity and deactivated the pulse. A mysterious vortex formed at least twelve feet in front of me. I wanted to enter, but an overwhelming fear gripped me, and I stepped out and pressed the spinning orb. The orb stopped spinning, and the blue light ceased. Sweat popped up on my face, and my pulse raced. Whatever lived inside the orb was otherworldly and evil. For now, I kept the vortex data to myself. I had a hunch the whirlwind was a door to Satan's realm. The SFT team inspected the bracelet and discovered it functioned as a transmitter, beaming signals high into the stratosphere through its orb-shaped design.

After I placed the orb inside the security safe, the blue light from the bracelet pulsed once more and stayed active. When I leaned forward to see why it continued to gleam, I saw Zerus within the glow.

He transmitted data to Zarzu Genesis. The hologram bracelet's active signal increased, showing he was ready to send more Nephilim through the wormhole portal if necessary. Zerus sent a message to his soldiers on Zarzu to prepare people and activate their bracelets once he got the primary hologram bracelet returned to him.

My efforts to keep the Nephilim from Earth had to work. If I fail in my efforts, humanity will face extinction. I had not forgotten my children, who were dead and gone to Heaven. One evening during the night, a dream of my sons lifting from the Earth to Heaven never left me. The vision gave me peace: Almighty God saved my sons and millions of people. I missed my sons and often thought of them and their father. He betrayed me and bore the mark of Satan.

AROUND 3 A.M., I joined Becky on the floor cushions in the computer room.

"Becky, the bracelet is ready for an exchange. No one else has the code to unlock my primary bracelet. Killing me means losing the device forever. I had to select a method to destroy the device and aid us in the battle. Once they leave, I'll tell you the password, provided I survive. If you read the Bible, the word for the password lies in Job 2:2. You must figure out the clue because the word in the verse is backward. I had to inspire you to engage in reading and praying again."

I reached over and hugged Becky. She blinked, and tears ran down her flushed cheeks. I stepped to exit her pod.

"Carmen, wait, please be careful." I pivoted. "Have you seen or heard from Zerus?"

"Yes, after I put the bracelet inside the Code Cryptex, I saw Zerus within the glow of the hologram. He told his people to prepare to send more Nephilim via a wormhole or the hologram. Either way, he is sending more aliens. We must tell Peter and the ISS to prepare to destroy the wormhole. Did anyone find the rogue humanoid?"

"Check your security text." I peeked at my wristband, and a red dragon appeared in 3D, then flashed on the surface of my wristband. "Becky, come and check out this pulsating message?"

Becky wandered over to her pod door and peered at my wristband. She gasped at the sight of the dragon and a new message.

Zerus's face came into view as I gawked, and his piercing gaze locked with mine. *"Be careful who you trust, Carmen. One of your trusted engineers is not human."*

"WHO'S THERE?" My voice trembling with a mix of fear and curiosity. A sudden blinding light flooded my resort room. A stark contrast to the serene luxury it exuded. The intense brightness illuminated every corner, casting long shadows against the walls. The faint hum of the city below seeped into my room, a constant reminder of the bustling life outside the resort on an early Thursday Spring morning in Dubai. But who intrudes at this hour? And why? The questions swirled in my mind, adding to my unease.

The resort room was elegant, with creme-colored walls adorned in gold, white duvet bed linens, ornate posh rugs, and a framed mirror hung behind the king-size bed with a gold headboard. Above the bed, a grand chandelier illuminated the room, adding a touch of luxury. The room boasted a stunning view of the garden pool, white sand beaches, and direct access to the Persian Gulf. Although I spent less time in the room, sleeping in a luxurious room gave me peace.

I had never seen such extravagance. I took a moment to enjoy my suite. Exhaustion weighed heavy on my eyelids; I'd spent most of the night working on the intricate hologram bracelet for Zerus. The aroma of brewing coffee drifted through the air as I struggled to awaken my weary mind. A clang and bang let me know Lita sent for my breakfast, and I must rise and start the day regardless of my exhaustion and grief. Despite my weariness, I couldn't shake off the nagging feeling of unease at the unexpected intrusion. A stranger invaded my room and not Lita. Adrenaline coursed through my veins, causing my heart to race and my stomach to flutter with fear and curiosity. Who was this mysterious trespasser? What did they want?

The massive brown bedroom door swooshed open. A spiral blue-gray portal materialized out of nowhere. Inside the portal stood a silhouette, but this was no ordinary figure. A dazzling gold entity shimmered, adorned with celestial characters. The man's arraignment of gold covered his feet, and he wore a gold crown. I couldn't look at his face but recognized the melodic cadence of his voice and his charm mesmerizing as if he were singing. A sense of déjà vu washed over me —I had seen this spirit before, on the distant planet of Zarzu Genesis. His captivating and unsettling presence added to the intrigue of the scene.

"Get that hologram from her. Don't let her trick you. She is clever and smart." His voice echoed, yet his angry baritone voice reverberated into the stratosphere. As I leaned closer to the portal, I felt my chest pounding, torn between curiosity and the need to stay concealed.

"Master, she confirmed her ability to fix the hologram while working on other projects this week in Dubai. Since she is in our domain, she has no security. Though her humanoid robot, Lita, has weapons, her humanoid is not strong enough to take on my Nephilim."

"Fools. Carmen's wristwatch tracks her location to Melekh and Peter; besides, my nemesis protects her. The Special Force Tigers crew will help. If she can't fix the hologram by week's end, then kill those boys. Zerus, move them to the moon pods today. Prepare to kill them. That wretched human is trying to trick us."

I let out a sudden gasp and covered my mouth. Tears formed, and I fell on the floor. Oh, thank you, God, they are alive. They were not among those taken in the rapture. I struggled to keep myself from shaking.

"Master Lucifer, if we kill her sons and her after the exchange, Mr. Melekh will kill us. He is powerful."

"Zerus, you are a wimp. Melekh will not kill us. Trust me. I have the entire matter under my authority and will crush anyone who inter-cepts my efforts to stop me. Now move those boys today."

Another shriek escaped my lips, leaving me surprised and exposed. I saw the man shrouded in bright white light, and Zerus whirred around and narrowed his eyelids as he leaned closer to the portal's entrance. I wondered if Zerus could perceive my presence, so I clenched my hands and spoke the words *Azar,* and a mesmerizing blue mist descended, enveloping me in its mystical presence. To safeguard my sons, I had to guarantee that neither Zerus nor Lucifer caught sight of me peering into the portal.

As they engaged in intense discussion, scheming their evil intentions, I crept towards the entrance, which stood open. I peeked through the gateway and marveled at the grandeur of the arch above me, embellished with radiant shades of gold and eerie demonic figures. Along the curved archway, these creatures swayed and danced in a mesmerizing, never-ending motion.

Then, I approached to witness a tall, powerful man with mystical abilities. He didn't move but guarded the arch with his flaming sword.

After further evaluating their remarks on the moon pods, a forgotten memory stirred: not the death trap moon pods. Oh no, not the experimental pods that failed, designed by UltraOnic Marketing International when they established a settlement on the moon. Not the failed project that I worked on with Emperor Zerus.

I remember Noah signing a contract for UltraOnic and regretting his signature because the pods didn't keep humans alive. Once the pods were complete, the air-penetrating equipment failed. Those igloo pods on the moon's surface were fatal for humans. Three years ago, a viral infection poisoned the air supply. Oh, no, that's where they put my boys. Jehovah, help my sons! I screamed inside myself.

Zerus drew near, his movements so stealthy that no footsteps vibrated. He came to a sudden halt, immobile. "Carmen, don't think I can't see you," he uttered as he glimpsed the subtle silhouette of my form. His voice echoed in my ear.

"Lucifer, who is that person listening to our conversation?"

"That vile Northrop woman."

"Can she see and hear us?" His face and body were motionless.

"Yes, and shut up, Zerus. I see her, but a mist of blue covers her. Did you notice her staring at us?"

"Yes. Carmen Northrop has the unique power to delve into our realm. But maybe I am mistaken; she has unknown supernatural powers. She possesses immense worth; we could use her to further our kingdom."

Lucifer, oh no, not the devil. My heart skipped a beat, and I felt my mouth drying. Dear Heavenly Father, please help me. I prayed. I was no match for the powerful ex-archangel.

Just as Zerus exited the ship's pod room, Lucifer's hand shot out and gripped his arm, causing him to wince in pain.

"No, Zerus. Carmen Northrop's power is real. Keep your vision on her as I affirm and authenticate her supernatural talents."

As Lucifer's vision blazed with a red inferno, his body underwent a startling metamorphosis, shifting from brilliant white light to the ominous coloration of an ash-colored demon. A wicked smirk stretched from ear to ear. Gone were the golden pipes on his chest, the cymbals, and the handsome face of a demi-god.

I jumped to my feet and stepped back from the portal, filled with anticipation and a hint of fear, unsure of his intentions. I had no choice but to defend myself from potential harm.

With a swift motion, Lucifer raised his hand, and the stench of sulfur filled the air as a bolt of pure energy shot out akin to a lightning strike, heading straight for me. Another brilliant blue-gold light washed over me, and my hands shot up in self-defense; in an instant, the fire-ball vanished into nothingness.

"Lucifer, you are correct."

Zerus's brows arched as his spheres grew grapefruit size. He opened his mouth, and I remembered his large teeth as our views met. He saw the radiant blue aura that encircled me, and his awestruck expression was priceless.

"Close the portal," Zerus's voice echoed through the chamber.

I realized the man or demon I was dealing with was no ordinary being. He was the devil. The portal dissipated as my prayers spiraled heavenward, leaving no sign the gateway ever existed.

Now, after ten years of dormancy, the revival of my long-abandoned supernatural gifts left me perplexed. I sensed a mysterious energy coursing through my body whenever I prayed. Father God had heard my prayers and added shelter for me when the gold light mingled with my blue light. The incident shook me inside, but my confidence remained strong. I had to succeed with the assignment; otherwise, my sons and I could perish.

One mystery left me puzzled, trying to connect the scattered clues. As my blue mist became visible to Lucifer, I couldn't help but recall my mom's words; she mentioned demons being oblivious to the blue aura. Were my mystical powers stronger than my mom's? Did my supernatural covering always have a blue mist to cover me regardless of whether spirit or physical?

My number one duty is to keep the bracelet away from the Nephilim. They were devils, and they wanted to kill humans. But why, after they helped us rebuild our society after the devastating earthquakes and tsunamis? I couldn't believe it; my wildest dream had become a horrifying reality: the Nephilim had descended upon our planet to wipe out humans. And as if guided by fate, a black hole appeared, consuming their world and its twin planet. It felt as if a sharp dagger had struck me when the shock hit, sending a searing pain through my stomach that compelled me to sprint towards the closest bathroom, where I emptied the contents of my unsettled gut.

With Zerus and Satan aware of my secret, I had to keep a constant watch over my life and the safety of my team. I had to confide in Becky and share my secret with her. What steps can I take to safeguard the hologram bracelet from harm and neutralize the Nephilim threat? The giant Goliath in the Bible had brothers who were tall, fierce, and muscular, and David killed them. I must now endure the same agony.

Yes, I thought. With Mr. Melekh's company involved in producing and installing moon pods, they could become an asset in accomplishing my mission. If I asked him to help, then he expected dinner with him. Rashid Melekh desired a deep connection with me beyond surface-level interactions. I had faith in his support. Well, I now must ask him. I must get my sons back before they die a horrible death.

THE BLISTERING sun had come over the horizon of the Persian Gulf. I spun around, stood at the window, and wondered why God had left me on Earth. After my alien abduction with my ex-husband, I discovered the great gathering of the saints had occurred, known as the rapture. I prayed multiple times a day, seeking guidance from Messiah Yeshua. It made sense why God left me behind on Earth. He had a greater mission to protect humanity from the Antichrist, whom Satan was controlling. My task was to stop the Zerus bracelet hologram from reaching the Nephilim aliens again. I still wondered who the Antichrist was because he had not announced his dictatorial power.

After what I saw with Zerus and Lucifer, I knew they could try to trick me into giving the hologram to them. My children were dying, and I knew it, or they were dead. I had to devise a foolproof plan to keep the 3DImage from anyone.

Testing the hologram requires me to enter the portal, and once I've done that, I'll let Zerus know the bracelet is operational. Yet fear gripped me. The bracelet's power had proved fatal for the Nephilim who entered the image, and if my calculations were flawed, I could die. My agony each day was grueling. I had to find the truth involving my sons, and I suspected Melekh knew the truth.

With Becky, my trusted friend, by my side, I had to ask her to unite and devise a plan with me to thwart the invasion that had transformed our once peaceful planet into a harrowing battleground of chaos and despair.

I poured myself a hot cup of sweet java and tapped my wristwatch.

"Meet me for breakfast in thirty minutes in the lounge," I uttered when Becky responded. "I will take charge and place the food order. A sudden emergency has occurred, demanding our immediate attention and swift resolution."

"What? Oh, okay. See you in thirty minutes."

My cell buzzed, and the name on the screen sent a wave of panic through me.

Chapter Nine

Melekh's sudden dinner invitation through a text message surprised me and filled me with anxiety. With limited time to prepare, I felt a mix of fear and anger that made the idea of eating or talking with him after the intense confrontation with Lucifer and Zerus impossible. Despite the inconvenience, I attempted to meet him and left Lita at the resort.

While en route to Cyrus Rashid Melekh's home, my mind raced with thoughts of the upcoming presentation on the extraterrestrial hologram. I wanted to capture each detail and imprint it in my mind. A swish sound echoed as the hovercraft lost altitude and stabilized as a few spaceships sped past me. What bothered me was the spaceships speeding past and landing in the water beside Rashid's home. Anxiety and fear welled inside me as more questions arose in my thoughts: why were the aliens at his home? Rashid's unnamed expectations for the project and my concern for my family's welfare heightened the stress weighing on my mind.

The hovercraft touched the heliport, and a pair of humanoid robots greeted me. They led me to an open-air veranda overlooking the Hatta Dam. Melekh emerged from his striking three-story glass abode nestled at the foot of the Hatta Mountain range. A waterfall cascaded over the hillside, pooling into a luminous reservoir, a sight to behold, located 90 miles from Dubai.

Massive glass doors opened, and the king of his domain stepped out. He wore a regal gold jacket that shimmered in the sunlight, paired with sleek black silk trousers. A cascade of curly, jet-black hair framed his face, and a wide grin stretched from ear to ear. His mere presence had a powerful effect, leaving me feeling suffocated and breathless.

"Carmen, I am so glad you decided to have dinner with me," he responded, a smile lighting up his face. "It crossed my mind that you didn't have any affection toward me."

You are right, buddy. Despite the mystery that shrouded him, his charm captivated me, trapping my thoughts and stirring internal emotions.

His long, muscled legs strolled toward me. I had not moved but waited for him to help me with my chair.

"Mr. Melekh, thank you for dinner. I brought notes and projected repair of the hologram for Emperor Zerus and his people."

"Keep your notes tucked away for now. We're friends. Let's enjoy our dinner first, and we can delve into the hologram project later. Call me Rashid, my dear." His words hung in the air, a subtle reminder of the dynamics at play.

We had a delicious savory dinner of seared salmon, rice pilaf, green beans, blueberry cheesecake, tea, and coffee. I wondered how he could secure such lavish meals with people fighting over food worldwide. We were privileged to have jobs and work for wealthy moguls.

"Let's stroll to the beach. I need to discuss something with you."

While we strolled, I spotted two humanoid robots armed with weapons in the distance. The water from the river splashed against the sand as the evening breeze stirred the air. I had forgotten we were in martial law since my job protected me from most of the violence and chaos.

He adjusted his stride, pivoted towards me, and took hold of my hand, refocusing his attention on our interaction.

"Carmen, I want to help you with the hologram. I believe Zerus is planning a military coup, and my people are ready to kill the Nephilim if they decide to take over the planet. I want you to stall on the project, so don't give the hologram to Zerus until I give you the okay."

He kept his focus on my face without emotion.

"Are you offering to help me? But why?"

"You are my employee, and I care for my employees' safety. But you are special, and the aliens have targeted you in particular. I want you to stay safe. Besides, I have fallen for you. After my conversation with Zerus, I requested you repair the Nephilim holographic bracelet."

His statement fell on my ears, an unwelcome sound. The double blow of my son's abduction and my husband divorcing me had left me feeling betrayed and lost. As I stood in front of the handsome man, my heart heavy with pain, I struggled to handle my anguish.

"Don't worry. I will wait until you are ready to date again." He lifted both my hands and kissed them. He released my hands, and we wandered towards his home. The massive mountains and sand were stunning, but I found it odd for a man of his wealth to live so far from the city. I focused my attention on the dam, and I could sense the vibrations of the rushing water as we stepped. He pivoted, grabbed my hand, and picked up his pace toward his home just as a silver spacecraft circled us several times and disappeared.

"Rashid, I never thought you'd agree to a deceitful plan to fool the Nephilim. I thought they worked for you. Why did you pick up your pace? Are you worried the aliens might abduct us?"

"No, my dear. The Nephilim aliens are clients, not employees. Without their help to rebuild our planet, our world might have collapsed without them, yet they brought misery."

Excellent answer, but I remained skeptical of him. I was still not on board with Rashid Melekh; even though he claimed to be a friend, a mystery circled him. The idea of having a romantic entanglement with him intrigued me. Yet my spirit and head said no. He was hiding his true intentions.

"I see Peter gave you the upgraded wristwatch?" He kept his face focused on the path and the humanoids guarding him.

"Yes, he did. The entire team has translucent blue smart band devices."

We extended our walk in the soft white sand, and I watched the horizon as the scorching sun closed over the mountain. While navigating the scorching desert sand, I was relieved to have worn tan boots and a tan spacesuit. The hot temperature threatened to scorch my body if I wasn't careful. Another spaceship appeared, shone a light over the water, and submerged into its depths.

"Rashid, I see the Nephilim live at the dam and around your home. Should I be worried that they might abduct me?"

He stopped and grabbed my hand. "They will not abduct you here. The dam is deep and gives them a place to keep their spaceships without the prying judgments of humans. You are safe with me." His handsome face and smothering eyes left me speechless. But I found my voice and continued.

"Peter mentioned that if someone kidnaped me, I could reach out to him. Rashid, I found it odd when the Nephilim abducted Lita and me a week ago. The wristwatch didn't signal Peter."

"That is not true, Carmen. We got a signal, but the Nephilim stopped it; their ability to cloak their activities is troublesome. Today, I have the power to detect their movements. I can protect you, my dear. So, call my emergency number when in danger and if you can't reach me. Press the red button on your blue smart band."

The mention of power caused his entire body to radiate with a fiery glow resembling burning coals. It was weird. The gold glow then vanished. Was there a hidden power within him? Was he aware I spotted the light around his body? I wanted to inquire but waited.

"Do you know the condition of my sons and ex-husband?"

He halted, gripping my hand and guiding me to face him.

"My dear, those vile aliens didn't tell you that your sons were dead?" His face softened, and a slight smile graced his lips.

His body closed in next to mine as he tilted his head and grasped my hands at that moment, his eyes never leaving my face. As the light illuminated his body, I could see his light aura swirling around me.

"My dear, they had custody of your sons. They seized them and tried to enclose them within a pod, but they vanished alongside millions of others. It frightened the aliens, and that is when they blackmailed you into thinking your sons were alive when they were missing or dead by a supernatural power. The vile creatures play tricks on you with supernatural powers to make you think they are alive but have been dead for days. I'm sorry, Carmen, but you must understand the betrayal of these creatures."

While his lips moved, my conscious mind grappled with his shared revelation. My sons were dead. Oh, God, please, no! Melekh told many lies, and I couldn't trust him. Was the vision I saw a lie projected by the demons to make me think my sons were still alive? I didn't know what to believe. No tears remained, only a burning anger and a desperate urge to avoid any interaction with the aliens and their covenant hologram. I had to receive the truth from Melekh.

"Carmen, my dear, please believe me when I say. Your sons are gone. Their clothes remained behind, along with millions of other captured individuals. We found the event disturbing. Even Zerus found the vanishing people mysterious. A report printed by a rabbi who believes in Jesus quoted: *For the Lord himself will descend from heaven with a cry of command, with the voice of an archangel, and with the sound of the trumpet of God.* Even I couldn't help but recognize the rabbi's statement. And remember my religious training, which I hadn't practiced in years."

My body braced as adrenaline flooded my veins, preparing me for the intense battle ahead. I blinked. A single tear slipped over my cheek. I heaved, breaking away from his grip, and leaned forward, gasping for air and trying to find inner peace. His arms encircled me, lifting and engulfing me in a bear hug that threatened to crush me. I found solace in the comforting embrace of his warm, muscular body and the warm scent of jasmine. The sultry look he gave me as I pushed back from him gave me the evidence I needed to justify my retreat.

Rashld Melekh lied to me. He had the jasmine scent I had smelled on the humanized Nephilim on the spaceship. Oh, my goodness. He lied and stood before me, claiming to be my friend—another betrayal. I sensed a fire surge inside my being, and I had to protect the hidden metaphysical power inside my being from emerging.

"Carmen, your behavior is surprising." He reached out to touch me, and I bristled at his touch.

"What of Noah? Rashid, please don't lie to me. You said we were friends, so be straightforward with me."

"Come, let's sit and drink a chilled beverage." He tried to hold my hand, but I retreated.

"I don't want a drink. Rashid, I want the truth." I ran towards his residence, but he caught up, grabbed my shoulders, and turned me to face him.

"Okay, let's slow the pace and stroll, Carmen. I didn't think we were in a marathon race," he stated, panting for breath.

We had reached the veranda. Rashid signaled the waitstaff to bring a fruity alcoholic drink as we sat in cushioned, reclining matching chairs beside the pool.

"Carmen, the less you know what happened to Noah, the better. Martin, your husband's work partner, and Abu work for me, but I did not know they were working with the aliens to sabotage my company. They received a payoff of millions of dollars split between them. When he signed paperwork to put your sons on the moon, he signed away his rights to his life. In the event the aliens wanted to conduct experiments on your sons. The aliens need people to live. They chose your sons. I told you the truth. Your teenage sons were alive, but they vanished along with others when the Nephilim put them in the pods aboard their spaceship."

"What do you mean, the Nephilim need humans to live? Are they conducting experiments on us?"

"Yes, each time you are with them, they take blood and use it for experiments to further their species' survival."

"You mean they take my blood and others to stay alive? These creatures are vicious. If the blood extractions continue, mortals will soon be extinct. Rashid, please don't lie to me. Is that the plan?" My vision realized if he responded yes to my questions. I had to complete my plan to lock out the Nephilim from the portal and keep the bracelet.

"They want to kill humans and start their species on Earth. Zarzu

Genesis is dying because of a black hole near their planet. Let's change the topic. I didn't invite you to discuss unpleasant topics."

Oh, no, my vision is true. We're doomed if I don't develop a foolproof action plan. I had to leave and complete the project. But the nagging thought that one of my SFT members had gone rogue and was working with the aliens made me keep my plans to myself and Becky.

"Rashid, the sun has descended. I have more coding to complete with the team. I appreciate your honesty, and now I trust you to help me. The code will be ready by Friday, and I await your call before I return the gold bracelet to Zerus."

"The true power of the bracelet is still a mystery, and it could threaten your well-being. You have two weeks to study the device and lock it in a safe place when not in use. It is an odd piece of jewelry. Please, my love, exercise caution. Its true potential remains unknown."

He leaned closer and touched the bracelet on my right arm, which came to life with a blue glow as the sapphire ball spun. I felt the clasp tighten as it hummed a melody, and then it affixed to my flesh.

"What a marvelous treasure. The bracelet emits a magical and lively energy."

I watched his eyes turn red as he rubbed his fingers over the gem. "Keep the bracelet locked and not on your person. The value of it makes it a potential target for someone to harm you. I have developed feelings for you, and I don't want to see you get hurt."

Rashid's eyes glowed, and a smirk formed on his lips. What made him touch the thing and the artifact respond to his touch? I was right. He had secret abilities I was unaware of, and he chose not to divulge his true self to me.

"Rashid, do you have powers?" He yanked his hand back and shot an intense frown as he clenched his jaw.

"What made you ask me such a question? Yes, I have powers. But I will never use them on you, my love. My mystical powers are used to protect you against harm." His narrowed brows let me know he still hid a secret. Rashid voiced his love for me, but I wasn't on board. I have a job to complete. Not interested in a love relationship.

Rashid, I need to return to the resort. I have work to complete.

I tilted my head and beamed at him. With a tender, lingering kiss on my palm, he goggled the captivating sapphire, his eyes shining with delight as if it possessed the secret to eternal happiness. Then Rashid let go of my hand and uttered a strange statement.

"Always be cautious of those closest to you, as they may harbor harmful intentions against you."

Peter departed from the conference terrace with a sly grin, tilting his head to the side as he conversed on his smartwatch. He sprinted through the conference hall and exited through the door.

Carmen observed Peter's swift movement through the conference room, resembling a cheetah pursuing prey. His brow furrowed in deep reflection, and he strode past Becky while absorbed in a digital conversation, only acknowledging her with a nod as he dashed from the veranda.

Peter's sudden departure and Carmen's rush to leave after a private conversation near the door surprised Becky. Intrigued by the mysterious scene, she was determined to uncover the motives behind Peter's unexpected exit.

"Talk to you later, Becky," Peter spoke as he exited the room.

Carmen ran in the same direction as she snatched a water bottle; her footsteps echoed as she sprinted toward the exit doors.

"Carmen, Carmen, wait," Becky's voice echoed through the room, her words dissolving into the thick air of suspense that now enveloped them.

She whirled around and motioned for Becky to follow her to the outside garden near the exit doors.

Tears turned Carmen's face red. What upset Carmen so much that she said meet me outside the building? The electronic doors opened when Becky's hand waved over the exit pad. Carmen stood beside the outside green garden with a delightful variety of flowers and a floral scent that circled their company's cylinder glass building, erected on stilts above the ground. Colorful birds chirped and flew across the sunny blue sky. Water lapped against the shore of the Persian Gulf. The impact of the warm sun warmed Becky's tired body.

"Are you okay? You want to tell me what happened?"

With a tissue in hand, Carmen wiped away her tears and observed Peter entering a black spaceship. The unfamiliar spaceship made her question whether Carmen had ever encountered the ship. Then, in disbelief, she watched as Carmen gasped, her hand jerking to cover her mouth, her eyes widening in shock.

"Have you seen this spaceship before, Becky?"

"No, I haven't, and I wonder who he met with that made him rush through our conference room. Carmen, what's happening?" She hesitated, then spoke. "Talk to me!" Carmen's face was a mask of anguish and fear, and her droopy shoulders only boosted her expression of anger.

Carmen placed her fists on her hips, took a large breath, and exhaled while moving back and forth in front of the fountain.

"Girl, you look as if you could kill someone. What's happening, Carmen?"

"Peter threatened me after fifteen years. He told me that this silver blue bracelet was my lifeline and my job if I couldn't get the hologram for Zerus working by Friday. Given the mistreatment I experienced, he could show kindness."

The conversation left Becky needing clarification and speechless. Carmen was brilliant, and she could stand her ground. But Peter ruffled her feathers, and she said he threatened her.

"What did he say?"

"The digital device is your vital link to life and survival on Earth. Afterward, Peter leaned in closer with a scowl. I was afraid and shattered by his response."

"Did he explain the added qualities of the upgraded bracelet? Don't forget, we will travel to Abu Dhabi over the weekend and then return to Dubai."

She nodded. Carmen calmed herself as she drank a bottle of water. Her tan face regained color, and her breath and speech were normal.

"Yes, but why the threats? Did you ever consider Peter to be a humanoid robot? His actions were not normal."

"Of course not. Carmen, what are you saying? Peter is part human and robot, similar to the cyborg humans that lost their lives and are machines. No, you're mistaken. Peter holds you in high esteem, and I conclude he wants the alien project to go away and you to finish the job so we can get to other projects. You are selfless and put everyone and everything above your aspirations." Becky patted her arm.

They stepped to the fountain to sit and talk.

The closer Becky and Carmen got, the louder the sound of water splashing became, and the air around the charming marble fountain was heavy with the earthy smell of damp stone.

Majestic gargoyles stood at the heart of the fountain, with water flowing from their detailed mouths, creating a stunning display of discarded coins in the circular design.

"Becky, you are mistaken. Peter shoulders immense pressure as a human to make our projects a reality. But if you're correct, someone will soon expose the truth. You didn't see his behavior. I want to go to heaven now. This project is causing me stress and a deep sense of sadness and despair. Mr. Melekh is making passes and wants me to be a love interest. My children—" Carmen started.

"What of your children?" Becky noticed her head bent forward as she placed her palms on her face.

Carmen jumped up and faced her.

"I listened to Zerus tell Lucifer to kill my children. They're dead, but not as Zerus and Lucifer claim. I'm sure.

"What do you mean?" She rocked back and forth with her arms crossed as she pulled on her lips.

"What's your opinion of the rapture of the saints? Is that possible?" Her trembling voice was soft.

"Are you serious?"

A deep sense of regret compounded Becky's anxiety when she learned people were missing. The idea of a saint's rapture in post-Christian church departure was unsettling. She regretted disregarding the predictions of the Tanakh and the Bible, a choice that now burdened her. If Carmen's assertion was correct, her parents were gone. Her parents believed in Messiah Yeshua's teachings. After hearing the news, she didn't call to check on them.

Carmen never took her eyes off Becky. Then Becky rose and hugged her. Tears flowed from both. Becky remembered her wonderful family, and now the truth was straightforward. The rapture of the saints happened, but maybe Carmen's sons survived.

"Carmen, what are you trying to tell? People disappeared from the Earth. And Zerus was not responsible for their disappearance."

"Yes."

Becky backed away from her and called her parents. Their cell line went to voicemail. Becky leaned into the fountain, cupped her hands, and splashed water on her face. Carmen called her grandmother, who always answered her cell. The voice attendant responded, but the message box was full. After drying their hands, Becky waved, saying they needed to return to work.

"Melekh told me that my sons vanished at the exact minute the Nephilim tried to put them into the pods on the spacecraft. Zerus and Lucifer lied and haunted my dreams to make me think they were still alive. When millions of people vanished, so did my sons. They are in Heaven with Messiah Yeshua. Yet Zerus is not aware I heard the truth from Melekh. But can we trust him? I have questioned myself. So far, I can. Melekh is candid with his judgment, and he hates the Nephilim."

Becky stepped back, her mouth wide open, and shook her head. Tears formed and fell as she realized she had missed the rapture. Those who had a genuine connection with Father God were the ones who transitioned. Was she correct that the rapture happened? Her parents warned her, and she fluffed off the notion. Was Carmen correct in her assessment of Melekh? He could be a friend, and he could help the team. Adding Carmen to join the battle to rescue Jews and Gentiles during the chaotic seven-year tribulation could be valuable. She had spunk and could use Melekh to save the team's life. Yet Becky's inner spirit pulled her away from Melekh. His aura was pleasing, but he had another side to his personality, and she promised to pay attention to him for her friend's sake and her teammates. Her fight to stay alive surged within her, and she implored Carmen to join her.

"Are you ready to join the Jewish Coalition and fight?"

"Yes, Becky, whatever I must do. I must stay alive and help others now that I know the truth that Zerus killed my sons."

"How do they serve?"

"The Jewish Coalition fights for Jews and Gentiles in Jerusalem. They are the Messianic Jews who minister to other Jews who don't believe in the Messiah Jesus. We have weapons and hide in various underground places in Jerusalem and other cities, which I can't discuss right now. We give money, food, medical help, housing in the new underground, and help Gentiles. Gentiles are the largest group, but soon will be the smallest. More Jews are coming to believe, and soon the 144 thousand men will preach the Gospel of Messiah Yeshua as we go forth in the Tribulation."

Carmen's facial expression was priceless. Her sullen face lost its ash color and glowed with sunlight. Her slouched stance straightened, and a smile graced her face.

"Girl, you still have to prove to me the rapture happened. Faith holds only value for me if you can offer tangible proof. The mere notion of faith implies skepticism in my mind. Are your sons still alive or deceased? Admit the truth to yourself and fight for the living. Did your sons vanish or on Earth with Zerus? Come on, Carmen, admit to one side and stand firm. Stop the flip-flop decision."

Carmen paused and shot Becky an annoyed glance as she cocked her head to one side and shook it, flung her hand in the air, and crossed her arms. Becky realized her limitations, while Carmen's naïve belief in the rapture fell short until more evidence confirmed her assertion.

"Carmen, I love you as a sister, but you must dig deeper into your heart and find faith before it's too late."

"Okay, enough religious talk. Let's get back inside before security sends those humanoids out to get us," Becky uttered.

"Wait, Mr. Melekh told me not to give the hologram bracelet to the aliens until he gave the okay. So, Friday is not on the table. What do I do?"

"Did you tell Peter?" Becky inquired.

"No, I was afraid after he threatened me. Let me ask him if I can get an extension. To support my claim."

"No, first, text Mr. Melekh and get him to authenticate your plans so Peter doesn't get suspicious. Let's use your proposal to swap the bracelet with the vacation hologram application but put the virus bot on the chip."

"Whatever you say, Becky."

"I'll be with you, whatever happens."

"Becky, I'm glad you have my back. You are a dear friend. I'm disappointed you didn't believe my story, but I forgive you and pray you will trust Messiah Yeshua soon."

"Hey, buddy, we are in this dilemma, and the team supports us no matter what happens."

As they approached the building, two robot guards with guns approached them.

Chapter Ten

After five days of intense work, I took a moment to catch my breath and asked for an extension. Understanding the intricate nature of the hologram project, Zerus and Melekh granted me two more weeks, doubling my original deadline to repair the bracelet.

The Western Wall in Jerusalem was a place where people from various backgrounds, including Gentiles and Christians, braved potential danger while seeking solace in prayer.

The heightened tensions caused by martial law led to the dispersal of crowds using tear gas, filling the air with a choking, acrid smell.

Grief filled my heart as the news report presented surreal video photos of death and carnage along the Western Wall.

Implementing military law turned Jerusalem into a fierce battleground, with the sights of armed soldiers parading the streets. Amidst the saturated air, the loud sounds of gunfire and piercing screams echoed through the chaos, a result of the clash between robot soldiers and defenseless citizens.

The reporter had to take cover to avoid being struck by a laser beam. The footage captured was disturbing and violent.

I decided that once our job site deployed us in Jerusalem, I could help fight the extraterrestrials if we were unsuccessful in destroying the beast. I must offer support to those who believe in the Messiah Yeshua.

THE DISTRESSING NEWS from Jerusalem filled my heart with sorrow. Then, I noticed a hologram call coming through on my wristband.

"Hey, Becky." I paused, then took a breath. "I saw the Jews and Christians seeking safety in Petra; they mentioned a secret timepiece collected by aliens. The reporter stated that the timepiece or bracelet was an ancient relic that protected them from Satan and his demons."

I leaned back on the sofa, put my laptop on my lap, and prepared for the unsettling news. Lita sat opposite me, engrossed in her holographic conversation with humanoids. But her attention shifted when I seized my laptop. She rose, stepped over, and sat next to me.

"Becky, listen to this: Jews and Christians sought refuge in Petra from a mysterious timepiece brought to our planet by the aliens."

She paused. "Carmen, they mentioned our bracelet in the article. Now listen, the journalist stated that this age-old artifact shielded them from the clutches of Satan and his evil followers. But now, they find themselves vulnerable without its protection."

"Becky, I experienced a vivid dream a few nights ago that shook me. In this dream, I saw a fierce battle between the Nephilim and ordinary people in a far-off land. The clashing of swords and the heavy breathing of the combatants filled the air as they fought over a mysterious piece of jewelry. Although I couldn't discern the exact details of the jewelry, it was a bracelet said to own mystical powers. In an impressive display, the Nephilim seized the precious bracelet from its glass case, even with gunfire directed at them. As bullets struck the Nephilim, they remained unaffected, overpowering and killing the security personnel using only their bare hands. The scene was grotesque and chilling, leaving me horrified. When I awoke screaming, I escaped from the nightmarish events that had unfolded before me."

"Becky was silent, and her face on the hologram turned red. She bowed her head and kept scrolling on her tablet, which annoyed me.

Lita sat and watched Becky and me interact. She didn't say a word. Yet, I knew Lita had taken mental notes and knew the tension between us. I worried she might tell Melekh the news of the bracelet, but I buried the thought and concentrated on getting Becky to expose her intel.

"What timepiece was he referring to in the report? Could our mysterious jewelry be from Zerus, who might have stolen from the Israelis?"

She stayed muted, focusing on her typing. Becky's actions made me anxious.

"Becky, I know you hear me, so please say something. She cleared her throat, um—" Her voice trailed, her eyes fixed on the ground.

What in the world? Why won't she answer my question and stop acting weird? She's got a secret, and she's too chicken to spill. Becky only acts strange when she has awful news.

"Yes, yes. The relic is the same bracelet that Zerus and his people stole. Okay, Bart told me not to say a word. But I have been busting inside to give you the latest intel. Zerus's hologram bracelet is both powerful and dangerous. To guard against Satan's influence, Israelis turned to an archangel for protection. The Nephilim wanted it so they could sabotage the plight of Gentiles and Jews to find safety during the Tribulation. Zerus stole it when they left for several years. He re-engineered it to deploy more Nephilim to Earth. I recommend you keep what I told you a secret. Keep the bracelet safe, and never give back the original. We must return it to the Jewish Coalition when we arrive in Jerusalem."

I was so overwhelmed that I sat there, mouth agape, for at least a few seconds. Bart Hall and Becky, who met at NASA, shared a bond of friendship. My heart skipped a beat when Becky mentioned Bart had told her to keep the origins of the bracelet secret. UltraOnic Marketing International hired Bart and Noah, and Bart took on the role of IT manager.

"What you have admitted means they lied to get me to repair the bracelet is a farce. They wanted me to fix the bracelet because it had a supernatural power and then use it on us. And you and Bart never told me the origins of the bracelet. Oh, my goodness."

Inside me, a wave of anger surged. With every muscle tensed, my body shook as I clenched my hands into a tight fist. Tears cascaded over my cheeks as I confronted the unsettling thought of other hidden secrets. Once again, betrayal sat before me; this time, it came from my friend. How could she betray me? I could never divulge the secret of the bracelet, but now I had no choice but to safeguard myself and the wretched artifact.

"I'm sorry, I didn't tell you. But I swore to secrecy. The underground coalition serves as the lifeline to Christians. The Jewish Coalition provides underground transportation to Gentiles and Jews to Petra as they flee from the Golden Nephilim, who have a more human display."

"Let me meet you outside to talk more freely."

We met by the waterfront, stepping and talking.

THE SCORCHING SUN'S sweltering heat against our skin didn't deter us from covering our heads with hijab and our bodies with long white dresses that were not hot under the sun. Although our jumpsuits had a built-in cooling device, we wore clothing appropriate for the culture to avoid potential arrest. We grabbed bottles of water and began to walk and talk.

"Carmen, please be aware that those without the required red dragon mark tattoo were at risk of being abducted by the Golden Nephilim. After being arrested, they took people to the mother spaceship for confinement. After that, the aliens had plans to transport mortals to Zarzu Genesis. They took citizens who disobeyed the orders during martial law to the electronic pool in abandoned warehouses worldwide. AI humanoids attached spider tentacles to humans and sent electronic shock waves through their bodies. After an overnight stay, they sent people home if they survived the shocks. The electronic pool warned those who rebelled against the new power, the NWP."

Drinking my water, the top-secret information Becky had privy to through Bart, amazed me.

"I heard three new members joined the coalition yesterday. Sophia, Jon, and Cyborg Nick. They had a run-in with Cyrus Rashid Melekh in Romala, Texas, when his oil moguls poisoned the water supply. He is a rascal. You must be careful with the hunk, Carmen."

I kept my head bent to the ground as my lips slid across my teeth. She was correct; Melekh was a hunk, and I trusted him with my life.

"How do you recommend I secure the hologram bracelet for safe-keeping?" Becky knew the team better and understood its politics. I had to rely on her wisdom.

"I'm clueless, but I'm positive you have thoughts to share. Remember, the team has more at stake than we imagined."

A musical interlude from the passing buildings echoed in the wind. The steady hum of air conditioning units, the occasional rumble of flying vehicles overhead, and the melodic splash of water against the shore smoothed my anger. I had to devise a foolproof plan.

What should I do to secure the hologram and keep Zerus happy? My time limit was going fast, and Melekh had told me to stall, yet he didn't acknowledge his motive. The depressing news from the security team left me hopeless since the Nephilim abducted individuals daily. I had neglected to support enough people in their fight for survival against the alien invasion.

The hungry beasts were hauling people into pods on the mothership for transport to either the moon or their planet as they abducted them. People were being eaten alive by the Nephilim, who used human blood to change their essence to appear more human.

***

AFTER A GRUELING DAY of coding on Friday, the team and I rested by going to the city marketplace, where we sampled local foods as we shopped.

Later in the afternoon, we delivered the vacation hologram to Ms. Bilal. When I delivered the vacation hologram bracelet to her for her high-powered customers, a satisfied smile spread across Qadira Bilal's face. The stress of completing Qadira's project and the Zerus bracelet had kept me under continuous stress. But with Qadira's project completed, I took a deep breath to relieve the tension.

Lita tagged along to keep me and the group safe from kidnapping since we had finished our projects for the week. Before the end of the evening, we visited several markets, including the Water Front Market, where locals came for fresh meat, fish, and produce. A local band was playing at one of the outside markets, and the team stopped and ate, then returned to the Melekh Dubai Hotel on the city peninsula.

As we crossed the walkway to the hotel, the wind stopped blowing. Flying vehicles tumbled from the sky and crashed into the ocean. We sprinted towards the building. I feared spaceships striking our building. Sirens screeched in the air, and cries and wails echoed. We had just entered the building when a giant spaceship hovered over Dubai and scooped up people on the streets and at the pools with the red laser. As we peered out the large pane of glass window, the chaotic traffic collisions merged with the terrified shrieks of individuals while the red laser plucked mortals and whisked them away into the spacecraft.

"Lita, what's happening?" As I tried to steady my quaking body, my voice trembled with fear.

"Carmen, Zerus, and his folks are angry with a transaction made by Mr. Melekh, and they are gathering people for replacement parts."

Everyone on my team turned and stared at Lita, their bodies suspended in place. I spun around and saw the terrified expressions. As I squinted at Lita, I glimpsed her body language when she kept her face turned away from me, suggesting she possessed more information than she was concealing. Undeterred, I pressed on with my inquiries.

"What do you mean, replacement parts? Give me details, and hurry."

"Miss Carmen, the Nephilim can't stay in our atmosphere without recharging their outward image. They kill humans and use their blood to restore their outward presence to appear more human and use the blood for experiments. Non-scaly Nephilim beings have not consumed human blood. But they will die soon if they don't eat the red substance found in their soil. Our atmosphere will kill them if they can't get human blood."

During the chaos of the Nephilim attack, individuals rushed from their offices for safety. Meanwhile, outside the building, vehicles became engulfed in smoke, spitting flames and emitting sparks. Fire spacecrafts soared overhead, dousing the raging fires with foam.

The humanoid robots, now acting as firefighters and first responders, faced the grim duty of clearing away the wreckage, retrieving the deceased, and transporting the injured to medical facilities.

Amidst the turmoil, a group of brave individuals sprang into action to rescue a man trapped inside his vehicle just moments before it exploded. The blast's force caused our building's front door to shatter and collapse, leaving a gaping hole in its wake.

My mind and body were in shock. At that moment, I found my answer to my plight, staring me in the face. The Nephilim must capture humans to stay alive. They had become blood-thirsty Nephilim. We needed to lure the Nephilim into the hologram and keep the people away from the aliens to survive. How could it be done? Although I had stayed in the entrance hall with the team, the terrifying sight of alien attacks prompted me to move to the computer room with the team as we hustled toward the room. Meanwhile, we plopped on the bean pods in the computer room and chatted until we heard another crash outside our building.

"The blood the Nephilim draw from us kills mortals. How long does a transfusion support their life, Lita?"

"From what I have calculated and watched them after they take the blood, they must refuel after seventy-two hours. They took your blood, Miss Carmen, but when they take humans on board their ship, they drain the human blood and store it so they can blend in with the population. The golden skin color happens because of a blood transfusion from a human. The gold color only happens for the Nephilim, who were scaly before being transported to Earth. Blood is unnecessary for the golden Nephilim we saw when abducted. They have adapted to our planet, yet they need the red dirt to stay alive. Zerus and his aliens didn't consider our atmosphere their ability to stay on our planet. The data I gave you is from a rogue alien."

Feeling weak and lightheaded, the news of the Nephilim stunned me. I slid off the bean chair and onto the floor. I touched the smooth surface beneath me, and as I looked up, I escaped, hitting my head on the floor. Lita grabbed me and placed me in the bean chair. My teammates were lounging on the bean pods scattered across the floor. I leaned my head against the pod, and Lita sat beside me, checking my vitals. Watching Becky's face, I could see her complexion had turned pale, and she reached into her pouch for her inhaler.

"Miss Carmen, are you okay?" I glanced at her and closed my eyes as I gathered my thoughts. I was glad Lita caught me.

"Yes, Lita, thank you for helping me."

The reason for the bloodbath was to re-surge their energy. As mortal beings, we needed to find a concrete solution to stop the Nephilim from taking more lives. A report popped up on my wristband as I sat in the chair, highlighting the military's alertness to outsiders who could threaten the new government. I had to regain my strength and continue pushing forward, determined to overcome any obstacles.

Lita had grabbed a bottle of water from the counter by the entrance. She pushed the bottle into my hand, and I drank. I glimpsed at Becky. The sight of Becky's trembling hands and chin made my heart ache. Fear had consumed her and the team.

"Becky, snap out of it." I clicked my fingers in her face as I leaned closer. A trance gripped her and the group. Lita's revelation had left the team paralyzed with fear. My teammates stared into space, not on their devices, as they sat on the bean pod chairs.

Then, I noticed a gray mist leaving our room. Only Lita and I remained unaffected by the time suspension. Either Lucifer or Zerus had suspended the staff. One of them eavesdropped on our conversation. I glanced at Lita. *"Don't tell your teammates, not yet. They are not ready to hear the truth."* Her telepathy gave me solace.

"Hey, buddy, we must find the rogue alien and get him to confess to hacking the vacation hologram. I plan to save our project."

Becky blinked, twirled in her seat, and focused on me.

"Carmen, where do you get your energy to recover so fast? I'm in shock, and you are planning an intervention to save humanity. Whatever you decide, I am in this battle with you. Please give me five more minutes to absorb the heart-wrenching data Lita gave us."

"Buddy, you got it. Let me tell you how Lucifer is using Peter to maneuver our projects. I saw Lucifer's spirit invade Peter to get me to send the hologram to Qadira. He had Peter hack the code. Peter disguised himself and gave the rogue Nephilim the new code. The Nephilim changed the lock, opened it, and then changed it back. I saw the deception in my vision last night as I slept."

"Hold on, wait, a minute… Are you sure our supervisor hacked the code and disguised himself?"

"Yes. In my vision, I saw Lucifer conversing with Peter hours after we completed our project. Now, I implemented a deceptive code to pinpoint any disguised hacking attempts. It wasn't just Peter who carried out the underhanded task. I couldn't see the Nephilim, but he was gold, which doesn't help."

"What? Carmen, what you are saying is meshuga. And, you are positive?" I leaned closer, and in hushed tones, I spoke.

"In my vision, Lucifer spoke with Peter. At our meeting yesterday, Peter read my thoughts, which had never happened since my employment. He tried to enter my mind, and his facial expression was not Peter's. His eyes were red, and I saw the demon inside Peter in a quick flash when I turned my head to peek at him. Peter has always been kind towards me, and I have never seen him give me a hateful look as he stared and bared his teeth. It scared me to the deepest part of my being."

Becky moved closer and leaned back in the chair.

"Are you saying you have a supernatural power to view into another realm?"

I nodded.

"Oh, my goodness!" She put her hand to her mouth as she uttered her words. "Carmen, you are a true blessing. If true, your sons have ascended to heaven. You know that deep within you since you have a supernatural power. I might not believe in Father God as you do, but I learned. A person has gifts when the Holy Spirit indwells them. The Holy Father left you behind to guide and strengthen those doubting our belief in Messiah Yeshua, who display unwavering conviction. How can we find the rogue alien?" Her lips twisted upward on one side.

"We set a trap to see what happens."

"Did you bring it with you? And what kept you, Peter? I gave up on you coming and started eating my brunch. I thought you had the Zerus hologram bracelet with you."

Melekh despised people's lateness, and Peter wished he didn't get perturbed. His abrasive tone and quick wit could level a person's confidence in seconds.

"Melekh, Carmen is still asking questions. She will become suspicious of my actions if I take it. She and Becky will ask questions. I can't risk their trust at this stage."

"We must upgrade your skin again, but your presence is flawless this time." The humanoid robot completed her task on his skin and left the cabin as another humanoid entered with a hypodermic needle.

"Peter, you look great. The upgrade to your weapons and skin is perfect. Did you tell your team you were in meetings this week?"

"Why, of course, Melekh? They will never know I am a human cyborg. My secret remains intact as long as Cyborg Nick keeps our secret from our days with the CIA. The Nephilim aliens saved my life, and I owe them gratitude for saving me after that dreadful shark attack three years prior. But why did you want me upgraded with weapons?"

"The Special Force Tigers are vulnerable, and I want them protected around the clock. My team of security humanoid robots will stay with them until they die or they decide to take my mark."

"Ouch, that hurts." The humanoid never stopped her duty. She gave him four more injections and then left the cabin. He turned and looked in the mirror the humanoid gave him. "Wow, I am handsome."

Taking a moment, Peter stared at himself in the mirror. A slender man with a tan complexion and dark hair with streaks of gray, Peter sported a groomed mustache above his upper lip. He pressed his hand through his straight hair and smirked.

"Yeah, enough bragging. Make sure Carmen doesn't give the hologram bracelet to Emperor Zerus. She's been reluctant to find a solution. For now, watch her every move. I told her to stall and not give Zerus the bracelet."

"Why did you say that? We need to move on the Jerusalem project."

"Peter, I am being set up by Zerus. But the hologram bracelet has powers that can change the world and enhance my supernatural powers. Zerus mentioned the hologram can transport people and aliens and alter the scenery."

Melekh stepped from his seat to the spacecraft's bar. He had kept secrets hidden from his staff of engineers, including one vital secret: his collusion with Zerus. Rashid Melekh, wise man, he thought. He knew he had to honor what Melekh asked him to do, or his lucrative job could vanish.

"Are you requesting a new bracelet for power harnessing? The SFT techniques are capable, but Carmen has intel on how to fix the alien technology. It could have been sheer coincidence, but she repaired their transmitter. She understands Hebrew and ancient hieroglyphics, and no team member has provided similar skill."

"No, not — Do you want a drink?"

"Yes, and make mine whisky, no chaser for me."

Melekh strode over and handed Peter the drink. He had his standard glass of red wine, which Peter drank in one gulp, savoring the smooth liquid.

"Qadira Bilal wants another vacation hologram once the team develops it; I want the schematics and the bracelet. Tell Carmen to make two bracelets. But if she could gather the supernatural power of Zerus's Nephilim bracelet, I could override his aim to surrender our planet. I own the planet, not him."

"You want to override Carmen? What happened to your affection for her? What happens with that part of your scheme?"

"She wants time. Time is not on my side. I have fallen for her, but now she must prove her loyalty. Otherwise, I will allow the aliens to kidnap her, and she will have to show us her authentic self or die. I suspect she has spoken with Becky, and if so, she will be a liability to my plans."

"If you double-cross Carmen, you will confuse her, as she won't accept your claims. She has grit, and I suspect she is a fighter. The way she has handled herself with Zerus has been remarkable. Melekh, it implies you are playing on both sides of the ship. Let Carmen complete her assignment. Then pretend with Zerus that you honored his requests."

"Yes, but let me make one thing transparent, Peter. You are my employee. Never try to override me."

The narrowed eyebrows and glare of fire in his eyes sent a chill through his body. "Remember, your life can end within seconds."

Peter's shoulders were tight, and his hands were clammy. He kept his spine straight and placed his arms on the armrests, not changing his forced grin as he gritted his teeth.

"Good, you understand."

"What is your next plan to keep the aliens from taking over the planet? I can stall the group after we arrive in Jerusalem. And I understand the complexity of the hologram bracelet, but what if Carmen can't fix it? Then what?"

"My, man, she will fix it because I told her the truth: her children are dead. They vanished the same day after bombing my oil fields. Don't get me started on that topic." He watched the veins in Melekh's neck pop out and his jaw muscles tighten.

Peter grabbed a plate of food from the waitstaff humanoid and ate. He kept his face focused on his plate and snuck a peek at Melekh throughout the meal. Melekh believed in God, and the people vanished into heaven when God snatched them. Melekh had a remarkable belief in someone other than himself. Peter never considered Melekh religious. Yet, over the past month, he has changed and become more compassionate and calmer since Carmen joined the SFT group.

He remembered when he felt complete, his Navy service a distant memory. His parents were no longer alive after their sudden disappearance. His sister had died at birth, and a thief one day killed his brother after the mysterious disappearance of humans. He had always questioned a higher power and found the notion of religion flawed. To him, life followed a simple cycle of birth, living, death, and then decomposition into worm food. The idea of believing in a god implied foolishness to him.

Fifteen years ago, after leaving the Navy, he applied for a job at P.J. as the engineer manager. Peter became the Special Force Tigers manager, allowing him to embrace his independence. He poured his heart and soul into the leadership role.

"Delicious Belgian waffles, coffee, and the savory smell of the western omelet are delicious. Please let the chef know." The waitstaff attendant bowed his head and left the cabin.

"My next plan of attack is to get rid of Noah and Abu. They are fooling with my clients and spending my money. I thought Noah honorable; he fooled me and became a womanizer and a cheat. Carmen is a better person without Noah. I hate to see her suffer."

Melekh patted his wristband. "Well, my dear Carmen is calling me. I wonder what she wants. I'll call her after we finish brunch."

Carmen had called Melekh. Interesting. Maybe he convinced her to be his love interest. If so, the bracelet might divide them when she finds out what he wants. He had to keep the peace, keep secrets from his staff, and keep a lookout for Carmen.

"Melekh, did you forget you told her to meet you for a 5:00 pm dinner?"

His stern stare across the table left him concerned that his anger might show.

"Yes, but I told her *to beware of who she trusts*. She is suspicious and convinced you have doubled-crossed her with Zerus."

He handpicked his words, wanting to avoid upsetting Melekh. His venomous comments were the last thing he wanted to hear today.

"I told her that Zerus is wicked, and she believed I betrayed her?"

Melekh grumbled, raised from his chair, cursed, flushed with a pursed mouth, and went to the spaceship's back for a drink. Peter watched him pour two hefty shots of tequila. Oh, boy, Melekh was in love with the woman to drink alcohol. He had not seen him take a drink since his divorce ten years ago. Carmen had gotten inside his blood, and he had lost control. Peter finished his last bite when the cabin lit up with a white light.

"RASHID MELEKH, what are you doing whining over a woman? Get back to your assignment. Add to your kingdom and let Carmen Northrop alone. She is poison to us. Get that bracelet from her and keep it away from those foul Nephilim. They have lied to me. I want the entire hoard killed."

As the spaceship's atmosphere shifted from peaceful to menacing, a subtle gray mist changed shape, revealing the evil angel's ominous presence.

The melodic tunes emanating from Lucifer's chest evoked eerie melodies while his imposing, soot-colored bodyguards loomed behind him. The overwhelming intensity of his presence paralyzed Peter with fear. Never had he feared anyone, but the spirit of Lucifer frightened him. He admired the angel because he could evoke fear and had an entourage that followed him as if he were a god. One thing is sure: Melekh admired Lucifer and had taken on many of the angel's qualities, making him uncomfortable. But Rashid Melekh still had a human heart and had fallen hard for Carmen, which controlled how much evil ran through his veins.

In a synchronized motion, both men sprang to their feet and bowed before the wicked angel. Melekh straightened his back, his eyes locked onto Lucifer's intense stare. Peter stayed rooted next to his chair, refusing to move.

"Okay, Lucifer, I will get the bracelet. I might have to trick her to get it, but whatever it takes to retrieve the relic. The bracelet has more worth to me than Zerus. Who gave the bracelet to the Jews?"

"Who do you expect, fool? Of course, their archangel, Michael. My nemesis protects them. I own Earth and its people. Get rid of Zerus, and the planet belongs to you."

A puff of smoke materialized, and Lucifer vanished. Lucifer left gray ash floating in the cabin as it fell to the floor. The heavy scent of sulfur and rotten bodies left a stench in the cabin. Humanoids hurried and activated the clean air supply, swept the ash from the floor, and departed.

"Melekh, what are you going to do? Will you pretend to care for Carmen to get the bracelet? You know I can get it for you tomorrow, and you can use it."

"No, Peter. She will suspect, and I want it fixed and ready to use when I gain my Antichrist power."

"Make sure Carmen repairs the relic, and I get a replica before the aliens grab it."

"Melekh, you are ruthless and wicked." We both exchanged a hearty, wicked laugh.

Chapter Eleven

I SMELLED chlorine on my skin as I entered my room after enjoying a refreshing swim in the outdoor pool at my workplace in Dubai. I felt a buzz from my wristband, and it caught my eye.

"Carmen, come to my office at once." Peter's message requested my immediate presence, leaving no time to waste. Without delay, I showered, changed into my work jumpsuit attire, and rushed to his office to see what he needed.

I had to calm myself after confiding a secret to Becky. Even though she was my friend, I found it hard to trust her with my secret. The thought of her revealing my secret to Peter, or worse, sharing my supernatural vision, made my mouth dry and sweat bead on my face as I hurried through the hall.

"Carmen, do you know that Noah and Abu replaced the counterfeit bracelet with the original vacation hologram we gave to Qadira for her customers? The bracelet Noah and Abu stole ended up being useless, and I received a text from Noah expressing his disappointment with its lack of authenticity."

"Noah, did what?" The betrayal was so stark it struck a physical blow to my being, and I struggled to keep my emotions in check.

Anger washed over me, and I sensed heat rising to my face. Noah's foolish actions embarrassed me and made Peter blame me, putting my credibility at stake. Answering Peter in a calm and composed manner was crucial.

"Peter, let me explain. Noah must have given Qadira the fake bracelet and said it was from me."

"So, you were aware they gave her a phony bracelet?"

"Peter, No. I didn't give a counterfeit bracelet to Qadira, who paid millions for the vacation hologram, but it wasn't fake. Noah and Abu stole my fake bracelet when they came to the office. The day you asked me to give them a demo. Becky and I tricked them and gave them a dummy bracelet. Noah's refusal to leave the bracelet on the table suggested something suspicious was brewing. Just as I looked away to grab my tablet, he seized the opportunity and placed it in his pocket. I caught sight of him swiping it while Becky remained unaware. But her intuition kicked in when she found the cheap, duplicated bracelet on the table. We called the guards. When guards searched them, the bracelet was gone."

Noah's unexpected deceit stunned me, and his once loyal demeanor morphed into an unsettling aura of hatred as he schemed to switch bracelets. Who was Noah working with that put him on the line to his doom? Now, Qadira believes I am a fraud, and my credibility is on the line until I save face.

"Those rogue men tricked Qadira with the fake bracelet. I am so sorry for the uncomfortable mess I put you in with your project."

"You didn't know, and I was suspicious, so I used counterfeit jewelry instead of the vacation bracelet. I must protect the hologram bracelet Zerus gave me to repair. It has dangerous powers. Now, Qadira thinks we gave her the wrong image. How do we rectify?"

"Don't worry. I have called and spoken to Qadira. She is coming by the office this afternoon to pick up another bracelet for her clients. She was furious with Noah. His actions with Abu resemble those of a criminal. Mr. Melekh has a special mission for him. He won't be a bother to you or the team."

"What happened to the vacation bracelet they switched with Qadira?"

"The text didn't cover that specific status. We need to retrieve Noah and Abu's vacation hologram. A bracelet that enables people to travel without protocols is not advisable."

"I am worried, Peter. If someone took the vacation hologram with nefarious intentions, we could be in danger as engineers. Will you tell Mr. Melekh? He must know what is happening."

"I'll be reaching out to Mr. Melekh within a few minutes. Unpleasant news isn't his thing. His temper is unbearable when people cross him. I have seen what happens to folks."

"Well, I hope Noah learns his lesson. I can't believe he has become wicked and betrayed me, our sons, and now my teammates."

Wow, the news of Melekh's temper set an alarm in my mind. I had never seen his anger, but if Melekh had a terrible temper. Noah and his buddy were on the path of Melekh's wrath.

"Carmen, your ex-husband, became wicked when he took the dragon's mark. Until now, we shielded your team from the mandatory dragon image. You'll have to decide whom to pledge loyalty to in due time."

I turned, and my forehead furrowed into a frown. But as I departed, I said.

"Peter, I will return with the bracelet for Ms. Qadira Bilal in five minutes."

Thank God I had a replica of the vacation hologram bracelet for Qadira. I uploaded the data from my copy to the mainframe, instructed the humanoid manager to make another bracelet, and texted when replication was complete.

Upon my return, I found Noah and Qadira in Peter's office, and their interaction was unpleasant.

"Carmen, you remember Qadira Bilal?" We shook hands; I remained standing, and she sat beside Noah. Qadira was a stunning, slender woman with a tan complexion; her long black hair cascaded along her back, and her piercing turquoise eyes captivated anyone who looked into them. Her demeanor was cordial, but an air of contempt circled her aura.

"Pleased to see you again." She was furious with me because of her icy stare and pursed lips.

"Mrs. Northrop, may I call you Carmen?"

"Of course." I nodded in response.

"Noah and his friend are untrustworthy, and I apologize for your unfortunate entanglement in their web of lies. Thank you for your hard work and the image I purchased. I know the aliens want my hologram."

She turned and cocked her head toward Noah, who bent his head to avoid her glaring face.

"Noah wanted my vacation hologram for money, and then he could pay off a debt he owes to the cartel and the aliens. His friend Abu deceived him."

I turned my face toward the scene and watched the tense interplay between Qadira and Noah. Qadira's deliberate actions made no doubt she wanted him to suffer in my presence. Her head swiveled from me to Noah until she stood and approached.

"I have my guards here to lock the bracelet at night. So don't worry if it gets into the wrong hands."

Qadira expressed her approval through a gentle nod and a warm handshake, softening her facial expression. I reciprocated by mirroring her gestures. I stuck out my hand, and we shook hands in agreement.

"No worry. As a scientist, you understand the relevance of our projects and the necessity to safeguard our copyrights. Again, nice to meet you."

Noah jumped to his feet and shoved his body against mine. How dare he think he could intimidate me? Besides, I had the upper grip on his game. He could rot in hell for the atrocities he did to his family.

She snatched the box from its resting place on the table and handed it over to her guards, who secured it in a combination sealed container.

"The same." Her turquoise orbs bore into my green eyes, and I nodded, and so did she. Then Qadira exited the office. I couldn't help but keep my eyes on Noah. His piercing stare bore into my soul, making me suffer within my spirit.

The man and his wickedness were repulsive to me. As I prayed for his wretched soul, my thoughts turned to the hellish fire that awaited him, and I yearned for it to be less severe at the end of his life. One tear descended from my eye. My love for the man I had spent two decades with raising children remained embedded in my heart. I had to release him to mend my broken heart. Noah meant harm to me and my job, so I had to forgive him. I had to rise higher and be an example of a faithful Christian. As I wiped a tear from my face, I sensed calm wash over me as I prayed.

I vocalized my words to myself. *"Poor Noah. Hell is waiting for you. Once again, another obstacle to keep me from getting the truth."*

NOAH STORMED out of Peter's office alone; his clomping footsteps on the marble floors echoed in the corridor. I saw him engage in a heated conversation with Abu near the exit. I sidestepped into the computer conference room and placed my tablet on the table in my pod when Noah's hand clutched my arm.

Noah had trailed behind me and ventured into the secure room, breaching protocol without me realizing it. I turned and faced the man I once loved, his presence evoking a mix of nostalgia and regret. I thought of days when we sat on the patio, listening to the animals, playing board games, and watching the sunset. Noah had ceased to be the man who loved his sons and me, now consumed by a poisonous darkness that condemned him to hellfire. He was a wreck, his trembling hands and unkempt hair revealing his inner turmoil. His face contorted with fear and anguish as I peeked at him. His web of lies had ensnared him, and now he pursued help from me. I stiffened and heard chairs scraping against the floor as my male teammates rushed toward my pod.

"Carmen, I... my dear, my apologies for the pain I've caused you. Please forgive me. I never intended to bring you harm. I had to hurt you to survive since you got in the way. Abu warned me that refusing the bracelet meant death."

"I think you are late with your apologies. But I hold no hard feelings against you. Where is the vacation hologram you stole from, Qadira? Be upfront with me; I'm not in the mood for lies.

"Don't worry; we used the bracelet to pay my debt. I don't have it anymore."

"What has happened to you?" I searched his face for any compassion and found none. "The vacation hologram is dangerous and could be fatal to anyone. You must retrieve it."

"What do you care? You left me standing on a cliff. I will never forgive you."

Out of the corner of my eye, I noticed my teammates dash from their pods and form a circle.

"Are you still whining? Grow up, man. Get that vacation hologram back, or you will see death earlier than you thought."

The sight of his distorted face and the force of his fingers triggered a memory of when the aliens snatched his foot. What a fool he had become. He jolted me from my thoughts.

"Hey, are you and the Melekh having an affair? Whenever I look at him, he never misses an opportunity to discuss you, and he has an unprofessional way Melekh licks his lips when he mentions your name."

My five male teammates locked arms next to me and didn't move. They sealed Noah into a semi-circle. Clenching the chair, I glanced and nodded at my teammates, attempting to conceal my anxiety. Yet I wanted the guys to stay close.

"Noah, my life is not your concern. You can leave."

Releasing his grip, I shoved his body away from mine. I strolled halfway over to my cushion recliner when he grabbed my arm again. This time, he dug his fingers into my arm. Before I could even prepare for what was happening, the guys had me in their grasp, and to my surprise, Lita joined them. Then, out of thin air, Abu dashed towards me, entering my field of view. How did he enter? A retinal scan was mandatory.

As I grappled with a dilemma, I was at a loss for navigating the tense scene while my teammates positioned themselves to guard and shield me. The tension thickened as Lita, my humanoid robot, settled in front of me, her expression unreadable. Noah was on my left, digging his fingers into my arm. Behind Lita stood Abu as he glared at me with murderous intent. My heart raced as I noticed Abu gripping a weapon, adding another layer of complexity to our dangerous predicament. My teammates had circled me, and the gun aimed to kill any of us. I didn't want my teammates to get killed.

"Carmen, give me the damn bracelet, the one Zerus gave you, or I will kill you within seconds." I could see Noah's lips twisting into a terrifying snarl, his clenched teeth visible as he yanked my left arm, his fingers digging into my skin and drawing blood. I could sense his breath near my ear.

"Noah, what are you doing? You can't have the image, and you will not get out of the building without someone shooting you for stealing. Have you gone insane? How much money are you getting for the bracelet from Zerus?"

While my body quivered with fear and anger, my teammates remained steadfast, holding onto my arms and shoulders.

"Zerus will get his share later, but the bracelet is for Abu and me. We made a false money arrangement, and the oil moguls want their money back or the bracelet. If I fail this time, they will kill me. Do yourself a favor and retrieve the code from the mainframe room. Carmen, I know that is where you hid your precious projects. You forgot we were married, and you told me everything."

"Noah, to begin with, that is not my issue. You are the one who caused this mess, so it's your job to unravel the lies you've told in your business dealings."

Abu moved closer, pushing Lita until he reached around her and pushed his weapon into my stomach. My teammates still held tight to my right side and shoulders.

"Guys, move back; I don't want you to get killed. Alert security, please, and step back." My voice quivered, and my body shook. My teammates moved backward but still had their hands ready to use their weapons. Abu wasted no time moving to my right side, and I felt the pressure of Abu's laser gun as he pushed it against me. Noah stepped back.

My teammates didn't give an inch. The courageous individuals were prepared to perish alongside me. I controlled my emotions and prevented the mist from emerging. I spotted Becky by the entrance, and she pressed her finger against her mouth. The exact moment of Lita's departure from in front of me was unclear, but I knew she had notified the humanoid robotic police.

"Hey, man, don't shoot her. She is not worth it. She is doing her job. We will get the bracelet another time. Look, Abu, more humanoids are coming. I hear them stomping through the hall." Noah let go of my arm and stepped back away from me.

Abu's weapon pressed against my ribs, and he shocked and scared me, but he was not getting the hologram, and neither were the aliens. What power did the hologram bracelet have? Men died to own the relic. I understood the controversy with the relic. Both man and beast desired its powerful possession.

A sharp ache surged through my left arm as we moved toward the network room. Noah's fingers squeezed my muscles when he clasped my arm again. Lita must have left in the commotion because she positioned herself at the door and aimed her weapon at Abu and Noah. When I reached the room and tried to enter my face with digital recognition, the door didn't open.

"Abu and Noah, the door will not open, and humanoids know you are trying to steal. Kill me now. I'm tired of playing games with you."

"Abu, let her go, or you will become ash within seconds," Melekh's voice echoed behind me.

Even though I recognized Melekh's voice, the jab of Abu's weapon against my side made me even more determined to avoid getting shot.

My cell buzzed.

"Don't answer it."

"Abu, If I don't, the security team will arrive within seconds."

"I said don't answer the cell." His grizzly face focused on mine.

"Too late. Security personnel are entering the door." Lasers flashed across the room, and everyone slipped to the floor to avoid the laser firing in my direction.

The potent smell of sulfur filled the room and clung to Abu.

Thoughts of Lucifer and his evil minions overwhelmed my mind. The odor of demons brings with it the essence of hell.

With a forceful shove, Abu pushed me to my feet. He fired his weapon as a blaze of lasers zinged above our heads and tore open a gaping hole in the wall, causing a fire. Humanoids rushed to the men. My teammates fell with me in a heap on the carpet. Abu extended his finger, pointing it at Noah. They disappeared when touched by the light. My journey in the new world of the Antichrist differed from what I expected.

Melekh was at my side within seconds, helping me to my feet.

"My dear, are you okay? I told you I'll let no one hurt you. You are our secret weapon. Noah is gone forever, so don't worry. He is where he belongs. In hell."

Lita supported my coworkers in regaining their balance after they stumbled while helping me. Becky rushed over to my side. Not a single word eluded her lips, but she wrapped her arms around me as Melekh supported and lifted me.

"Did you kill Noah? You sent the burst of light?"

"Yes, but he is not dead. He is away from you for now. His punishment in hell will make him think twice before he threatens you again. As for the missing bracelet, I will find it and return it to you."

We moved towards my workstation, and he pivoted and sprinted towards the exit. When I peeked at his swagger, he had disappeared. My thoughts swirled. Melekh had the power to disappear, and his power puzzled and frightened me. He was a mysterious figure, always shrouded in secrecy.

To protect myself from the man's cunning maneuvers, I had to uncover his true allegiance, wary that he could be a double agent in the supernatural realm.

―――――

THE ATMOSPHERE BUZZED with excitement as I entered the room and sat next to Adam, the team leader for our satellite project. We were in our usual computer meeting room, a familiar space filled with whiteboards and computer screens, where we often discussed our projects. Adam, an outspoken guy I had known for ten years, had a gentle yet honest spirit. His medium build, pleasant smile, and curly brown hair made him handsome. His skills in programming, mathematics, and linguistics made him exceptional. Mr. Melekh found a seat at the front of the room, and Becky, our manager of the entire team, stood next to Peter, taking notes on a tablet.

"Hey, Adam, what's with the sad faces? Did we miss out on receiving the bonuses?" The atmosphere grew heavy with despair as the number of deaths and arrests caused by rejecting the dragon's mark increased. The company promised us bonuses and vacation but delayed everything, leaving us disappointed and frustrated.

"Carmen, no vacation." He kept a downcast face as he acknowledged my questions. "But a potential project is in the works, Becky will explain. I guess we have another day to dedicate to coding and problem-solving. We will stay in Jerusalem, a city on my bucket list for years. Despite the ongoing war in the city, with its constant sirens and wailing of grieving families, we will need to exercise caution."

Adam's words stuck in my brain and alerted me that every day we lived was a blessing. The tribulation had been horrendous for people. But team SFT, shielded by a supernatural force, protected us from gruesome deaths and apocalyptic weather worldwide.

The office in Dubai provided a luxurious work environment with a dedicated suite for the team. Complete with individual bedrooms, an equipped kitchenette, a bathroom, and a spacious living room doubling as a computer station, we had everything we needed to work on projects around the clock. A skywalk and hall separated our quad suites. Our conference room was next to the computer room.

Becky stepped to the whiteboard and wrote a new schematic on the screen.

"People, we have a new project due next week on Friday. Qadira Bilal, a wealthy associate of Mr. Melekh, has requested a second hologram for her clients. The hologram must allow clients to stay inside it for one week. Qadira's vacation hologram enthralled her, but now she yearns for a comprehensive experience that allows her to explore the universe and major cities, complete with realistic weather effects. The first city is Jerusalem. Read the specs and pay close attention to her requests."

Peter joined Melekh at the table, symbolizing the team's unity. He folded his hands behind his head and leaned back in his black cushion leather chair. His deep-set eyes darted back and forth, taking in the expressions on our faces. At the front, Becky remained focused, light pen in hand, capturing every vital point. Melekh kept his attention on the team as he scrolled and tapped on his device. He glanced often in my direction, and I averted my eyes to keep from viewing the sultry stare he gave me.

"Carmen."

Oh, no, his warm and inviting voice changed to a chilled breeze on a summer day. He needed my Zerus hologram program. I could see his stark, icy stare piercing my soul. His mind locked onto mine, combing my thoughts, and that unknown piece disturbed my spirit. Had Peter changed into a demon? Peter never tried to delve into my thoughts in fifteen years on the job.

"Yes, Peter."

"Your specs for the alien hologram need to be altered for a vacation hologram. Before circulating it on Friday, we will change the hologram. Share your schematic with the entire team, allowing them to choose the segments they want, while Becky oversees the rest of the application. Will you upload your data right away?"

Before Peter could finish his statement, my fingers zipped across the keyboard and uploaded the schematics to my teammates.

"Of course, Peter. The shared server synchronized the data on every laptop."

"Excellent. The team will handle the Bilal project. Becky, you will complete the alien project with Carmen. Questions?"

His face showed no expression as he moved his hands from behind his head onto the desk and pressed his fingers into a praying position.

"Great, get back to work. I will check on progress tomorrow at noon."

Upon rising from their chairs, Peter and Melekh approached the exit, halting their progress. Melekh turned to glance in my direction. I raised my head to glance at Peter and caught a stare from him that froze my fingers on the keyboard. He knew of the hack from the rogue alien, so why was he giving me death glares? Melekh's sizzling stare made me curious. What thoughts raced through his mind? Melekh's passionate interlude stirred my heart; a fleeting moment ended as Melekh and Peter departed.

In front of me, a shimmering portal appeared out of nowhere, captivating my gaze. My supernatural power showed me an image of Peter and Lucifer talking in his office. Lucifer's spirit entered Peter, and he proceeded to our conference room. The image disappeared, and another person appeared; viewing Noah took shape before me. I watched a gray mist shroud Noah as Satan's evil spirit occupied him. I gulped in a sharp gasp of air. Lucifer possessed Peter.

Lucifer knew I was on to his evil scheme. What was the reason to show me, Noah? I didn't have time to contemplate. Time is not on my side.

My teammates helped me complete Qadira's second vacation code, duplicated the design, made changes, and were ready for a beta test by the Friday deadline. With my help, we secured the hologram code's front and back end to lock and unlock. We tested Qadira's hologram, and it worked without a flaw. I used our vacation code to match the alien hologram.

I inserted a virus code into the Nephilim program. It enabled the removal of aliens attempting to transport creatures from a different dimension into the 3D simulation. From my analysis, the strategy could neutralize intruders in case of hacking. A wave of relief washed over me as I completed both projects. The thought of the entire plan failing and losing both Qadira's and Zerus's bracelets, not to mention my demise, worried me.

FRIDAY MORNING CAME FAST. Qadira picked up the new translucent hologram wristband, eager to explore the world with the travel picks we programmed. The moment she made her choices, islands and countries came to life as holograms, offering her clients an immersive experience of traveling across the globe.

Two hours later, we received a call from Qadira. The hologram was not working. Noah had gotten stuck inside the Jamaican vacation and could not exit.

Someone left me a cryptic note in my email.

"Carmen, beware of those who want to hurt you. An extraterrestrial operative, hired to disrupt the project, hacked into your vacation hologram. Be cautious with individuals you choose to trust."

After contacting Becky with no response, I dialed Melekh's number. When I called, Melekh picked up first.

"Rashid, someone hacked into the server."

"Carmen, did the email leave an Internet Protocol (IP)?"

"I tried to seize it, but AI's functioning in the computer environment erased the network identifier."

"Let me get my folks to check on this threat. Send me the email, and I will find the culprit."

"Rashid, thanks so much. Let me know what you find."

Becky and I searched my server side and found an untraceable IP identifier pointing to an alien hack. We determined the alien sent a cloaked threat.

By mid-morning, I had completed my notes for the final installation of the alien hologram. Becky had called for a meeting by the ocean to chat. The topic of concern is the Jewish Coalition in Jerusalem. She had a virtual call from Bart from Jerusalem, which wasn't satisfactory news.

My wristband vibrated, and I saw an unfamiliar number.

"Hello, Carmen."

"Mrs. Northrop. Emperor Zerus. We lost another Nephilim today when the vacation hologram, you, and your team coded a program to lock Noah inside with seconds to live before the hologram disappeared. Noah escaped, but my comrade died because of your careless coding. Your repair of our code is due next Friday. Guarantee safety, or you and your team are dead."

With a muffled growl, Zerus ended the call.

My nerves were a wreck, and my failure to succeed with the project had plummeted. Noah's near-death reopened my anxiety and confidence to code. I had to find the alien who sabotaged my project. I notified Lita to recheck her sources. She hurried inside the computer room. What puzzled me was why Zerus and Noah were with Qadira. Were they collaborating? The conspiracy against me and the cursed bracelet grows stronger.

"Miss Carmen, the alien you are searching for does not exist. The species you are looking for are part human, alien, and cyborg. The master humanoid robot and AI master confirmed my data. Do you know your saboteur?"

"No, Lita. I don't, and you don't know who stole my project? I don't believe you."

"Miss Carmen, the person must be in your inner circle. Use your telepathy to find the culprit."

"Okay, thanks, Lita, for the update."

She spun around and turned to her security station outside the computer room. While pressing the keys on my computer, the screen turned blank and reappeared. The message on the screen ignited a rush of emotions within me.

"Beware who you trust!"

THE WRISTBAND'S incessant dinging and buzzing shattered the peaceful Saturday morning, jolting me from a deep slumber and another dream. I slapped my wrist and fell back across the bed.

"Carmen, Peter asked for us to meet in the conference room. He has another project for us. I believe the project might save your assignment. Hurry and meet us in the conference room."

"But Becky, do you realize we have a day of rest on Saturday?" I listened for a reply, peeked at my wristband, and saw Becky close the call.

As I started out the door, I snatched my papers and laptop and realized I needed to dress. It took me three minutes to dash through the ornate hall of plush purple rugs and chandelier lights toward our modular conference room.

Moments before I reached the door, a hand covered my mouth, dragging me into the computer room. Noah removed his hands from my mouth.

"What are you doing here?" My breaths came in labored spurts.

"You fooled Abu and me. But you will not fool us again. Hired assassins are out to kill us because we promised the bracelet, and you gave us a fake bracelet. Now, if you want to live, give me the bracelet."

He pulled out a laser weapon and aimed it at me. His crimson irises, perspiring brow, restless eyes, and wild beard, accompanied by his foul-smelling attire, made him appear deranged. The thought of him possessing the bracelet filled me with dread, knowing it could spell the end for our planet. I had no time to waste. My mind raced to create a diversion on the spot. I rubbed my hand over the red button on my wristband and prayed the activation worked.

"The bracelet is in the mainframe room. If you kill me, you get nothing. So come with me, and I will give you the alien hologram bracelet. Just remember, if you take it, Emperor Zerus and his people will kill you within seconds. What happened to the bracelet that you stole? Those Nephilim are not our friends anymore. They mean business. Don't you remember our children and how you sold them for money? What has happened to you?"

The demons changed his personality. I had read that the dragon's mark twists spirit and soul, turning a person into a demon. Noah's once handsome face sagged with wrinkles, the white of his eyes was blood red, his hair was shaggy, his clothes had soot on them, and he wreaked of sulfur.

"Shut up! Enough of your yapping. Let's go. You're dead if you make one wrong move, my dear Carmen."

I lurched forward as I entered the computer conference room, taking in every detail around me to elude him without death. My focus was sharp, my senses alert, and I was ready to navigate any challenges. The room fell silent as Noah stood by my side, his laser weapon drawing everyone's attention. At that moment, a tangible sense of evil presence and power filled the air.

"Afternoon, Noah. How can we help you?" Peter's calm and confident response showed a slight twitch in his eye, which showed that he had spotted the weapon.

Noah nudged me as he pushed me forward with the weapon aimed at my temple. Everyone in the room stopped typing and watched my trembling lips, chin, and swaying body.

"Peter, I want that bracelet now. Despite Carmen's struggle to deceive me with a fake, I am still determined to gain the original Zerus hologram bracelet. We exchanged a hefty sum of money, and now Abu and I are in mortal danger unless we surrender the bracelet to ruthless bounty hunters employed by oil tycoons."

My teammates didn't move. Yet, I spotted them reaching for weapons we carried in case of attack. After the alien invasion, the team had laser guns supplied to us. The SFT team aimed their weapons at Noah to fire. They stood ready to shoot, their eyes fixed on the horrifying sight before them. I noticed Becky standing beside Peter; she hid her fingers pressing on her wristband.

"Carmen, give the man the original bracelet, and we can continue our meeting."

"But Peter—"

"Do as I say. Do you want to live? So, give him the alien original hologram." His eyes widened as he spoke the word original. I got Peter's hint I should give Noah another fake bracelet. I moved toward my workstation and handed him the bracelet. He always kept the laser fixed on my left temple. I feared one slight mistake, and I was dead. Terror to die by a laser horrified me as I trembled and prayed.

Noah snatched it from my hand, and when he released me from his grip, a humanoid robot was behind him and shot him dead in the head. Noah collapsed onto the marble floor. The horror of his death left me numb as I slumped on the carpet surrounding my desk. In a horrifying moment, blood sprayed across me and my workstation, causing me to fall to the floor in a trembling heap. My teammates surrounded me and pulled me away from the blood splattered on the floor and workstation.

"Carmen, are you alright?" I heard a familiar voice.

Melekh and Peter were present. Their footsteps echoed as they made their way forward. With a tilt, Melekh's firm grasp sent me stumbling into his arms. Trembling and anguish, I felt the near-death effects as death's spiny fingers wrapped around me. Terror engulfed me. My heart raced, and my palms became sweaty. The moment I embraced Melekh, a sense of relief washed over me as I felt his warm embrace. I leaned into his chest, feeling the strength of his arms as he kissed the top of my head.

The humanoids picked up Noah and took his body away. As another team of cleaning humanoids entered the room, the powerful scent of disinfectant circled, overpowering the lingering smell of splattered blood. On the large, cushioned sofa, Melekh held me close, and as I turned my face towards him, I glimpsed his warm, caring expression. I didn't realize he had carried me to the sofa.

"Carmen, we saw Noah when he entered the building after he had accosted several humans to gain entry. After you pushed the red button —Peter and Becky notified me. We saw everything on the hidden security screen in the conference room. You were safe the entire time. We had to wait to get you away from him to keep you safe."

"Melekh, I've never been so glad to see everyone. I feared his ability to kill me at any second. I can't believe my ex-husband sunk so low as to take the lives of his children and then mine."

Noah's sudden demeanor shifted upon receiving the dragon's mark. His once noble nature weakened him. I never imagined he'd turn his rage and thirst for vengeance towards me. An unknown evil force consumed his mind, leading him to a dark path. His allegiance to Satan transformed him into a demonic figure. The Nephilim aliens and demons Noah now worshiped expected the Antichrist's arrival in his terrifying glory within days. It's heartbreaking to witness the man I once loved succumb to such darkness.

The overwhelming sadness made me long to weep, but my tear ducts ran dry. A job awaited me, demanding I eradicate the Nephilim and prevent their intrusion on earth.

I heard Peter's voice echo in my ears. "Get the bracelet."

Chapter Twelve

Carmen squirmed before moving from the edge of her desk to the food counter. As Becky watched her, she assembled a plate with cheeses, meats, vegetables, cookies, and a fruit drink and then returned to the cushioned floor.

"Carmen, the team identified intriguing facts with the alien bracelet. We support you and will help your efforts. If you merge Zerus's hologram into the vacation hologram for Qadira, they won't be able to detect any discrepancies. Your idea can seal the Nephilim's fate as the hot volcanic ash from the Earth mixes in the air chamber. It unleashes a deadly virus and poisons their nervous network. They will collapse and die. Gather the research you seek from the central server and make a backup for security reasons. The enemy is always lurking, hiding in the shadows, unseen and unknown."

"Becky, your analysis is correct. I will grab my notes from three years ago, study the specs, see what I captured, look for other weak spots, and then add a bot code to the chip."

The food smelled terrific to her, and she felt hungry. Carmen lowered her plate to the computer table, eased herself into the chair, and took a bite. Several of her teammates reached the counter and loaded their plates with food. At first, Becky could hold off, but seeing the guys taking so much food made her change her mind. She rushed to the counter and grabbed a plate. Becky joined Carmen at the computer table. The circular room had a large table where they could eat and code. Their wristband-activated digital keyboards made it effortless to store away equipment unless they relied on physical hardware to code intricate programs.

The brief respite was a welcome break from the intensity of their mission, allowing them to recharge before the next phase of their plan.

"We need to concentrate on Jerusalem. Our next assignment will lead us to Israel. Peter hinted we travel to Jerusalem after finishing the 3D Image hologram project."

Becky leaned closer to Carmen, creating a privacy shield as they engaged in hushed conversation. The animated discussions of the Special Force Tigers echoed across the room.

"I wanted to discuss the Jewish Coalition with you. They will need our help once we leave for Jerusalem. Jon, Sophia, and Cyborg Nick are underground. They help transport more individuals to the south. I can't talk here, but we must talk offsite soon."

Becky, after work today is perfect for me. "Work on the hologram. That's my evening, and I need a break."

"Excellent. Carmen, meet me in the lobby at 5:00."

We met in the lobby and strolled towards the market, discussing plans to protect fellow Christians from alien harassment. Few or no aliens were in Dubai.

"Becky, I find it strange that we haven't seen Nephilim aliens or their spacecraft since arriving in Dubai. They're invisible."

The term "invisible" resonated with me. Zerus' sudden disappearance during the demonstration instilled a sense of dread, leaving us afraid of his powerful display. Carmen's complexion became dull gray as the deceitful Nephilim alien lizard man executed his mischievous antics.

"Carmen, I had paid no attention until you spoke of it. You are right, except for the visits you encountered with Zerus. They are hiding or choosing to stay undercover. Do you suppose the devil has an underground meeting place nearby, and that is where they live?"

Carmen stopped walking, turned, and stared at me with tight lips and a scowl.

"Becky, you still don't believe in Messiah Yeshua. Do you realize we are in the throes of tribulation, and you still don't trust God? What's wrong with you?"

Becky reached out to touch her arm, and she pushed her away. She crossed her arms, and the frown on her face was not pleasant.

"Hey, I am sorry. Please help me with my unbelief. I listened when the rabbi spoke and knew the scriptures, but they never stuck. You can help me believe so I don't end up in hell."

"Hell is awful, according to the Bible. Becky, you must have faith in Yeshua. Belief is more than thinking of living in hell for eternity. You must love, care, and have a genuine relationship with Messiah Yeshua; otherwise, you are fooling yourself and could end up in hell because you faked your belief. Girl, you send yourself to hell and remember that fact. El Shaddai never sends humans to hell. We choose. How did we get on this topic?"

Carmen's animated hands synchronized with her words as she conducted her speech. Her words stirred her spirit for the first time in years. Becky desired a genuine relationship with the Messiah Yeshua. Zerus had scared her to her core. Carmen's anguish shifted into heroism at every stage under her watchful gaze. She was determined to rescue her sons, but after she learned they were dead, she still had a fire in her spirit to save the bracelet and help others. She admired her tenacity and grit. Carmen was still talking, and her voice interrupted her thoughts.

"Are you listening, Becky? Oh, my goodness." I watched her shrug her shoulders and her dazed facial display. "Becky, I thought you drifted off to sleep."

"Oh, I heard you. Just soaking in what you said."

"Yeah, right? Girl, I can only pray with you and give you scriptures to read. Your decision to believe is up to you. Friend, believing in

Yeshua is crucial based on our past three years. The news outlets and social media have announced martial law and will expose the Antichrist in a few months. A perspective change will help you reorient your faith. Then again, contact with Zerus, a wicked alien, will force you to seek the Messiah."

We strolled again and ended up at the candy store by the water. After we bought a mixture of candies, cookies to share with the team, and a bottle of water, we walked to the shore, found a bench, and relaxed.

"You are my best friend, and Bart tells me I am doomed to hell unless I hurry and repent and confess my love of God. The hologram project and the aliens' chilling return have unsettled me. I picked up a Bible over the last week and read a few chapters. I owe that feat to your kind words, giving me room to think. Thank you."

"After following my difficult struggle with Noah, he took a dark path towards Satan, and as a result, I ended up losing my sons. I am ready to fight for others and myself. If the Nephilim aliens win our planet, we're doomed."

"Okay, I will tell Bart. He is in Jerusalem working. Let's revisit the topic in a few days. I cloak our correspondence to keep our calls secret from prying ears. Bart wanted a relationship with me, but with our hectic schedules, I pushed away and regarded him as a dear friend."

Carmen nodded and ate, deciding to keep her opinions to herself. Her cell phone buzzed.

"Let me see who is calling. It's Melekh. He wants to meet. My workload leaves no time for him. But if I refuse, he will demand a meeting. He hates the word no."

"Meet with him. Sent a text and see what happens?"

Carmen sent a reply to meet, but he didn't respond.

She made a mental note to hold off discussing the Jewish Coalition further with Carmen. Carmen remained true to her word, which made her happy. Becky was glad that their team was supporting Carmen in the fight of her life, despite the unknown cost to their existence to die if they didn't eradicate the aliens. She needed to rally the rest of the team of coders to support Carmen's efforts.

"Does Bart meet with Melekh now that he owns the company?"

"They only spoke once, and that's it. Bart insists on conducting conversations within the secure room of our prepper home to protect his employment."

"Tell me more. What does Mr. Melekh have to do with our company except supply the monies to keep it running?"

Carmen jumped to her feet when the stray dog ran up to her, and she patted the shaggy animal. It ran away when its owner called its name. The owner was at least seven feet tall and had a gold hue to his complexion. His countenance was strange and not human. He straightened his back and watched the water splash along the shore, and the salty scent of the gulf encased her nostrils.

It dawned on Becky: the man was an extraterrestrial. Did Carmen see the strange glow and his eyes change to ruby red when she approached him? She had to warn her, and then she stopped and waited for her to catch up as the man ran after his dog. He turned around and licked his lips as if we were dinner. A chill of fear shook her body.

"Hey, girly, let's go." Carmen pivoted and went on with her inquiries. We lost not one beat in our conversation. Becky didn't want to mention Carmen's name in the alien's presence. The way he interacted was eerie.

"Becky, Mr. Melekh owns everything on the planet. He is now selling parcels of land in the Middle East."

"How is that possible?"

"Carmen, he became wealthy when the aliens helped rebuild our planet after the collapse of the earthquakes and tsunamis. Did you forget?"

"No. The man wasn't on my radar. Becky, do you remember I worked for hours to help Emperor Zerus on the moon pod projects that have now returned to haunt me? I hate I helped him and his people. I never fathomed the aliens' return to Earth in a million lifetimes. The Nephilim's sole purpose of eradicating humanity and seizing control of our planet terrorizes me. Aliens, not a fan!"

"Becky, Becky!"

She heard someone calling her name, and she turned around and saw Peter jogging along the shore.

"Hi Peter, what a surprise?" She responded as she whirled around to greet him.

Peter appeared out of nowhere as they turned around to watch the waves splash against the beach. No one was on the beach except them. Peter's sudden arrival instilled fear in them. Carmen's face lost color as her eyebrows darted upward, and she drew a sharp breath. Peter's body was wet from running, but from where? They didn't want to believe Peter had cyborg tendencies, but Carmen had a point. His behavior was uncommon, and they could not pinpoint when Peter's personality had shown supernatural tendencies.

"Glad I caught both of you. I need a run to release my stress. I spent two hours meeting with Mr. Melekh and Emperor Zerus, discussing the actual release date of the Qadira hologram."

He stood with his back straight and arms crossed and approached Carmen. She peered up at him. She let out a slow breath.

"Make sure you finish that blasted hologram by next Friday. I am tired of Zerus and Melekh. The best course of action is to complete the project. It is not only your job; it is your life. Stop stalling and find a solution fast. Those aliens are sending more Nephilim to our planet, from what I understand. There are signs the Earth is facing an aggressive takeover by those beasts. Keep what I am saying to yourself. When I ran past the Nephilim man with the dog, I spoke, and he leered at me as he licked his lips as if I was his next meal. Those beasts are hiding in human bodies, waiting for the chance to kill us. Our existence hangs in the balance if they take over the planet."

Becky wanted to run, but her feet stuck fast in the sand.

We stood fixed with our mouths agape as we looked at each other in shock.

"LITA!" I screamed when I saw her inside the test hologram on the ground. "Lita, please speak."

An intruder accessed the Cryptex puzzle, activated the Zerus hologram bracelet, and abandoned her to her fate. The bracelet rested on the floor of the lit computer room while the hologram continued to portray Lita's motionless figure enclosed in the image.

"My loyal humanoid robot, who had been my guardian amidst a looming power threat, fell victim to a malicious act orchestrated by an individual seeking vengeance against me. Who could commit such a heartless act? I had my suspicions, but earlier threats from Zerus established them. The identity of the culprit remained a haunting enigma. An evil force bypassed the impenetrable cipher lock. By disabling the 3D image, the perpetrator activated the hologram of the Zerus bracelet.

The culprit hacked into Lita's most recent software update, manipulating her to appear in a holographic simulation of a tranquil Australian beach. Lita lay amidst crashing waves and strong winds, in danger of being dragged into the ocean inches from shore. The SFT team heard my screams and ran to help retrieve Lita from the fading hologram.

"We rescued her within seconds. Who motivated someone to hurt her? No, someone is sending a message to me."

"Don't worry, Carmen. We will find the culprit. You have one choice."

Becky and I turned and gave each other a knowing stare.

"Zerus, that scum. I need to tell Melekh so he can find her saboteur."

After five minutes, a humanoid robot team came, picked up Lita, and took her away. I knew I needed to prepare for the worst with her, and I kept checking behind me for Zerus. He and his people needed to leave. The abductor damaged Lita's circuits, chips, skin, and metal parts. Since she had a human brain and her chips to the brain worked, she remained alive. She communicated with me through telepathy.

"Carmen, the humanoid master, and the emergency team will fix me. I'll be back at work soon. Miss Carmen, you have questions. I didn't perceive the person or entity who activated my concealed button and covered my vision. The abductor was mindful of my inner workings and covered my eyes to prevent me from identifying them. Whoever

tried to get rid of me was clever. Please inform Mr. Melekh, who can help you with your search."

"Lita, thank you so much for your intel. I will find the person who sought to cause you harm."

I joined the SFT team and left her with the on-call humanoid. He picked her up, and the door closed. I felt remorseful as I noticed my choices had once again inflicted pain upon someone dear to me. Anger flamed my body as I sensed my supernatural power energized me. I said a prayer to calm my spirit. My mystical powers didn't need to activate.

The weather was terrible. After a month of no rain, a three-day downpour occurred, accompanied by scorching weather of 98 degrees and high humidity.

I worked to name the intruder who tried to steal the image from the computer and secure rooms. Despite my efforts, today was a failure. I didn't finish adding the virus attachment to the code. We had computer problems, and the humanoid robots had to stop a bot virus placed by an unknown entity from spreading to other mainframes.

The chatty and jittery humanoid robots expressed uneasiness as they kept to themselves. They glanced in my direction and then turned and whispered to their comrades. An entity must be near because I sensed an evil presence, and a faint scent of jasmine drifted in the air.

My intuition told me that one of them was a team member who assisted Zerus. I had no proof of my suspicions; my visions were inaccurate. Lack of sleep had caused my exhausted body to block dreams in the past week.

I pulled up the bracelet hologram to work on the final touches offline. The vacation hologram was still missing, which worried me. We had two devices to secure: the vacation hologram and the Zerus hologram bracelet. What bothered me was they looked alike, except the vacation hologram had an amethyst stone and the Zerus stone a sapphire. Both shared a gold bracelet and had a dark display.

"BECKY, I am ready to try one more beta test on the bracelet and see if the power I thought we had is taking something vital from Earth."

While the team worked through the day and afternoon, they discovered the Nephilim were taking volcanic ash from our volcanos and testing to see if their red volcanic ash had the same properties as Earth's.

As the day progressed, I noticed the volcanic ash covering the Earth was different, signaling that the Nephilim alien's timeline was expiring since the red ash and human blood were the key to their survival on our planet. To stay alive, they resorted to keeping humans alive and then extracting blood from them when necessary, often resulting in the unsuspecting humans' deaths. Coexistence with the Nephilim for an extended time became a concern, enduring their relentless attacks on humanity until they experienced a significant biological transformation at a molecular level.

I rubbed my eyes to get another view into a fading portal when I saw Noah and Abu giving the vacation hologram bracelet to men wearing white robes with white turbans. They looked furious as they grabbed the bracelet and stalked away. The bodyguards shoved Abu, who bowed his head. Noah kept his hands in his pockets, turned, and walked away.

It surprised me that my visions were working again but were quick and fuzzy. I had forgotten to offer my prayers, praise the Messiah, and express gratitude for the gift of another day. Sliding downward on my knees, I closed my eyelids and prayed. The weight of my words filled my soul. I didn't care who saw it. If I were to perish, then let fate decide.

Later in the afternoon, Melekh sent me flowers and dinner for the entire staff. I listened to him, eager to uncover his insights about the Nephilim and their relentless assaults on humans. I scrapped my thoughts of him and continued to work when Peter called.

"Carmen, afternoon. I need an update."

"Peter, I'll deliver the bracelet to Zerus on time. We stopped working to allow the humanoids to discuss a virus problem while I remained focused on my work. The humanoid robots are too chatty, and they want to expose the rogue robot. Fear might be present among the humanoid robots. When I peered at them, the robots ceased their conversation, twitched, bowed their heads, and stopped their tasks."

The erratic behavior of the humanoids led me to believe the rogue humanoid was nearby. I didn't want to signal to Peter that one of our team members might be the traitor. So, I did not complete my analysis because I suspected Zerus was behind the virus on the mainframe.

"Do you know which robot is rogue?"

"No, but the humanoid robots know. I miss Lita. She could point out the culprit."

"Do not fret, Carmen. I have implemented a security protocol on the mainframe that can detect changes in the computer configuration. Focus on finishing your tasks and getting ready for our trip to Jerusalem."

"Peter, do you know where the missing vacation hologram might be? If I don't get it back—"

"Yes, I am aware. Let Mr. Melekh take care of that problem."

"Okay, Peter. I am eager to start on our next project."

"Wonderful to hear." Mr. Melekh called so I could give him an update and keep Zerus away from our building.

While we were talking, Peter emitted a groan.

My day became baleful after Peter's hologram signal. "Emperor Zerus's spacecraft landed on the helipad. Prepare if he asks for an update and offer details. He has called and sent urgent messages the entire day. Give that devil alien something he can use at this point. If Zerus needs another demo, then do it! Delays are costly for the company, and Melekh is unhappy with constant harassment from Zerus."

The groaning fell to me this time.

"Of course." I reclined in my seat and let out a deep sigh.

Chapter Thirteen

Monday night slipped upon me, and the scheduled hologram bracelet dominated my thoughts. I peeked at the moon, casting shadows as the clouds crossed the ocean. The spicy Middle Eastern food's aroma and salty night air were refreshing. Chaos and stress filled the past fourteen days. Unable to reevaluate my life, I sank into a patio recliner. Next, a shadowy presence took shape.

"You thought you were safe after Noah's death. You're mistaken. I am the one who sabotaged your project."

As I turned around, Abu stood before me, his nostrils flaring, and his face twisted into a menacing snarl. He wore a black spacesuit, boots, and gloves; he carried a weapon that wasn't a laser. I had never experienced such terror from a creature. The odor of death wafted through the air as the sulfurous stench encircled his body and emitted a subtle reddish tint. I didn't bother to answer or question him but pushed the red button on my wristband. I allowed myself to engage him in conversation to bide my time, or at least die trying.

"What do you want, Abu? The bracelet belongs to Emperor Zerus and his alien people. If I fail to turn over the bracelet, people will die." I figured out he was dead when Melekh vanished him to wherever, and now Abu is back to harass me.

"What do I care? Give me the damn bracelet now or die."

I had to think fast to survive. As Abu edged closer, he had a hypodermic needle in his hand.

"Abu, I must go inside the computer room. I don't keep it on my person. Since you can disappear and reappear, you could get it yourself without me."

"No, because the entire computer room has alarms that will go off, and you have the bracelet locked inside a new Cryptex combination lock. Get up, let's go. Otherwise, I'll poison you and move to Becky's room to make her open it. I have been watching you and your tricks. Melekh can't help you, and I know you have summoned him. He is part of the scheme. No one will come and help you." His cackle left goosebumps on my arms.

I rose from my chair, grabbed a jacket, dashed through the hall, and aimed my bracelet at the scanner the computer room opened.

"Welcome, Abu. I had a hunch you'd escape and return to steal the bracelet. It's not for sale by anyone, and especially for you."

BEFORE I KNEW what was happening, Abu shoved me to the ground, and lasers fired across the room, just missing my head. I ducked, scrambled under the nearest table, clinched my hands, and spoke 'Azar' as the blue mist materialized while watching Melekh and Abu battle. Within minutes of the zinging noises, humanoid robot police arrived, shooting as they entered. Fear of getting shot engulfed me; I rested my head across my arms as the last laser shot above my head. Abu cursed, and then came a heavy thump. I raised my head to peer at Abu, dead on the floor, as blood oozed from his still body and computer chips sizzled before a minor explosion erupted from his body.

Abu, a cyborg human, I was stunned by the revelation and sight of his mangled frame on the floor. Then, within seconds, a mist of gray formed around his body, and his spirit entered the fog and evaporated. I couldn't shake the feeling that Abu might appear again, filling me with dread. I uttered '*Enough*,' and the mist disappeared.

"Carmen, Carmen, are you hurt?" Becky's voice echoed, and the thundering footsteps of the Special Force Tigers team and medics dashed toward me.

"Guys, I am fine." They pulled me from beneath the table. An intense shiver ran through my body as sweat clung to my clothes and blood slipped into my mouth.

"No, Carmen, you are not okay. You are bleeding on top of your head."

I touched the side of my right head and felt the blood above my right ear, just missing my temple. I had a minor wound, but it required attention from the medical team.

Everyone huddled around me as the humanoids placed me on a gurney and worked on my wound. I had not heard from Melekh since the shoot-out and wondered if he was okay.

"Becky, where is Mr. Melekh? He disappeared." My heart dropped as he showed no concern for my well-being.

"Let's get Carmen back to her room and allow the staff to clean it and prepare it for tomorrow," uttered Becky.

The humanoids tucked me in my bed, brought food, and left as my comrades stayed and ate pizza, salad, fruit, and sodas with me. While scanning my messages, my wristband buzzed.

"Hello Peter, I thought we had the evening off to relax. How can I help you?"

"Carmen, I understand you had a dreadful evening. Your visitor crept up on Lita and locked her circuits. But I am glad you are alive and doing fine. Mr. Melekh called me, and he will come by later this evening. He had an urgent meeting to attend. So, expect him soon. Get rest."

"I will, Peter, and thanks for calling me."

"Okay, team, give her space," Becky uttered. "Don't stay too long. We have a busy day tomorrow. Lita and two other humanoid police guards will protect Carmen. I will be glad when that bracelet returns to the Nephilim aliens, and we will finish the project. It has been a thorn."

We trudged back to the suite, and I plopped on the bed and closed my aching eyes. Lita sat next to me in a chair. Lita examined my wound, bandaged it, and gave me antibiotics; then, I slipped under the sheets into the bed.

Everyone left, and I was alone with Lita until a knock at my bedroom door startled me. Lita jumped up, opened the door with her weapon ready to fire, and greeted Mr. Melekh.

"How is my dear friend feeling? I am so sorry you had to endure the wrath of Abu. You had me worried, Carmen, and I am glad Abu didn't cause you serious pain, just a minor skin wound. I tried my best not to shoot you when I saw Abu with the laser pointed at your head. Carmen, I blame myself for putting you in harm's way."

His voice broke as he spoke. He was genuine in his apology. He snagged my heart. I kept my distance from him for my well-being, as I knew of his true nature. Despite this caution, I developed feelings for him, with an unexpected flutter in my stomach and a racing heart each time I saw him or heard his name.

"Never again will I let my business impede protecting you. My security guards work around the clock to protect you, Carmen. You will not see them, but they are watching. Abu was in a place where he broke protocol and ended his earthly life. Abu was part human, alien, and cyborg. He was the real culprit who tried to break inside my office building, steal your Zerus bracelet, and ransom more money from me. I told you a lie on purpose to protect you. My security people snooped around, looking for clues. Abu killed two guards at the entrance. My team told me he was the saboteur. Please forgive my lie."

"Rashid, thank you for coming. I'm tired and must put the finishing touches on the alien bracelet tomorrow." I had to dismiss him because he had lied to me, and that mattered to me.

"My dear, I will stay with you until you fall asleep." I noticed tears in his eyes, and it shocked me.

"Carmen." He hesitated. "I have fallen in love with you and don't know how our relationship will work."

He paused, clasped my hand, and kissed it before sitting on the edge of the bed. His shoulders and head bowed as he laid his head on my chest and sighed. I rubbed my hand over his silky hair, closed my eyelids, and enjoyed the affection and tender embrace. Whenever he was near, I knew he cared for me. He always grinned and stared. His bewitching cologne lured me deeper into his web. Yet, I cherished the moment to forget my troubles and enjoy his company.

"Sweetheart, I must go. I'll return to check on you. Lita will stay in your room with you and remember—"

I didn't have time to respond. Rashid leaned in and kissed my forehead, then placed a smoldering kiss on my lips. Smiling, he bid Lita and me goodnight and exited through the door.

WEDNESDAY AFTERNOON SLIPPED UPON ME, and the scheduled hologram bracelet dominated my thoughts. The intensity of my dreams heightened, causing me to wake up every few hours, unable to sleep for extended periods. Everything I tried to keep from Zerus failed; the hologram bracelet did not work correctly. My anguish and failure to succeed at the assignment still left people dying in the streets.

The bracelet still emitted power, but the red glow was diminishing. I notified Astronaut Trish to decide if they could locate Zarzu Genesis and update me on their climate.

An urgent message from Trish Berg, the ISS Science Officer and doctor, asked me to call her. Becky joined me in my room while we made the video call.

"Carmen, I wanted you and Becky to learn the latest data on the planet, so I called you via secure video." Trish, the Science Officer and Medical Doctor. She was an exceptional woman aboard the ISS space station. She possessed a trim, athletic frame and olive complexion. Her ash-brown curls flowed over her shoulders as she donned a form-fitting, blue spandex spacesuit, emphasizing her petite frame. Her striking turquoise eyes and warm smile drew you in, captivating your attention.

"Zarzu Genesis is falling into a black hole and will be gone by week's end. The faint red light from the hologram bracelet is the only power or energy left for the Nephilim. Once the planet is gone, they will announce a total invasion. Those wicked creatures will seek to kill humanity."

Becky and I looked at each other and dropped our heads in anguish.

"No wonder Zerus was running a raid on the planet and wanting me to hurry and complete the hologram. The emperor had an entire planet of millions of Nephilim to transport, and the quicker I got it working, the more aliens he could transport. Zerus could not return to Zarzu without being pulled into the black hole's gravitational pull."

I stood and paced for a minute. My mental juices flowed.

"Okay, guys. Trish, I need Commander Marc Zacker to aim that laser at those Nephilim ships and destroy them. Those Nephilim that are left on earth, if I give them bracelets with the virus in them once they enter, they will try to return to their families, but the virus will lock them inside, and they will die in the holograms."

"How many bracelets do you have?"

"Two now. But can I get the humanoid robots to help me produce at least one hundred of them and disperse them around the globe within ten minutes? I can get Mr. Melekh to help. If true, he said he had supernatural power to capture and move the aliens into the holograms. We can lie and tell them they have only one day to save their people. Codes are ready to go; attack day is Thursday. What do you think?"

"Carmen, it sounds great. Let's see if we can rid ourselves of the aliens. If not, we die, but let's die trying." Trish waved and disappeared off the screen.

Becky jumped to her feet, stepped to my table, grabbed an apple, and took a bite.

"Our plan sounds dangerous, but if we fail, that's our job. Let's keep the plan between the three of us and Marc. Get those bracelets made tonight. I want everything done and ready to start tomorrow. If you must stay up to complete the task, do it. If you need help, please tell me. I want to double-check your codes, so get me to order food and plenty of coffee."

"Becky, you are a wonderful friend." I strolled over, hugged her, and went to my room to pray. Having neglected prayer for days, God's guidance in my prayers became crucial.

I needed to investigate the demonic realm to visualize what was coming, and as I tried to open the portal, it remained locked. Without my power, I did not know how to fight the aliens. I prayed and pleaded, but God remained silent. After thirty minutes, I rose from my knees and entered the living room. Becky had ordered food, and the waitstaff had arrived and gone.

We sat and worked out our plan, then called Melekh.

We completed our design strategy by late Thursday morning. Lita helped us with the bracelets for the Nephilim dispersal, a crucial step to support peace in our realm; her help was invaluable. Her return brought me joy as she supported and protected me and the team.

The skilled humanoid master transformed Lita. They installed brand-new circuits, computer chips, synthetic skin, and state-of-the-art weapons. Thanks to her enhancements, she recovered her capabilities, transforming into a warrior ready to support me.

Melekh had not returned my calls, leaving me in a state of anxious anticipation. I had returned to my suite to shower, change clothes, and prepare to meet Zerus. Moments stretched forever as I placed the computer research on the table, feeling restless before deciding to shower. Then, a sudden knock at my door jolted me from my reverie.

I hurried and opened the door to be greeted by Rashid's grinning face. Then, to my surprise, he grabbed and hugged me so tight I thought he was trying to break my bones. His unexpressed love for me showed when he kissed me, leaving his essence on my lips long after our lips parted.

"I missed you, and you thought I forgot to call back. Despite the fires I had to handle, I opted to see your stunning face instead of going home."

He reached out and gripped my hand. As we passed Becky, she was fast asleep on cushioned pillows on the floor. We strolled to the veranda. Birds chirped, filling the warm air, and his passionate breath caught in my nostrils when he nuzzled my ear as we strolled.

His arms tightened around me, pulling me into an embrace that left no space between us. Our lips met, and at that moment, I sensed a fiery collision of longing and passion overwhelming our senses.

"My dear, I am sorry. I should have asked to kiss you, but you looked sexy and stunning. I couldn't help myself." The dimples in his cheeks deepened as he brushed back curls off my face.

"How can you say that? I've been awake most of the night with messy hair and smelly, wrinkled clothes. You have a remarkable sense of humor, Rashid."

He cuddled me, then released me as he stood back, and his countenance changed, devoid of a grin but still holding my hands.

"My love, excellent news. The rogue Nephilim is dead. The rogue humanoid robot and one of Zerus's Nephilim were working together to get the key to your research, steal the data, and give it to Zerus. My people spotted both rogue characters attempting to enter my office overnight. Security didn't ask them what they were doing because I had informed them to kill them on the spot with no questions. I guess they thought I had the data, but they are no longer a threat to you and my projects."

The news of the alien and humanoid's elimination from Rashid left me troubled. I was unaware that both the alien and humanoid were working together. I knew the humanoids were chatty. Peter had said he had secured the mainframe.

"How did they die? Was it a laser?" His head tilted to one side, his lips forming a stern line, raising suspicion in me.

"My dear Carmen, does it matter how they died? Zerus and his hoards will not get your hologram bracelet."

His smugness left me wondering what else he knew and kept secret. His humanoid robots were formidable, armed with weaponry unparalleled in the entire galaxy.

"Zerus is causing problems throughout the globe. I called an emergency meeting with my investors to see what we could do to stop the invasion. Your genius idea of utilizing atomic lasers to launch and exterminate the Nephilim is remarkable. Your idea poses a problem - the ISS is at risk because of Zerus' advanced weapons."

He moved to a cushioned chair near the pool and motioned for me to sit beside him as he patted the chair. I didn't tell him my recommendations, but then I remembered surveillance in our office. He heard my plans, even conversations I deemed personal.

"What do you suggest? I am ready to disperse the hologram to Zerus, and his entire species will die once they enter the hologram. I fear the Nephilim left on the planet will continue to hunt and kill humans. You were aware they were taking human blood to live?"

He turned his head and kept his face pointed toward the ocean. With Rashid's head turned away from me, understanding his expression had become impossible. Rashid's lack of honesty was palpable, and I couldn't shake the notion of deceit. And the reason behind his betrayal remains a mystery. He had a hand in the Nephilim abductions to save their species. My inner spirit kept whispering that he was deceiving me, a faint warning in the depths of my being.

"My dear, I realized their deception two days ago, which has been upsetting. You must know someone else is working against you: your ex-husband and my point man, Abu, for my projects. They wanted to kill you because of me. Since Noah is dead, I have only Abu to kill. My attention to be your loyal friend angered both men, and now I must kill Abu."

For the first time since Rashid and I met, I realized he was an individual no one should cross for any reason.

"Will you be able to protect me and the team? I have no power to keep Abu and Zerus away from me."

"My dear, sweet Carmen. You have my word to protect you always. Let's return to the Zerus problem. Let me create a distraction in the interstellar space that will allow Zerus a route toward the wormhole once he and his armies head in that direction. By deploying atomic lasers from the ISS and targeting the Zerus's spaceships as they blast into space, we will destroy Zerus and his armies through a wormhole. I can finish the job and annihilate Zerus and his horde with my powerful supernatural weapon."

"Rashid, I saw your display of supernatural powers. Whatever you ask. Lita will help me distribute the bracelets to Zerus, who will give them to his people this morning."

Rashid's overwhelming power and commanding presence filled me with fear, yet I prayed Satan did not own him. The thought of him being the Antichrist sent me a chill, a foreboding reminder of my bond with him. My emotions grew toward him. Despite this ominous possibility, he showed his genuine concern for my well-being and warned me of the lurking threat that could whisk my life away. The bracelet symbolized my determination to protect humanity from the Antichrist and alien forces.

"Very good. Now, be careful, and don't get Zerus upset if he tries any of his tricks. Press that emergency red button on your digital band, and help will come within seconds. I must prepare for the day, and so do you, my love."

He placed a warm, soft kiss on my forehead and hurried through the living room and out the door. I followed behind, but he was nowhere in the hall when I opened the door. How weird. Rashid had powers, but this was the first time he displayed his secret. He possessed supernatural abilities that gave him the power to disappear. His enchanting jasmine fragrance circled the room. Aliens emitted the jasmine scent. Yes, I remembered, and Rashid was partnering with the aliens because his scent matched theirs. What was I going to do?

AN URGENT WARNING came in on Thursday morning, informing us that aliens were abducting humans. Security advised the Special Force Tigers to stay indoors.

The aliens carried out brutal attacks. The onslaught persisted for a quarter of an hour before the extraterrestrial beings departed as fast as they had arrived.

I knew Zerus was behind the attacks, and I warned the team to hurry and put the finishing touches on his hologram.

"Becky, let's give Zerus a program sample and see if it works before we give him the completed project."

"Fantastic idea, but if he gets stuck inside, we'll have blood on our hands with those creatures. It will be my head for allowing you to go ahead without permission from Peter and your death."

"You have a point, but if we can find the correct signal to send to the code from Zerus's master activator on his wrist, then we code a replica. We use the carbon copy to give to the aliens and send that bracelet to Zerus." I needed the team to understand what was at stake once Zerus had the false bracelet.

"Becky, Zerus intends to spread his Nephilim across the globe, and the deadly virus code embedded in the bracelets will prove their demise. The key to eliminating Zerus and his followers lies in accessing the hologram, making them helpless because of their dependence on the red soil from their home planet."

I depended on the SFT to make a network, which could lead to the Nephilim's downfall—a perfect plan.

"Their survival depends on the red soil. We must consult with Trish from the ISS to confirm my theory."

"What of the rogue alien? Should we track them? I believe aliens could give us answers. Becky, the rogue alien, is dead, and the humanoid, according to Melekh. He came by this morning while you were asleep. I see your mystery man has feelings for you, Carmen. Be careful."

I twirled, waved her off, and reached over the table to gather my research so we could leave.

"No, he's only a friend. We must concentrate on keeping that code from Zerus at any cost."

"Okay, call him and see what happens."

Two hours later, Zerus appeared, and he wasn't happy with my suggestion to beta test with him inside the image.

"Carmen, if I die inside that hologram, I have alerted my security team to kill you on the spot."

The moment he mentioned "security," two formidable Nephilim materialized, brandishing their weapons in my direction.

"Emperor Zerus, I understand, and you will not get stuck. I give my word."

I gave him the bracelet, and he placed it on his arm and activated the blue button. The hologram appeared, and he stepped inside the 3D image.

The landscape of mountains and green grass appeared as coded. Zerus pressed the button again, opened the portal, and walked out.

My heart raced as he stepped inside the visual effect. I uttered a prayer that he had emerged intact. I needed him to survive so I could complete my mission. If he died, his scaly Nephilim guards had their weapons aimed at shooting me, then Becky. The scene was far from pleasant, but I knew my daring plan had triumphed. Becky remained oblivious to the potential consequences if I failed. I had not shared the grave plight that awaited the team. With a simple button push, a vivid green light appeared. My program code had captured his signals, which I needed to rid our planet of the beasts.

"Carmen, well done. I admire the landscape; it is a pleasant touch. Have this ready by Friday. The digital clock is counting to your doom."

Zerus placed the bracelet in my hand, its gold circular clasp glistening in the light. The touch of his hairy fingers on my palm made me cringe in disgust.

He waved his hand, and the creatures followed him to the exit. He entered his awaiting spaceship, and we watched the spacecraft disappear from the overhead skylight.

"Glad he is gone. Carmen, your plan worked, but I was worried."

"Both our lives were on the line, so..." I hesitated, my heart pounding. I wanted to tell Becky her life was on the line, but I kept my worries to myself.

"Zerus is cognizant of your managerial position and understands the potential consequences if I fail."

"Are you saying he had evil intentions against me?"

"Yes, my friend." I tapped the image on my laptop and arranged the transfer.

I looked at the bracelet and inserted the chip into the laptop, and the alien code to their ship and its secrets appeared. Becky leaned over my shoulder, and her eyes were wide with excitement when I glanced in her direction.

"Carmen, we now have the ace card, and let's use it."

I swore to overcome any challenge, including Zerus, to avoid failure and death.

"Are you ready to release the bracelet?"

FRIDAY DAWN in the computer room came with a flash of dread and horror. We hurried to the atrium and waited for Zerus's arrival. Golden sunlight streamed through the skylights, bathing the atrium in a warm glow. Peter and the Special Forces Team members stood beside me as I unveiled the intricate 3D image bracelet to Emperor Zerus. As they arrived early, his faithful lizard bodyguards positioned themselves on either side of the emperor, creating an atmosphere of dread and distress within the group. As I took a moment to pay attention to my team-mates, it became noticeable that a sense of tension filled the room. Each person displayed a sense of defeat, with their posture showing slumped shoulders, lowered heads, and clenched fists to prepare for a confrontation.

"Carmen, thank you for restoring my bracelet." His hideous voice sent a chill through my spirit. "Let me remind you. If you have tricked me, you and your entire team will die. Your planet will be ours, and you will serve us, so prepare to be a servant." His once-human presence had transformed into that of a scaly beast, with scales stretching from his head to his scaly feet. With a snarl, he turned and vanished, along with his creatures.

PETER'S once-fiery anger had diminished, replaced by his usual calm demeanor.

"Carmen," Peter began, his voice filled with regret and awe, "my sincere apologies for yelling and losing my cool. Becky told me how you had stuck your neck out to save everyone, and your powers had saved the entire team. Have you always had this unique gift?"

His keen eyes bore into my soul. A sense of suspicion gnawed at me when Peter disclosed my supernatural powers, making me question Becky's silence. Yet I knew she had kept my secret. Peter lied. Who told him? Only Rashid Melekh glimpsed my display as he took Abu's life. My body filled with anger, and sweat appeared on my upper lip, but I maintained my composure.

"Yes, since childhood." I was cautious with my response. I had adopted Becky's approach of waiting and analyzing my thoughts before speaking, which proved invaluable.

He cocked his head and locked his gape on me. His intense, glassy-eyed stare, devoid of emotion, caught my attention.

"Alright, everyone, let's grab food at the Hanging Gardens, then work." Peter stepped closer to me.

"Carmen, have breakfast with me at the Hanging Gardens. I appreciate your dedication to your work."

"Okay, Peter. Lita will come with us."

Everyone wandered to the cafe overlooking the gulf and ate spiced chicken, crepes, and mimosas. It was a pleasant meal. But I didn't trust Peter after I saw him in a dream. He was being way too nice.

I thought of having Lita conceal herself, allowing her to watch while I conversed with Peter. I communicated what had happened in my vision with telepathy, and she vowed to keep me safe. Lita followed us as we crept in the sand to the chairs in the Hanging Garden Cafe. Lita remained a constant presence as we dined beside the water, always beside me.

After we finished our meal, we strolled along the beach. Lita remained two feet behind me. While Peter and I chatted, the waves crashed against the shore, creating a calming ambiance. My teammates relaxed on the veranda, enjoying the picturesque scenery.

Out of nowhere, Abu manifested in the early morning. His sudden presence left me speechless, my mouth agape in disbelief. His now gray frame scared me to my core. After his passing, the sight of blood was so gruesome that one could not divert their eyes. I couldn't shake off the unease after Abu's deliberate comeback, as if my intuition was trying to communicate a hidden message.

Peter's surprised eyebrows arching upwards, jaw hanging limp, didn't fool me, and my supernatural instincts covered me. I uttered, 'Azar,' and the supernatural mist covered me. This time, my mist was translucent, and I didn't see the mist but accepted the warmth surrounding my frame.

"Morning, Carmen."

"Abu, how can I help you? I thought you died. How is it you're alive?"

"You don't understand the mystical world of Satan, so don't question me." His ashen, scaly face and red eyeballs scared me inside my spirit. I sighed with constricted breaths. "I understand you have the key to the alien bracelet hologram, and since the vacation hologram you gave Ms. Bilal didn't work, we want to buy the product."

"Who are we, and why are you asking me for the artifact? Mr. Melekh owns the company; any work I do belongs to him." I rotated and presented Peter with pursed lips and squinted. He said nothing and stood mute. As I gawked at Peter, I saw an unmistakable darkness— Lucifer's spirit, not Peter's, staring back at me. My dream had become déjà vu.

Panic set in as I scanned the beach. My eyes darted back and forth, looking for any sign of Lita, but she had disappeared without a trace. Glancing out at the veranda, I realized my teammates were nowhere to be found. With no one to rely on, I switched to combat posture, prepared to do whatever it took to stay alive. Refusing to let fear and failure hold me back, I embraced an empowerment mindset. I found hidden bravery and strength within myself.

I straightened my back, held my head high, and clenched my hands into a fist. If they wanted to kill me, then at least I was going to fight to my last breath.

"Carmen, you're not afraid of me. You have changed and are fearless. You will turn over the hologram bracelet. We have paid millions to get the device."

"Peter, I never expected you to betray your country and your adored Special Force Tigers. What happened to you?" His countenance changed; his eyes sparkled red, and a smirk graced his once handsome face.

"Give us the code, Carmen, or die in the gulf."

I stood my ground, feeling the tension in the air. Abu must have snuck up on me unnoticed while Peter moved, seizing my hands to prevent me from closing them. The shroud of mist that had once cloaked me had dissipated, leaving me exposed. After I said the word *Azar*, I questioned the sudden disappearance of the ethereal blue mist that has always accompanied me. Regardless of the reason behind its vanishing act, I knew that this was my ultimate opportunity to either confront Abu or succumb to defeat.

But I was determined to emerge victorious. As I struggled to get away from Abu and Lucifer, their menacing laughter echoed in my ears, and blood filled my mouth when I nibbled my lip. I experienced a moment of mental confusion as my mother's voice reverberated in my head. I forgot to pray and put my trust in my power. Praying and hoping for the mist to appear was no longer a choice. I prayed.

Abu ripped the counterfeit bracelet from my right arm with Peter's help. As I glanced over at Peter, my jaw dropped in awe. He had morphed into a stunning eight-foot angel, accompanied by cymbals and pipes adorning his chest as the wicked angel Satan sang a haunting melody. Several demons and black angels were poised by his side. As the wind blew, the nauseating stench of sulfur filled the air, making me gag. The wicked demons pulled me across the sand towards the hotel's cliff, causing me to regurgitate a blend of blood and vomit onto the sand.

Abu and Satan escorted me toward the edge of a high ledge that led to a deep drop-off into the gulf, placed zip-tie devices on my wrists, and let me go as I plunged into the gulf. I descended deeper into the sea. I pressed the red button on my wristband before they released me to drop into the depths of the water. My blue aura activated and circled me in a cocoon, allowing me to take quick breaths and stay alive. I am thankful that God has responded to my prayers.

"Help!" I screamed, my desperate plea piercing through the silence. I tasted the saltwater engulfing me, suffocating me as I fought for my last breath.

I prayed an earnest prayer in my mind. *Please, Messiah God, help me! I have done nothing wrong. If I die, I will be with you.*

Tightness constricted my circulation as I struggled to release my hands from the zip ties. My lungs filled with water. As I took a long breath, I clenched my fists, and the remnants of the dissipating mist vanished. I fought against the force of the water, my lungs burning as I struggled to break through to the surface. Then, a miracle happened. A dolphin glided under me and pushed me up into the air. As I caught my breath, I splashed and crashed hard into the sea. The dolphin caught me once again; I landed on him. He nudged me to the shore. Then, the dolphin dissolved when I touched the sand.

As I crawled up the beach, struggling, coughing, and breathless to free my hands, I clenched my hands into a fist. The zip ties broke free from my aching wrist as blood oozed from the deep gashes on my wrists.

Once again, I prayed and noticed people were absent on the beach and hotel. Was I dreaming, or did someone put me inside a hologram? My wrist cell buzzed and appeared to stop working. When I tapped the timepiece, it remained blank. Peter claimed my device was waterproof. Then I blinked and noticed the missing blue orb bracelet; the devils had taken the wrong bracelet. I wore two identical bracelets to keep the original safe. They snatched the deadly virus bracelet. My security bracelet and the duplicate hologram device for Zerus looked the same. If Abu entered the hologram, then death. If he died, I could live once again with no threat from Abu.

Next, out of nowhere, Rashid arrived; I collapsed in his arms, grabbed him, and held him tight against my chest. He lifted me fast as we exited the hologram with a single fluid movement and placed me on my bed. As I stopped sobbing, my gaze locked with his, and I realized they had trapped me in a holographic illusion in another realm. I sniffed his body, and the jasmine scent was strong and virile. Rashid had the same cologne as the Golden Nephilim, who drank the blood of humans. Was Rashid in control of the Nephilim?

"Rashid, did you create the hologram that transported us to another realm? What is happening? Don't you dare lie to me? I am no fool."

"Carmen, your signal came to Peter and me. I told you protection surrounds you. Lita had signaled me seconds before they hit her on the head. She is alright, and I will make sure we restore her."

"Who hit Lita? Wait a minute, Peter told you what? He was part of the scheme. Abu has taken the activation bracelet, but the virus contained within will be fatal for him. Is Peter a rogue humanoid robot or a cyborg? He tried to kill me, and I am devastated. Although, I realized it was Lucifer who was inside Peter. Is that true? Give me the truth, and don't you dare lie to me!" My voice raised an octave higher than usual.

His deep, penetrating expression as he searched my mind made me hesitate as he sat on my bed. Rashid grabbed my hands and patted and rubbed them.

"I know, but don't worry. Peter, a human, is being used, as you mentioned. After saving you, my supervisor evaluated my performance through a series of tests. I will take care of Abu and make sure he no longer causes you any annoyance. With a rational mind, Peter will extend his apologies, acknowledging his mistakes. I will make sure he does, my dear."

"It is not within your power to guarantee that, but I can safeguard myself. Who is your supervisor?"

"Carmen, I must go, but we can talk and have dinner later this evening. Rest or sleep to get your strength." He leaped up from the side of the bed, kissed my forehead, and strolled to the door.

Once again, he ignored most of my questions. A golden glow enveloped him, and he glistened with every movement, as if a faint haze followed his body. Rashid transformed from a mysterious figure into someone with extraordinary metaphysical capacities. But he sounded willing to support me. His declaration of love for me two weeks ago must have had a deeper meaning. I moved the idea out of my thoughts.

"No, I must stay awake because until the Nephilim are gone, I can't sleep. But maybe later we can meet for dessert." I had to lie; I didn't want to involve my heart further with Rashid.

As he twisted and turned, his eyes lingered on me before he exited the room. An eerie laughter hung in the air, marking his aftermath.

Chapter Fourteen

Pandemonium ensued as the Nephilim spacecraft lit up the heavens, using their firepower to abduct humans and transport them into their ships. During the chaos, the alien military forces commandeered the battle, their spacecraft darting and evading amidst a shower of lasers and plummeting vehicles. Lasers darted through the air, filling the atmosphere with shrill cries. Alien military forces tracked hovercrafts as their ammunition blasted them into oblivion, creating echoing screams and moans in the surroundings. The stench of blood, sulfur, and scorched circuits created a horrendous odor.

Many team members, both men and women, were grappling with injuries. The atmosphere resonated with the shrill sound of nuclear bombs hitting the extraterrestrial spacecrafts, yet the tenacious ships advanced undeterred, akin to a relentless pack of wolves chasing their prey. After witnessing the devastating scene, my spirit plunged as I saw hundreds of people sacrificing their lives to protect our planet.

The humanoids tended to our injuries, wasting no time providing medical care to staff members who had rushed inside during the Nephilim attacks. I used my wristwatch to watch the combat while the dynamic media screens inside P.J. provided live updates of the action in Dubai and around the globe.

After the fight with Abu and Lucifer, I suffered painful cuts and scrapes. As I walked through the hallway, the medical team greeted me and escorted me to the main conference room upon seeing my bleeding wounds. The humanoid robots had transformed the conference room into an emergency hospital to treat the injured staff members.

I observed the shimmering radiance coming from Zerus's central bracelet, signaling that the bracelet had activated. Upon scrutinizing the holographic bracelet, it pricked my wrist. I had given ten sensor bracelets to my buddies. These bracelets notified the team when the aliens infiltrated the hologram to trigger the virus. It became plain that the virus had penetrated the Nephilim nation through the hologram. Once exposed to the virus, it takes hold of the lungs, resulting in death within moments of inhalation. Their end is swift and unforgiving.

My teammates met me in the conference room and waited for me. "Guys!" I screamed from my gurney, my voice echoing through the hall. "Let's go!"

I hopped off the gurney, now bandaged and ready to fight. My Special Force Tigers team pulled out our laser guns, and we headed toward the atrium. We proceeded to the first floor with helmets, eyewear, and gloves. I set the pace at the front of the pack, Adam keeping stride with me while the rest of the team fell in line behind us.

The sounds of intense emotion and rage filled the airspace. My heart raced with a conflicting blend of strength and fear. "The Nephilim have activated the bracelets. Examine your bracelets as the glow transitions from a cool blue hue to a fiery red. The Nephilim will seal their fate when the color shifts to red."

"Shoot now." My voice echoed through the breeze as I called out. With a sudden whirl, Becky fixed me with a piercing glare.

"Why are you with us, Carmen? You can get more injuries."

"Becky, I can protect the team if I am with you. Don't worry, I will stay inside the atrium."

Lasers sizzled against the pavement and various massive buildings. Arab military joined in the fight, and their weapons desecrated the spaceships as they exploded and crashed into the Persian Gulf. The cruel beasts presented an endless supply of spaceships as they kept turning up one after another. Astronauts sent live startling video feeds showing the Nephilim launched a surprise attack on the ISS, filling the space station with chaos and fear. No serious injuries, but they needed more help as they had lost power, and NASA was working on repairs to put them back in orbit.

Reports kept coming in from the ISS. Aliens released dead and dying captives from moon pods into the stratosphere. As the space-suit's oxygen caught fire, dead bodies floated in the skies, exploding with a loud boom. The aliens engaged in a deadly game, killing individuals before opening the pods. Then, they threw their bodies into the dark outer space. The cruelty from the aliens was unprecedented. 3D images splashed across the sides of buildings, depicting the carnage on the moon.

We continued to fire until the mothership turned and vanished.

"Hey, guys, maybe the virus is taking effect." My heart raced as adrenaline coursed through my body.

"Let's hope so. If not, we are losing," screamed Becky amidst the chaos.

We breathed a minute of relief and thought our ordeal was over, but then a bright light fell upon me, encasing me in red light. The sound of Becky's terrified screams reverberated through the air as the light surrounded me.

"Azar," my mystical mist appeared to shield my teammates as I clenched my fists. A dense blue mist surrounded us, blocking our view of our surroundings, except for me. I could see the action.

Fire bolts rained downward upon us, shaking the ground beneath our feet. "Everyone duck and prepare for impact," I screamed.

The sound of glass breaking filled the air as time slowed. I crouched to my knees and pulled my hands next to my body to avoid getting cut by the flying shards. The air filled with human screams, cries, and groans that pierced through my ears. And just as quick as it began, the chaos subsided. I realized my mist protected us, keeping my team safe from harm. Their eyes spoke volumes of admiration and gratitude as I turned and gazed at them. I knew an explanation must follow.

Out of nowhere, the threatening red beam pierced through my blue mist and locked onto me. How did that happen? A whirlwind of thoughts fills my mind, a mix of curiosity, fear, and a strange emptiness. Amid the chaos, Becky's panicked voice pierced through the air as the team shouted my name.

"Carmen, Carmen, oh God, help her."

My body lifted off the ground, and I experienced a rush of exhilaration as I landed in a pod on the mothership. In the turmoil, a piece of shrapnel from flying debris grazed my left arm, and I let out a cry of pain. As I materialized onto the pod deck, I sensed pressure mounting as I peeked and glimpsed at Zerus. Within seconds, I had to think my way out of trouble.

My dreaded fear turned to horror when they snatched me. I had to think of an escape plan using my supernatural power or die this time. My mystical powers had failed me once, and I needed to activate them fast. I realized my powers were more potent than my mom's, and I had other qualities she didn't gain. The virus in the hologram didn't kill the Nephilim right away. But why? Now, the creatures seized me instead of my companions.

A group of gold human-appearing Nephilim strapped the belts to my arms and struggled to clamp my wrists, but I clenched my fists, and a blue cloud surrounded my frame. Despite the hypodermic needle being inches away from my arm, the Nephilim were unsuccessful in drawing my blood and carrying out their plan to kill me.

With godly strength, the aliens grappled with my clenched fists, their efforts futile against my unwavering metaphysical power, and they retreated from the pod. They surprised me when their hands went through the mist and grabbed my hands while the mystical power covered me. The golden-colored aliens had human blood. They could bypass my shield and touch me. This revelation stunned me, and I remembered the factors in my mind for future attacks.

If my thoughts were correct, my power against the Nephilim who drank human blood might be useless. They tried to remove my wristband, but it clung to my skin tighter and became a part of me. With sheer strength, a paranormal force snatched them and launched them to the opposite side of the room. The surreal sight of the aliens hurled into the air and landing on their backs sent a spine-tingling wave of satisfaction through my entire being.

I didn't believe I could keep the deadly hologram from the aliens, but now I had to succeed in my battle to rid the Earth of those creatures and help humanity. The mysterious light helped me, and I said a quick prayer of thanks because Father God helped me during my battle.

Zerus hastened up his steps to my side and tried to remove the mist, but when he touched it, an electrical shock zapped his body and sent him flying across the room. He scrapped his feet across the steel floor. The haunting scraping of his nails made me clench my fists tighter; he returned.

He had a laser look-alike weapon, and the fierce scowl and gritted razor-sharp teeth he showed scared me. Yet anger sizzled inside me for taking my sons, and revenge fueled my resolve to fight until the Nephilim died. I had to get revenge, and if it meant my death, so be it. I knew I had him when he pointed the weapon at my face. When he fired, the laser backfired, struck the perimeter of my pod, and set it on fire.

Nephilim surgical team screamed and ran, begging Zerus to stop. Yet the blaze on the pod was hot, and I felt its burning heat. A golden Nephilim sprayed liquid on the pod, and the flames subsided. The flames licked at the edges of the blue mist, but it held firm, preventing any injury to me. As blood trickled from the shrapnel embedded in my arm, waves of agony coursed through me.

"Stop the firing before you kill us, Emperor."

Nephilim quelled the spreading fire on the floor and other pods.

"I need to kill this woman. Since the beginning, she has been a persistent irritant. The room and hall overflowed with the echoes of his feet scraping and the unintelligible language he spoke, creating an eerie ambiance.

Everyone left, and no one returned to check if I was alive or dead.

A faint voice spoke to me. "I have saved you. Now finish the job assigned. Remember, I will let no one hurt you." The voice was so familiar and soothing. I believed Melekh spoke to me. Was he on board and stopped Zerus from killing me? I couldn't figure out for sure why Melekh concealed his identity.

"Kill her now." I heard a commotion in the hall and angry voices speaking in a dialect unknown to me. I had to vanish or die in the clutches of the Nephilim beast.

The mist still circled my body. I prayed and asked God to remove me from the mothership and send me back to Earth. I had to flee the spaceship before they returned with a more lethal weapon. Their bracelet became a lethal device to humanity. I will destroy the bracelet once the Nephilim dies. I raised my hands towards the sky, and then I disappeared into thin air.

A supernatural vacuum sucked my body into a holding place as I fell into a trance, where I felt nothing but the blood in my body sway and gurgle through my veins. I still needed to figure out my location and destination.

A voice broke the silence and called out my name, sending me shivers. I perceived an angel dressed in white, his face unseen. His booming voice echoed through the air, reminiscent of the rush of water over a waterfall. He assured me of my survival, for my mission had just started. I could save others from El Shaddai's impending wrath, which will occur within the next seven years. Before me, he vanished, leaving behind a fragrant medley of gardenias, flowers, and herbs that filled my nostrils. The sound of screams and moans jolted me awake from my temporary slumber.

When I landed back at the atrium on the floor where I left, the full scale of the fighting confronted me, with debris scattered everywhere and the air thick with tension. The atrium had caught fire. Humanoid creatures sprayed a substance to contain the spread on the first floor. The building rocked back and forth. I became fearful the building might collapse since it sat on an enormous elevated steel platform.

What I watched next horrified me.

Those Nephilim aliens had shot Becky in her right arm, and she was on a gurney with the other ten members of my tech family, injured with shrapnel and laser skin burns. I rushed to her side, my heart pounding in my chest, a fiery sweat breaking out on my forehead.

"I apologize, Becky, for the harm I caused you and the team."

"Carmen, I'm fine. I will continue once the humanoid finishes binding my wound."

"Please take a moment and pray, Becky. We need divine intervention."

As the humanoids grabbed me, I felt their firm grip on my arms, their touch sending waves of discomfort through my body. They wasted no time in placing me on a cool gurney. Although the numbing medicine eased the pain, the acrid scent of burning flesh lingered in the room as they removed the shrapnel and stitched my wounds. My voice quivered as the humanoid smoothed the ointment onto my wounds. I winced at the sting.

The heavy, stifling atmosphere reeked of the unmistakable odors of blood, corpses, and the remnants of buildings consumed by fire. The distant cries of my injured teammates floated in the atmosphere. To aid our employees, P.J. Waxit provided humanoid robots for medical care. Warm blood trickled to the ground from gashes on my right wrist, where I had wrapped my wound with my teeth.

When I evaporated from the spaceship, my molecules changed and reassembled. As I reappeared in the main hall of the building, everyone cheered and questioned what had happened to me. I answered their questions amid my medical pain.

"Carmen, we were fearing the worst, but now we can breathe a sigh of relief," Becky uttered, grateful I was back and safe.

As Becky looked up at me, her face was blotchy and tear-stained, revealing her emotional turmoil.

"Don't cry, Becky. I'm scared but fine, but the aliens are still fighting us."

Thankfully, my teammates' injuries were not severe, and they expected to recover. I watched in fascination as the efficient humanoid robots tended to everyone around me. My thoughts turned to Rashid Melekh's fate.

Later in the afternoon, our intense battle in Dubai continued; as spaceships vanished, the team retreated to the conference room, but we kept our armaments beside us.

I told the team that Zerus gave up but expected another round of assaults to pursue. Becky and the two other female engineers on the team sent me air kisses while they cheered for me to continue. I strolled to the rear of the conference room, sat in a cozy lounge chair, and gazed up at the sky, letting out a contented sigh. Gradually, my colleagues gathered around me as the doctors completed their discussions and set them free.

"Carmen, Mr. Melekh had to leave, but he and his demon hordes sent the final blow to Zerus's Nephilim aliens and saved the city and our lives. I think it's pertinent to express gratitude to him. Right after the aliens took you, he vanished."

As Becky paused, I could see the glimmer of tears forming in her eyes.

"Carmen, I thought you were dead, but we kept shooting at the spacecraft. You can't go to sleep, or Zerus and his hoard of Nephilim will catch you when you least expect. We have taken turns watching for lizard Nephilim man until his entire family of extraterrestrials enters the hologram and dies."

"You're right. We must stay vigilant until Melekh arrives and the ISS gives us the okay. I don't know why the virus didn't kill the aliens when they entered the hologram. Keep your eye on the sensor bracelets. Once the blue light turns to red, the aliens are dead."

"Melekh attacked the Nephilim spaceships. His mother ship and smaller fighter spacecrafts soared into the sky, disappearing in the afternoon's expanse. The sheer number of ships was overwhelming, making it impossible to keep track." Becky kept her face glued to mine. Her facial expression never changed as she pulled out a tissue to wipe her eyes.

Then, I felt an ominous presence surrounding me; if I were to guess, Satan.

"Carmen, you are correct. I have not finished my fight. It has only begun."

"Be careful who you trust," Lucifer called out to the heavens, his cackle echoing in space. The powerful sound of his voice echoed through the sky, capturing the attention of all who heard it.

As we searched the sky, Becky, my close companion, mirrored my exhaustion with heavy breaths. But I couldn't help but notice an increasing sense of threat as the hair on my head stood upright, reaching toward the vast expanse of the sky.

Zerus must have concealed himself in the shadows; within seconds, he and two Nephilim who resembled Zerus seized my arms, but it was too late for the Nephilim.

An electrical surge shot from my hands and sizzled their beings. Zerus pressed the activation bracelet, and he vanished. As he disappeared, I heard wails and screeches.

A supernatural portal opened, and I saw Zerus and his entire team of Nephilim rush into the hologram portal. He signaled them to press their bracelet buttons, and they vanished.

I pressed my hologram wristband to view the heavens. The terrifying sight of thousands of spaceships filled the sky.

I sent an emergency signal to the ISS as I spoke to my wristband. "Commander Marc Zacker. Can you inform me if you noticed the anomaly on the console screen? An enormous UFO vehicle is exiting our galaxy."

"Shoot now! Kill them. Don't let them escape." I heard his voice echo over my hologram.

The atomic laser fired, and it was a dead-on hit. The wormhole dissolved before a ship entered, and the thousands of spaceships exploded as the ISS and Melekh's team of demon spaceships fired on the Nephilim crews. I watched the mothership and Zerus Nephilim crew explode with firepower. The Nephilim, wearing their bracelets, collapsed and perished on Earth when Zerus activated the master switch. The electrical shock from the computer chip and the virus killed them.

Before me, I saw the horrifying spectacle of colossal giants plummeting to the Earth, shaking the ground with a resounding thud and leaving behind gaping craters. I was relieved to see them die and my troubles eliminated. The fear and anxiety became a moment of calm over my being.

A fiery ball shot skyward from Earth. Nephilim screeched, echoing the words of dying Nephilim. *"We are dying. Stop and retreat."*

The Golden Nephilim, with the blood transfusions, collapsed and died. We had dispersed enough bracelets around the globe to kill the Nephilim. Without a hologram bracelet, the Nephilim faced their demise since they could not communicate with their spaceship, which was necessary for collecting the red dirt and mist from the volcano on their planet to keep them alive.

As I exited the hotel, I realized that my journey to survival and aiding others was only beginning. I prepared for the day to reunite with my fellow teammates at the café where I had disappeared at the Hanging Gardens. The humanoids were working to revitalize the city's streets and structures.

The crowded skyway in Dubai occupied lively sounds as the sun rose higher in the mid-morning sky. I saw robotic vehicles spraying, cleaning, and removing road debris. The panoramic window in my suite offered a breathtaking view of the busy skyway, where people zoomed in on their jetted vehicles. Hovercrafts flew overhead, adding to the bustling atmosphere. A satisfied expression filled my face and spirit. After we freed ourselves of those Nephilim for good, I renewed my faith in man and God. In my darkest moment, when my hope failed, God came to my rescue, bringing a renewed sense of truth and strength. I lost my husband and sons in my ordeal, but I gained faith in myself to succeed and not fear.

I used my supernatural power to fool the aliens into entering the holograms around the planet, and the moment they entered, God killed them at once. It was a special moment in history for me and the team. Melekh had been a great help, and I trusted and loved him.

Melekh's mysterious demeanor cast doubt in Becky's mind, making her question his true intentions. With a tone of worry, she cautioned me to exercise restraint and advised against placing my trust in him.

The Antichrist remained elusive, and our anxiety was mounting. The time had come for his mass meeting, and we were ready with the hologram we had developed earlier in the year, capable of being transmitted across prominent networks, media channels, and telecommunications devices. I remember several conversations with Becky.

"Carmen, I recommend you avoid any entanglement with him. Mr. Melekh, or Rashid, as you call him, is dangerous. The data we have gathered on him over the past three years makes me wonder if he is the Antichrist."

It pained me to believe her since I had gone through much sorrow at losing my family. But I kept an open mind, and if Rashid was the Antichrist, I accepted his friendship. Now, I had to approach him with discretion when alone with him.

***

THE RADIANT SUN illuminated the sultry morning of Shabbat without a single cloud in the sky. Preparations were taking place on the Temple Mount platform in Jerusalem for the expected arrival of the Antichrist. Meanwhile, our team remained in Dubai and found ourselves seated alongside Peter in a glass conference room adorned with a skylight that showed the celestial realm.

Peter expressed remorse for his actions and pledged never to involve himself in a deceitful scheme against his team of engineers again. I still harbored doubts and concerns following his disrespectful behavior towards me. The breach of trust with Peter left me feeling cautious. I entertained the notion that he might be an extraterrestrial being or an advanced cyborg possessing extraordinary technological capabilities known to humanity. Melekh's dismissive manner towards my questions left me puzzled and intrigued, wondering what secrets lay beneath the surface with Peter.

"Hey, guys, does anyone know the Antichrist's identity?" Becky's voice pierced the silence, filling the room with tension.

Peter's lack of interaction with the staff led team members to suggest he could be the Antichrist. The waitstaff gave us snacks: popcorn, chips, candies, pretzels, and fresh fruit. People munched on snacks and engaged in conversations, creating an atmosphere reminiscent of a lively movie chat. We encountered a pivotal moment requiring us to adopt a rigid mindset to guarantee our continued existence.

When I glanced in Peter's direction, I noticed his emotionless expression; his face fixated on the large screen above the floor. He didn't appreciate the joke. We carried on with our laughter and banter, and with excitement, we awaited the new leader's arrival on our virtual screen.

Screams, yells, and chants of "Messiah" echoed, creating an eerie scene. We looked around and saw people at the company chanting, yet our Special Force Tigers team remained silent. We watched in amazement. The world celebrated the Antichrist, but we had to be careful since most of our eleven-member team were Christians.

The massive screen pushed upward from the heliport deck displayed the Western Wall and Temple Mount with its gold dome. Many gathered at Temple Mount, where a grand platform stood. They pushed protestors back from the mount, and we saw many people shot dead on the spot when they tried to storm the platform. The grizzly scene was horrific.

"Attention people, today we are announcing peace throughout the world. Our fearless leader has made a seven-year peace treaty with the Jews, and he is ready to greet you."

A tall, muscular, handsome man in an Armani black spacesuit with raven shoulder-length hair and a face that made women swoon stepped up to the podium. My mouth dropped open, and my heart pounded against my ribcage. The rhythmic flow of my blood resonated in my ears. Cyrus Rashid Melekh, the owner of our company, was not only my best friend and love interest, but he was the Antichrist. He had fooled the entire team, especially me. Becky tilted her head and gave me a knowing look of sadness. She grabbed my hand and squeezed it.

"Becky, you were right. I am sorry to report that Rashid is not someone you can trust. For heaven's sake, he embodies evil, the Antichrist. After seven years, the man's fate is hellfire, highlighting the necessity of mindfulness in every word and action."

"Yes, that is true, but since he cares for you. You have the dominant hand and will know his weak points. It holds value for us and the Jewish Coalition. Peter leaned closer, straining to catch every word of our conversation.

"You should be careful, Becky. Peter is a spy." I hesitated to speak, worried that Peter may have overheard our conversation. But I noticed his eyebrows raised and his mouth tightened. He presented a drastic change in his demeanor. Peter's transformation overshadowed our success in finding the bracelet, leaving me perplexed by his sudden shift in behavior.

"Carmen, how could you utter those words? Could he be nosy? Yes. But a spy for Rashid Melekh. Maybe."

I signaled Becky with a shake of my head to stop talking. Peter sat at an angle from us, and I sensed he could watch our actions from now on, no matter what we coded. It made sense Peter worked for Melekh, and of course, if we had any interaction with the Jewish Coalition, Melekh needed the intel. My former friend is gone, and he once helped me. Now that he rules the world, how will I approach him? Melekh stepped back from the podium, and another man stepped forward. He raised his hands toward the sky, and the sky darkened as fireballs of sulfur fell to the ground and burned everything in sight. People ran and screamed from the podium. With his finger raised, Melekh pointed to the heavens. The sun appeared, escaping the clouds. The people cheered and clapped when they realized what had happened.

I strained to see Melekh's right wrist and gasped. He had the missing gold bracelet on his arm. "Becky," I nudged her shoulder. "Look at Melekh's right wrist." A gasp eluded her lips. "Girl, is that the missing Qadira global hologram bracelet? Is he using it to produce a hologram?"

"From what I see, yes. Rashid Melekh used our device to create a virtual reality image, making people think he is their God. Oh, my goodness."

"What are you going to do? Will you ask him to return it now that you know he is the Antichrist? Carmen, that might be dangerous." Her raised eyebrow and pursed lips made me think of the advice she had given. If Rashid had the global hologram, he could use it against humanity. Although the Nephilim were deceased, the Antichrist possessed unparalleled power to unleash unimaginable wrath upon humanity.

My wristband buzzed when I peeked at the message. Rashid Melekh, the Antichrist, had asked me to dinner. A chill of fear ran through my bones. My heart beat faster; my hand drew moisture, and his smooth baritone voice caressed me. I had fallen in love with him. He could see through my thoughts. What was my next move? Go to dinner or refuse? I was bound to face a negative outcome, no matter my decision.

"Carmen, dinner tonight, my place or yours. Please respond. I have much to tell you."

Chapter Fifteen

"Lita, have you heard from Mr. Melekh? His silence since his public announcement of world leadership is unnerving. It's been a week, and today is Friday. He has always been prompt, responding within three days. This unusual silence..." I trailed off, my voice knitted with worry. Lita and I had weathered a catastrophe together, and Mr. Melekh's silence was worrisome. I accepted his dinner invitation, and then he vanished without further contact.

Our team of engineers packed our bags and flew to Abu Dhabi for a week. After a week of chaos and destruction during the alien war, a conflict that tested the limits of our resilience and ravaged our planet, we escaped to the capital city of Abu Dhabi. The peaceful landscapes and enchanting aromas of Abu Dhabi were a welcome sanctuary for our battered souls.

"Miss Carmen, he hasn't responded. I'm sure he will call soon." Lita spun around, left the kitchen, and rested in a chair in the living room while I poured coffee. Our unity as a team was our strength in these uncertain times.

After much thought and discussion with Becky, thoughts of Rashid and his betrayal clouded my mind. I was in a predicament, unable to respond to Rashid's dinner date invitation. His betrayal of taking the Qadira global hologram bracelet had left me in fear and confusion.

Two active vacation holograms now exist. Qadira's company advertised the first vacation hologram. As a bonus, she added her new global hologram device, a guaranteed to relieve stress—travel on a lifetime vacation to any place on the planet. We were fortunate to have created two global holograms as a precautionary measure for emergencies. These global holograms, including those sold by Qadira, are a product of our team's innovation and have no malicious intent.

I couldn't grasp why Melekh had taken the global bracelet from Qadira, and she stayed silent. What had we done as a team?

I tapped my device and signaled Becky.

"Hey, Becky. Girly, do you want to go shopping with the girls from the team? Sounds wonderful. I want to relax for a few hours and eat breakfast. I called because we still have a problem with the hologram bracelets. Since Qadira is selling her vacation of a lifetime to people, do you think she is part of Melekh's wicked team to get people inside the hologram and then lock them in forever?"

"Wow, slow down, Carmen. I never thought that far. It is possible, and we are the designers of a weapon, to murder innocent people. Keep that thought under wraps for now. We leave for Jerusalem on Sunday. I will alert the underground Jewish Coalition. Let's meet at noon today."

"I need to refresh and experience new things. Meet you in the suite living room."

As I took a moment to collect my thoughts on the veranda, I found solace in the turquoise waves kissing the soft sand. I savored a delectable breakfast spread of eggs Benedict, fresh fruit, and sizzling sausages on the private patio of my extravagant hotel. The rhythmic sound of footsteps echoing on the stone pathway caught my attention, and as I turned, I saw Rashid approaching, his silhouette framed by the rising sun.

"Morning, beautiful; you are as enchanting as I remember. I am sure by now you have seen the televised show of my kingship."

He sank into the plush patio chair with a gentle grace, his eyes never leaving mine. I was glad I had nothing in my mouth; otherwise, the food might have flown across the table. I was stunned and without words. He was not supposed to care for me, but why was he nice to me? Oops, I forgot he could read my thoughts.

The Scriptures, once he became the Antichrist, he hated Jews and Gentiles. Did his heart override his conviction to carry out his wicked deeds? Maybe his love for me was an act to get me to take the dragon's mark. Genuine love means being honest and not asking me to take the mark while still ensuring my protection from him.

As Rashid locked eyes with me, a shiver traveled up my spine, the intensity of his gawk stirring a whirlwind of emotions inside me. The intoxicating fragrance of jasmine filled the air, pulling me deeper into his supernatural emotional trap. As he slid his hands across the table to hold mine, I became frustrated with my feelings for him.

"My dear, I have not changed, and I will care for you wherever you may go. I heard your thoughts."

"Why are you here with me?"

"Because you never doubted me and didn't judge me from our first meeting. Which meant you trusted your life to me."

As always, I had questions instead of words. Rashid's sudden presence after a week of silence didn't sit well with me, and that mischievous grin gave me hesitation.

"Carmen, I am ready to answer your many questions. The answer to your first question from several weeks ago. Who oversees my work? Of course, I am the one who always brings a burst of energy and vibrant personality to any room."

His laughter lingered in the atmosphere, echoing long after it had ceased. His grip on my hands tightened. But I wiggled my fingers from his grip and finished my breakfast.

"Your second inquiry of who I am is most troublesome. The display of my kingship answers your concerns. The one who controls my thoughts is none other than Lucifer himself, my supervisor, and he expects me to persuade more people to join his sinister team. My priest will show miracles, and you will join me sooner or later. But just in case you don't, I will not kill you or cause you harm. Not now or ever."

He took a moment to pause, inhaled with a sigh, and glanced towards the waterfront before proceeding.

"The Nephilim were not my idea. Satan had deployed them to kill humans before my transformation. You were never in danger from me. Once again, my supervisor reproduced the fragrance of the jasmine essence to my extravagant cologne as a ploy to trick you. I fought for our planet and you. As I told you before, I will never harm you, but someone else might."

His eyeballs changed from a soft gold to a brilliant red. He pushed his chair away and got to his feet, leaning in so close that I could sense his breath on my skin.

Oh. I pushed back from the table as the gasp slipped from my lips.

"Carmen, enjoy your vacation in my country, but my eventual seat of glory will be in Jerusalem. I will avoid you in Jerusalem because my power is not as strong in the holy city as in the United Arab Emirates, but in a few weeks, my full power in Jerusalem will prevail."

"Rashid, is the throne of Satan in Babylon?"

"Yes, my dear, for now, but soon in Jerusalem."

"And the bracelet?" As my gaze fell upon his right arm, the sight of a dazzling bracelet captivated me. I couldn't help but stare at the replacement clasp. The sapphire dazzled, and the gold bracelet stitched to his skin, adding an intriguing detail.

He caught my stare, and I averted my eyes to my plate.

"The bracelet has been mine since my money bought it in Egypt when Sophia McFadden found it in the sand. I believe you know her?"

His inquiry stunned me and left me speechless. With each movement, his raven locks of hair swung from his shoulders as he leaned closer, angling his head for a better view of my face. Next, he kneeled and directed his attention towards my face. Rashid's essence made me uncomfortable, and I wanted him to leave.

Despite never meeting Sophia, he was aware of the difficult

circumstances she faced in Romala, Texas. He had the water contaminated to gain wealth when his oil refineries polluted the Gulf states. Then, he set out to kill her and the mayor. Did he think I didn't know his underhanded business dealings?

"And yes, it was a virtual reality hologram created to fool the people of our planet when the lightning struck the earth. I altered the molecular pattern of the bracelet to mimic my desired design. Sweetheart, the bracelet is in capable hands. Never will I use it against you."

Rashid grasped my hands and kissed them. He was at my feet, beaming.

"My dear, I love you. Say the word, and we'll be together forever. Take the dragon mark, my love."

Oh, no. I was on the brink of surrendering my heart to Rashid until he ruined the moment by bringing up a disturbing dragon mark while professing his love. With his cunning plan, Melekh intended to lead me astray from my Christian faith, causing a rift between me and Adonai. Never! I prayed he heard my thoughts. Wickedness had taken its slimy grip upon his soul, and Rashid Melekh was more dangerous than before his rebirth.

"Rashid, never will I take the mark. I am a child of the Almighty Father, the ruler of all kings and the master of all lords. Not you or any deceiving wicked spirit."

He never took his direct focus from my face, and I felt his power. His radiant glow transformed into a brilliant shade of gold, overpowering me with its intensity. I had to tilt my head to shield my eyes from the blinding light. With a swift motion, I released my hands from his clasp.

"Carmen, how long have you had that supernatural power of yours?"

"My entire life. The Messiah Yeshua protects me."

"Yes, I see that now. I am the Messiah, the world's king.

Buddy, not in a million years are you the Messiah.

His lips released a burst of gentle laughter while he crouched and enveloped me in a robust hug. With an endearing gentleness and passion, he leaned forward and kissed me before disappearing right in front of me.

A rush of relief washed over me, leaving me breathless. The project to save the world from the Nephilim and their ancient hologram bracelet had been enough for the past two months, but now I had to negotiate with Melekh and his antics.

I now must use my hidden powers to stop him from reading my thoughts, so I bow my head in prayer and pull up my Bible app to the Psalms. I need Adonai's protection as a shield against him.

***

Lita took my breakfast tray and helped me pick clothes for the day. I asked her to unlock the room safe and give me the Cryptex box cipher. She waited for further instructions, but I dismissed her to stay in the living room.

I opened my suitcase to the security box with the Cryptex box cipher that held the key to Zerus's hologram bracelet. When I entered the password and opened the box, it contained the remains of the original bracelet, which had disintegrated and left only the red dirt from Zarzu Genesis. What an odd occurrence. Destroying the relic brought me a sense of immense relief.

I signaled Becky to come to my suite and gave her intel on the bracelet. "I had a visit from Melekh, too. Now that he is the Antichrist, he can open any of our codes without us knowing it. He reconstructed the global hologram and changed its architecture. We must be careful to notice whether we are in a virtual reality. Melekh's powers are beyond this world."

Becky pursed her lips as she examined the dirt, but not before she grabbed gloves, a mask, and a magnifying glass from me.

"Yes, but remember, he loves you; otherwise, he could not visit you. You have power over him, so use it with discretion. Carmen, I'm so glad you stepped up and stuck your neck out to save us. Otherwise, our vacation might not have happened."

Becky stretched her arms above her head and uttered, "I have a change of plans. Meet me at the spa. I need to relieve the stress from my body."

"Okay, see you in thirty minutes."

Becky hurried out the door to her suite to change clothes.

Rashid Melekh blended into the shadows, observing her with intensity. "Yes," he confessed. To himself, "I am captivated by Carmen and committed to keeping her by my side."

AMIDST THE RECENT chaos in Dubai, I sought solace in Abu Dhabi as I completed my digital paperwork and coordinated my upcoming journey to Jerusalem with my friends. My life was the opposite of what I had experienced in earlier months when the loss of my family troubled me. The haunted fears and defeats no longer tormented me; instead, I dismissed any thoughts of aliens or a sinister presence. Despite feeling haunted by dreams of evil forces, I found comfort in knowing I had support to help me endure the challenges ahead over the next seven years.

My bravery shone in steadfast belief, a guiding beacon, and unwavering turmoil. With resilience, I accomplished the incredible feat of eradicating extraterrestrial beings alongside my comrades.

An alert from my wristband showed it was Rashid.

"Hello, gorgeous. Are you ready for breakfast on the sand with me?"

"Rashid, do you realize the sun hasn't risen?"

"Yes, my love. The hovercraft awaits you, and my humanoid robot is at the door. Allow her to come in for five minutes, get ready, and join me. I have something important to tell you."

My hesitation led to questions, but I went to meet him.

"Okay, give me ten minutes. See you."

I hung up and hurried into the luxurious bathroom, had a quick shower, threw on my blue spandex spacesuit, covered my hair with a scarf, put on sandals, met the humanoid, and raced to the hovercraft.

As soon as I entered the craft, he was waiting with open arms, hugging and kissing me, and we were on the sand within minutes. I had fallen for the Antichrist man. How did I let myself get involved with him? Any further time with him was a one-way ticket to hell. I made the tough decision to end our time together today. I must tell him to stop calling me, and we can't meet. Yet, I sensed his relentless determination to persuade me to keep in contact with him.

The fiery sunrise created eerie silhouettes across the sun-kissed sands, as though concealing a foreboding secret beneath their shimmering golden hue. We lounged on purple linen pillows with breakfast assortments of Arabic coffee, kosher beef and chicken, waffles, omelets, fruit, and mimosas. The waitstaff placed two tiki torches on opposite sides of the rectangular portable pallet.

We watched several camels paced with their owners through the sand. We then reclined in a posh, connected recliner and ate in silence, except for the birds flying above and the grunting of the camels. He made life vibrant and carefree despite his sinister aura. He might change if I pretended long enough, but who was I fooling? Rashid, now the Antichrist, had one last trip with me before we parted.

"Carmen, I'll be absent for a while. My new company assignment involves global travel, so you'll see me. I will make sure you and Lita have around-the-clock security. Don't worry. You will not be in danger, but if you are, remember to call me."

As he passed me a small purple box, I ripped off the wrapping paper and let out a gasp as I unveiled the contents of the petite black box. Inside was a stunning gold ring with an intricate and exotic design that shimmered in the light. A breathtaking 20-carat diamond oval ring sparkled with a white light that blinded me. His smile widened as I gasped in astonishment at the sight of the ring. The gesture left me speechless, unsure of the significance behind it. Was this ring a symbol of marriage or engagement? Ultimately, I knew I had to decline his proposal.

"What does this mean, Rashid?" His face beamed with a radiant smile. He inched closer, his breath tickling my skin.

"Not an engagement ring, my love. The ring notifies me worldwide, and I'll be by your side. Try it on for size. It will adjust to your ring finger." Rashid peered at me, and I put the ring on my right finger.

He leaned back and laughed, his voice echoing over the sand and air. He kept his focus on me.

"Okay, my love. I understand your hesitation. As I stated before, it's not an engagement ring."

"Thank you for the ring. I will use it when necessary."

I angled my head to kiss him on his cheek. He edged closer, gripped my shoulders, and pressed his lips against mine. We talked for an hour and exited the magical sand above the hotel golf course.

Rashid gave me one more passionate kiss at the hotel door, strode through the hall, and vanished. He overwhelmed me. I pulled out the ring in the box and stared at it. I saved the ring for a future emergency. With the box snug in my pocket, I hurried to my suite.

After spending a week in Abu Dhabi and enjoying breakfast with my friend Rashid, the city's serene ambiance captivated my teammates.

My teammates and I immersed ourselves in the elegance of iconic attractions, such as the Louvre Abu Dhabi. During our visit, we indulged in golfing, swimming, shopping, and exploring other remarkable landmarks.

Our respite at the spectacular Melekh Hotel Suites provided a much-needed break from the perpetual hustle, serving as a rejuvenating pause following the exhaustive task of cleaning up the Natas Dubai Hotel following alien attacks.

We enjoyed breathtaking views of towering skyscrapers from the luxury hotel, indulged in posh amenities, sunk our toes into soft, white sand on the beaches, and savored delectable meals.

As the sun set, we wandered through the city of mirrors nestled in the desert's heart, admiring the translucent glass buildings surrounding us. The sunlight danced off the architecture, casting a mesmerizing spectacle. The translucent city was a sight to behold, with its unique design divided into two distinct sections - one perched atop a pedestal, the other half resting at the water's edge. This futuristic marvel of engineering exceeded our wildest dreams.

The next day, the female members of our engineering team

indulged in a delightful shopping spree. The male counterparts embarked on an exciting trip to Ferrari World Yas Island, Abu Dhabi. They shared photos of their thrilling experiences at the theme park.

As the week-long trip progressed, I sensed myself drifting away from my earlier life with each passing day, except for the unwavering presence of my beloved sons. I cherished them and held their memory in my heart.

The tormenting memories of my late husband gave way to tranquility. My children's sorrow remained, but with time, my heart will heal. One night, I had a dream in which the triplets reached out to me, assuring me of their joyous state in Heaven and their excitement to see me again in the future. It was a welcome change. God prepared me to be a warrior for my people during the Tribulation.

In our tight-knit group, the Special Force Tigers, loyalty was the foundation that bound us together, surpassing the level of mere friends. Determined, everyone promised to step up and save more saints from the Antichrist's wrath, which became our quest.

On our last day before heading to Jerusalem, Becky suggested we call Bart Hall for updates.

"Hey, Carmen, let's call Bart. We need to get intel on what to expect when we arrive in Jerusalem."

My heart filled with exhilaration. Being in the famed city where Jesus had walked gave me goosebumps.

"I can't wait to meet Bart in person. You have often spoken of him, and he recommended me for the Special Force Tigers team. I must speak with him. Let Bart know Rashid gave me a ring to protect the team. Becky, you were right. I have fallen in love with Rashid, but I ended it today, except for the ring."

"A ring?" Her eyebrows shot up, and her mouth dropped open. She halted her steps before she sat on the cushions.

"Yes, an emergency ring for security only. I will not wear it. It's just a token of his infatuation with me. That's it." I bought a necklace for the ring, hung it around my neck, and slipped it inside my jumpsuit.

"Carmen, once again, be careful. The ring holds greater significance in his mind. Be cautious, my friend. That ring can entangle you, making you forget why Yeshua left you behind on Earth. So let me see the ring."

I retrieved the ring from my side-zippered pocket. She gasped in surprise.

"Carmen, are you serious? This ring holds immense value, and he gives it to you. It is worth millions. How many carats is it?" Her voice was now an octave higher, and her eyebrows furrowed.

"It's 20 carets that what the inside box quoted."

"Oh, my, be cautious, my friend. We may need to grasp the depth of meaning that the ring holds for Rashid."

"You are right. Let's stop talking and wait for Bart." She handed me the ring. I pushed it inside my right pocket. I could no longer ignore the ring's unmistakable presence; a tingling sensation coursed through my right leg, confirming its existence.

As we dialed the number, I sank into Becky's plush sofa cushions. My mind buzzed with anticipation of our new assignment and the upcoming meeting with the Jewish Coalition.

The story continues in Venial (Debacle Series, Book 2)

**Join the Mailing List For
Perfidy, Book One, Debacle Series**

If you enjoyed reading this book, please share your thoughts with a review on platforms such as Amazon and Goodreads. Your reviews are crucial in connecting me with other enthusiastic readers like yourself.

The website is https://drmozart18.com/

Afterword

As I developed the six-part series, the first book became a story about the strategic use of perfidy, a term in military law. This unique concept, which refers to deceiving an adversary to kill, injure, or capture them, added an intriguing layer to the narrative. It represents a breach of the enemy's promised boundaries cloaked in deception. Developing the characters and their plots was a joy for me. I even took creative liberties by deliberately misspelling the fictional city's name, Arvvada, to showcase my creative writing freedom.

I used Hebrew names in the story, and the last name Melekh means king, which alluded to the fact the antagonist, who bears this name, will someday become the king in the six-part novel series, posing a significant threat to the protagonists and their mission.

And to my dear husband, Michael, I am grateful for your unwavering support and encouragement in my writing journey. Your dedication and feedback have been invaluable to my launch team and beta readers, and your guidance and patience have been crucial to my developmental editor. Each of you made this possible for me.

This Christian Sci-fi Fantasy novel, which delves into future events from the Bible, including the Tribulation and the Rapture, is a project

I'm deeply passionate about. I can't wait for you to dive into it, and I hope you find it enjoyable.

"We who are still alive and are left will be caught up" (Latin translation, rapio, from the Koine Greek) "together with them in the clouds to meet the Lord in the air" (1 Thessalonians 4:17, NKJV).

The story continues in Venial (The Debacle Series, Book 2)
Click here to get updates on the next book in the series.
https://drmozart.com

About the Author

Ardith Arnelle Price is a talented writer known for her captivating stories in the Christian inspiration and Christian sci-fi apocalypse futuristic/fantasy genres.

She weaves narratives deeply rooted in faith and spirituality in the Christian inspiration genre. In contrast, in the Christian sci-fi fantasy genre, she explores futuristic and fantastical elements within a Christian context. Using her pen name, Ardith A. Price, she has created an exciting Christian Sci-fi novel series. However, her love for creating new and engaging characters for her novels defines her.

Devoted to her faith, Ardith is not just a writer but an active member of the Christian community. Her work, which reflects her beliefs, is driven by her desire to inspire and uplift others. Ardith and her husband live in the metropolitan region of southern Michigan.

To learn more about her work and be part of this inspiring journey, Join Ardith's mailing list at drmozart18.com for news about upcoming books, giveaways, and appearances. Follow her on Facebook, Instagram, and Goodreads. Contact Ardith at info@ardithaprice.com or visit her website at https://drmozart18.com.

<u>Follow her on social media:</u>

Facebook: facebook.com/ArdithPrice18

Instagram: instagram.com/ardithaprice

LinkedIn: linkedin.com/in/ardith-arnelle-price;

Amazon Central: https://amzn.to/3DvxUWN

Goodreads:goodreads.com/author/show/20689122.Ardith_Arnelle_Price

Also by Ardith A. Price

Just the Edge of God

Looking Through the Sea of Glass

Mayim

Exalted - Not available

The Grave is Licking its Lips - Not available

The Narrow Door Blazes with Fire - Not available

Epilogue

"And then shall many be offended, and shall betray one another, and shall hate one another. And many false prophets shall rise, and shall deceive many."

— Matthew 24:10-11 KJV